The Flayer
Vol. 1

By Joshua K. Koehn

Hope it's everything you thought it would be.

— Josh K. Koehn

Authored by: Joshua Koehn (Twitter: @koehn_joshua)
Cover By: http://abe7280.deviantart.com/
Original Cover Concept: Cassandra Sigsworth
Edited by: Ashley Owca

Dedicated to:
My Mom

The Flayer:
One Shot

<u>Chapter 1</u>

Perfect. That was the word many people would describe the situation that Andrew Mullen found himself in. His clean-shaven chin rested idly in his hand as he stared out into the hustle and bustle of the restaurant. His mind drifted in and out as he watched the waitresses and waiters bringing food and clear the tables. He wondered what their lives were like. He wondered if they were as "perfect" as his.

"Andy," a female voice snapped him out of his daze.

"Huh?" Andrew turned his attention to the blonde sitting in front of him. Her blue eyes stared at him, expecting something to come from him. The eyes waiting for words that he had not prepared.

"Were you even listening to me?" The woman's voice hinted at her subtle annoyance.

"Bride's maid's dresses," Andrew took a shot in the dark. The ease of tension on the woman's face was the bell that told him he was right. "Sorry, I was just lost... thinking about... which would look best with your dress."

"So, which one?" The quiz master fired back at him. Andrew cursed in his mind. He had hoped she would have let him slip back into his own mental world.

"Go with purple," Andrew silently prayed to any deity that would listen to help him pull something out of his butt. "That is your favorite color, and it might as well be present if you're going to be wearing white."

"That…" Moment of truth. "Was not something I thought of. Good idea, Andy."

Andrew wished he could have let out a sigh of relief, instead he would have had to settle for wondering which deity he now owed his soul to. He watched his fiancée slip back between the pages of her bridal magazine. That cursed little book that was telling her every way to make their wedding perfect.

"You guys ready to order or do you need a few more minutes?" The waitress, who cordially greeted them with a slight southern drawl, said when she finally came to the table.

"We're ready," The woman set down her reading material. "We're ready, right Andy?"

"Yeah," Andrew picked up his menu and flipped the pages to remind himself of what he wanted to order. No, that wasn't right. What he wanted to order were a burger and fries. A humongous, greasy burger with everything, and fries with nacho cheese and bacon. However, the diet Erin had the two on was supposed to better for their health. Got to walk the future daughter down the aisle was what Andrew was told. He also wanted a beer. A bathtub filled with it to soak in and drink. "Yeah, Erin. I'm ready. I'll have the chicken sandwich and a side salad instead of fries."

"And I'll just have the large Caesar salad. Thanks." Erin smiled as she handed the waitress the menus.

"Drinks, or are the waters fine?" The waitress finished jotting down their order on the little pad.

"Water is perfect," Erin responded for the two of them, and the waitress walked off.

Andrew took note of her. Couldn't have been more than a few years younger than himself; 22 or 23. Not bad on the eyes either. The tight uniform didn't leave much to the imagination on her shape. A supple yet firm behind, thin legs that just made you want to slide your hand across over and over looking for any hairs missed while shaving. What really caught Andrew's eyes was how her soft red hair fell down the side of her neck and into her large cleavage. He shook the thoughts from his mind. He was about to enter the peaceful bliss of holy matrimony. He shouldn't be looking at other women with lust. At least that was what the pastor at the perfect little church where the perfect little wedding was going to take place in, had told him.

It didn't help that's what he was supposed to do. He had to tell himself this, many times over. Go to school, get a good job, get a wife, get a house, get two point five kids, and then die. His parents' generation did it, their parents and so on and so forth. It was just what normal people did.

"I know how hard it must have been," Erin interrupted his train of thought once again. "I saw you looking at the page of alcohol. I'm very proud of you for not ordering one."

"Yeah," Andrew leaned back against the plastic cushioned seat and faked a smile. "It was pretty tempting, but I stayed strong."

"Well, I got a surprise for my big strong man." Erin smiled. Andrew had twenty bucks in his pocket, and he would bet it all that it wasn't a blowjob, or any form of sex, another vice that his future wife didn't want him to have. At least until the wedding night, that is.

Andrew drifted back to watching the waitress do her thing. He envisioned her swaying her hips over to the table, with a savory double bacon, half-pound cheeseburger with all the fixings. She would bend over to place his beer down on his table, and her delectable breasts would almost be in his food because she had left a few too many buttons unbuttoned. As she would put a huge mug of beer in front of him, she would give him a wink, and go underneath the table where she would unzip his pants, look up and him from underneath and seductively say…

"Aren't you going to ask what it is?" Erin snapped her future husband back to reality.

"A blowjob?" Andrew couldn't stop himself. His mouth fired it off before his filter caught it. He quickly went to hoping that deity from before could pull another favor for him.

"Andrew," Erin scolded him quietly. 1 out of 2. Andrew was still getting better odds on prayers answered than with most gods. "There are kids here."

7

"Sorry," A quick look around from Andrew showed that either the parents hadn't heard him or just didn't care. "It just slipped."

"Well," Erin smiled to herself. "You are a recovering potty mouth. Anyway, Daddy wanted you to have these."

Erin reached in her purse and pulled out a ring box. Andrew took it and opened it up. Inside, two cuff-links glimmered. Each one shaped like the emblem of Andrew's favorite superhero, Justice Hammer. A green hammer on a red background looking like a shield. The hammer of justice, shielding the innocent. That was his motto. Andrew had gotten a high five from the hero as a child when he came to speak at Andrew's elementary school. Since then, he would do anything he ever needed to get his hands on the comics which told of the man's exploits.

His eyes grew, and he felt a slight smile escape his lips as he pulled one from the box, to closely examine it. The warm joy of opening a fresh comic from his childhood washed over him.

"Daddy knew you loved reading those comic books and had them made for you. Do you like them?"

"Do I? I love them." Andrew fumbled with the buttons on his white shirt trying to undo them to put on his new cuff-links. Erin promptly snatched the links from him and stashed the velvet box away in her purse.

"Not till the wedding." Erin grinned enormously at the crestfallen stare that Andrew gave her. It was as if a child that just had his new favorite toy taken away.

"I was going to wear them to work," Andrew protested. "Mike would love them."

"To an auto repair shop?" Erin was confused for a second, then let it pass. She leaned in closer. "Well, I have better news. Daddy also told me that he was able to get you a job at the plant. No more working in that dingy mechanic shop. He wants you to be one of the engineers at the auto plant. He even got you a selection ties. Isn't that great? No more tiny apartment for you. With the money you'll be making, we can start looking for a house right away. If we find one we really love, we'll have the keys in time for the wedding!"

"That's great," Andrew smiled. He couldn't tell if it was real or if he was faking it. He found it to be a mixture of both. "But what about Mike? I can't just leave him there alone. It's just the two of us running that shop. Could your dad pull some strings for him too?"

"Andy," Erin's voice became much more somber. "Mike's not really what you would call..."

Chapter 2

"Not office friendly? She really fucking said that shit?" A heavily tattooed bald man, roughly Andrew's age, sat across from him in the dim lit bar. "She sucks. Doesn't she suck? I told you she sucks. Tell me you told her to fuck off."

"I haven't…" Andrew started.

"It's the fucking cuff-links," Mike slammed an open palm on the table then leaned forward to his friend. "The bitch can't give you head, but she can give you some fucking cuff-links and you just melt right into her. I'll tell you what; I can do better than cuff-links. You can have my virgin asshole… ok, semi-virgin asshole. There was that stint in county…"

"Shut the fuck up," Andrew laughed as he sipped on his soda. "I don't want your semi-virgin asshole."

"Not good enough for you?"

"No, no, your asshole is just fine. A little used but still good." Andrew reassured him.

"Damn straight it is. So, what did you tell her about the job?" Mike downed half of his beer in one drink.

"I haven't said anything," Andrew informed his friend. "I just agreed to sit down and talk with her father about it and see where it goes from there."

"You're serious," Mike leaned back in his seat in the booth. "You are actually serious."

"It's just to talk," Andrew assured him. "It's just that with all the changes, the uptake in money might be good?"

"Yeah," Mike smiled. "I see your point. House, kids, retirement fund, all that shit. Got to look after yourself and the missus."

"Yeah," Andrew looked down at his beer. "Got to look after my future family. Responsibilities, all that jazz."

"Means you got to suck some old, fat, guy dick," Mike flicked his lip ring with his tongue. "Take it if you want. Shit's not for me. I ain't sucking no old guy dick. I don't care how stable it makes me. I'll eat instant noodles and the neighbor's cat my whole life if I have to. Hell, I'll even suck dick on the corner, but I ain't gonna suck dick."

"How many have you had?" Andrew questioned. Normally a field of glasses would have been between the two of them, but Mike insisted on buying the drinks tonight, and kept returning the glasses as they finished. "The fake homosexuality usually doesn't come out until you have a good buzz going."

"Long past that point, buddy," Mike smirked and raised his glass to his lips, finishing another. "I hit that point about the time I started having the bartender add a shot of whiskey to your little sodie pops."

"And that's why I love you, brother." Andrew grinned and raised his glass in a cheer. Andrew had tasted the booze in the drink on the first one and knew what his friend was doing. Now the buzz of drunkenness had slowly begun to take its hold and there was no point in stopping now.

"Hey," Mike clinked his glass. "You needed a fucking drink. When you're telling me about fantasizing about waitresses and the first thing you think about is a beer and not getting head, you need a fucking drink."

"Got to say," Andrew stared down at his glass, before finishing it. "I miss this shit."

"Easy way to fix that," Mike just put the glasses on the side of the table so he could finish his thought before getting another round. "Tell her to fuck off. No, tell her to suck you off, then you tell her to fuck off."

"You know what she said when I suggested that one time?" Andrew got a small chuckle. "Sucking dick is too degrading."

"You know a lot of our conversation has had to do with dicks and the sucking of them." Mike stood up and went to the bar. He returned with two pints of beer and slid one to Andrew. He almost downed the whole thing in one tip of the glass. The allure made him too eager to even taste it.

"God damn," Andrew wiped the head off his lips with the sleeve of his shirt. "That is so much fucking better."

"You're damn right it is," Mike reached across the table and clapped Andrew on the shoulder. "Cause now you're acting like a fucking man. Fuck that controlling Jesus freak."

"Can't," Andrew laughed and made a masturbating gesture with his hand. "That's why I keep chaffing my cock."

"Fuck that bitch," Mike laughed. "I mean, seriously, fucking is awesome."

"Ain't that the truth." Andrew finished off his pint while Mike had barely touched his.

"Seriously though," Mike crossed his arms and leaned back in his seat. "I am not about to tell you what to do and how to live your life, but have you ever even thought about not going through with it? Think about it. Here you are, about to go and get married to this little sweetheart, and then that's it. End of the story. Have a few kids, go to some shitty kid recitals. Fucking die. I mean, you know what you used to tell me?"

"What'd I used to tell you?" The lack of tolerance and the copious amounts of alcohol had now really started to hit Andrew.

"Mikey, you used to say," Mike pointed at his friend with his forefinger and his thumb straight up. "Don't you ever let me get boring. Fucking shoot me before I get boring."

"Yet here I am," Andrew's tone began to get somber. "I'm about to get boring, aren't I?"

"Bang." Mike dropped his thumb hammer. Silence fell over the two drunken friends.

"I don't want to do this." Andrew finally broke the silence.

12

"You ain't gotta." Mike again reached over the table in front of them and put his hand on his friend's shoulder.

"Yeah," Andrew agreed. "Now how do I tell Erin that?"

"I'll do it," Mike jumped at the chance. "Give some money for the payphone. I'll do it."

"As much as I would love to see that," Andrew laughed breaking his somber mood. "That is not going to happen. I got to tell her."

"Ok," Mike began digging in his pockets for change. "I'll even pay for it."

"Put that shit away," Andrew waved his empty glass to wave away the offer. "I mean when I'm sober."

"Or better yet," Mike smiled. "Pick up a girl here take her home. I'll snap some pictures and drop them off at her place. *'Look what I caught Andrew doing last night.'* **'Why is he thumbs-upping the camera? Is that your hand giving him one back**?' *'Why no, Erin, not at all.'* Come on, it'll be awesome. Dude, you can even make it an Asian chick. You know how you've always wanted to bang one of them."

"Nah," Andrew began to stand up. Placing his arms on the booth seat to try and hide his slight stagger; he began to head to the door. "I'll just call her when I sober up. Take her out and explain everything to her. Not much more to do. I got to get some rest if I'm going to do it. I'll catch you at the shop tomorrow."

"Go home," Mike stood as well and wrapped his arms around Andrew and hugged him. "Get some rest and think about it all. Jerk off, call her, and do what you got to do."

"Why jerk off?" Andrew laughed.

"Never make a decision about a woman with your balls full," Mike smiled. "Now go home and get some sleep, brother. And remember, I only tell you this shit because I love you, you fucker."

"Yeah," Andrew smiled nodding. "And that's the only reason I listen."

13

<u>Chapter 3</u>

The city of New Hancock was usually pretty hit and miss for its size when it came to safe walks home at night. Street gangs rarely prowled the streets, due to a large mafia presence that kept them at bay. So, the chance of a drunken college student, or in this case, a drunken auto mechanic named Andrew, getting mugged were slim to none.

Andrew's apartment was a short jaunt from his favorite watering hole. He patted the pocket of his pants to find the key in the front door. After locating them, he tried in vain to figure out which was the right key for the lock. In frustration, he threw the metallic bundle to the ground and enjoyed it jingle out in pain.

"Damn right," He scolded the keys. "Remember who is the boss. I'm the boss! You know that TV show? Yeah, the answer was me. Fuck, I'm rambling. I am rambling at keys."

Andrew reached down and grabbed the disobedient keys. In his mind, they were now fearing for their lives. He realized that they must have responded to negative reinforcement as he found the correct key right away. After a few flights of stairs up he knew the keys were still feeling the hurt as they coughed up the correct key again.

The door to his apartment creaked open and he tossed the keys to what he thought was a table by the door, but with a combination of too much to drink and the darkness, the keys only found the floor.

The sound of the keys hitting the floor was responded to by the sound of four sets of toenails tapping on the hardwood floor, getting closer and closer to him. Andrew reached down and found a soft furry head, which he eagerly took in his hands and began to rub vigorously.

"Hey, Shithead," The owner sat down on the floor to allow his dog to begin lavishing him with loving licks. "You hold down the fort while I was gone?"

A simple bark gave him his answer. Andrew took off the brown jacket he had been wearing and tossed it to the ground. He clicked on the light to reveal a blue studio apartment. A simple couch, facing a small TV sitting on a milk crate sat in the middle of the room, along with a bookshelf pressed up against one wall.

Andrew walked into the bedroom where a mattress lay on the floor with a sheet and some pillows and blankets on it. The blankets were in a jumble as a four-legged friend had decided to rearrange them to make a nest.

The medicine cabinet in the bathroom gave Andrew a good look at himself, as he began to urinate into the grimy toilet. He hated to say it, but he always felt so plain. Brown hair, brown eyes, nothing that really stood out about him. No chiseled good looks, no ugly scar. Maybe a new haircut, maybe that would spruce things up. He zipped himself up after a few shakes and took a moment to appreciate the piece of "art" he had hung in the bedroom. He had placed it there as he felt the wall looked boring after Erin had told him to take the bikini model poster down.

Andrew found his way to the bookcase that was a little bit taller than him, but nothing was sorted out of his reach. He reached for an old looking book on the shelf; something written by H.P. Lovecraft, his favorite author. He staggered his way over to the couch and set the book down.

Next to the dingy, stained, and checkered couch sat a box of tissues and some hand lotion. Andrew began to reach for them and stopped. He looked down at his hands, he looked around at the small apartment. Was this really what he wanted to do with his life? Sit in a small apartment, and jerk off to the same porno tapes until

15

his wedding day? Then have some shitty kids, and go to a shitty recital, then just die?

Or did he want the other path? A path of uncertainty. A path where instant noodles were cheaper than regular food on the salary of a guy who worked in a failing auto mechanic shop with his best friend? Did he want to live a life with no plan, and almost assuredly no future? Or was there another way?

He wasn't sure what made him grab that book. He wasn't sure exactly what made him open it. He wasn't even sure why he had hollowed it out in the first place. He still didn't know why he had hidden a gun in the book. Why he had pulled it out and loaded the gun was eluding him too. Was it the booze? Was it the thoughts of not being able to escape his current situation? It was alright though because the deafening sound of gunfire against his skull brought on a blackness that silenced all the questions in the end.

Chapter 4

"You got to shake the shit out him," Andrew heard a familiar voice. "Like his ass has a bad hangover."

Was this Hell? Darkness enveloped Andrew. No matter how hard he opened his eyes he could not see anything. However, he felt something press on them and they burned unless he closed them. Something warm held his body tightly on to whatever it was that he was laying on. It was soft and actually kind of comfortable. This was probably the waiting room before all the torture, or maybe the splitting migraine he had was the torture.

Then, without warning two hands grabbed Andrew's shoulders and with violent force shook him hard enough to rattle every bone in his body.

"Wake the fuck up," That voice from before shouted at him. "Wake up, you stupid mother fucker. Wake up, wake up, wake up!"

"Get back, you demonic piece of shit!" Andrew used what strength he could muster and threw his hands at whatever attacker was ready to drag him off to probably be flossed with a piece of smoldering barbed wire. "I've been in a church recently! I'm good!"

"Holy Father!" Another familiar voice filled Andrew's ears. "That…that actually worked."

"You just got to know how to work him," Mike. That was Mike's voice. "Didn't you get the instruction manual? Some girlfriend you are."

"I'll go get the nurse." Andrew could hear Erin's footsteps rush out of the room.

"Tell her to bring me a fucking lab coat. I know more than that dumbass doctor about waking a coma patient," Mike shouted as Andrew felt him sit down on the edge of the bed. "Morning fuckface. How was your nap?"

"Nap?" Andrew tried to sit up in bed but found that his arms no longer had the strength. He felt his friend twist and help him lie back down. Then with a small motor noise, the back of the bed began to set him up.

"Yeah," Mike affirmed as he made Andrew comfortable. "You've been out for about three days."

"Where am I?" Andrew tried to turn towards the sound of his friend but found that this exasperated the pain in the side of his skull. The violent pounding was almost more than he could bear.

"Saint's Pass Hospital," Mike moved back in front of the bed. "Where else should we take someone that tried to kill himself?"

"I thought I was in Hell." Andrew, with great difficulty, felt his face and found that the thing burning his eyes was a ton of bandage covering the top half of his head.

"Wouldn't touch that if I were you." A new female voice entered the room. Andrew guessed that this was the nurse.

"You forgot my lab coat," Mike pointed out the omission, "Don't give me that look, Erin. I'm sure your daddy could afford for them to put that on the bill too."

"How do you feel, Mr. Mullen?" The nurse began to check him over.

"Like I've been hit by a freight train," Andrew began to convey his pain. "Right in the side of my head."

"More like a 9mm round," The nurse gave him a better idea. "You're lucky whoever made it forgot to put a bullet in it."

"I know," Erin chimed in. "We're all very lucky. God was looking after you, Andy."

18

"Very, very, minimal damage," The nurse informed him. "Bad burn mark on the side of your head. Other than that, nothing physically wrong with you."

"Then what are the bandages for?" Andrew wondered aloud.

"Like I said," The nurse slowly began to peel them back. "Bad burn mark. I need to take a look at it. Try too slowly open your eyes after I take the bandages off."

White blinding pain was all that Andrew could see when he could finally open his eyes. After a few attempts, his eyes adjusted to the light and the white antiseptic look of a hospital. His fiancé, an older Philippino nurse, and his friend seated in a chair, with a very stern look on his face, greeted him back into the land of the living.

"See?" The nurse used a small mirror to show Andrew the burn mark on his head. A large red mark where hair should be behind his ear. "No broken skull, just that burn mark."

"I did a number on myself, huh?" Andrew reached to touch it but thought better of that idea. It hurt enough and touching a wound like that would only make it hurt worse. "Three days?"

"Shithead was laying right next to you when I found you," Mike spoke up.

"You found me?" Andrew inquired as the nurse began to put some sort of ointment on the side of his head.

"You didn't show up for work," Mike leaned back in the only chair in the room. "Came to check up on you, see if your hangover made you oversleep…"

"Hangover?" Erin interjected. "You were drinking?"

"Take your panties off and get them out of the twist," Mike snapped at her. "He needed a drink, so I spiked his pops. Back to what I was saying before I was interrupted. Your door wasn't locked, and I found you on the couch slumped over, gun in your hand. So, I called for a paramedic and when they found you alive, they rushed you here."

"Should have told them to leave me," Andrew laughed. "I ain't got the insurance for this. Might have to try again to get out of it." The room was silent.

19

"Daddy said he was going to pay for your entire stay," Erin informed Andrew.

"Awesome," Andrew enjoyed that feeling of relief. "So once the doctor checks me out, I can head home."

"Afraid not," The nurse told him. "You're going to be under psychiatric evaluation and be moved to the mental ward after the doctor determines you're safe to move."

"Right," Andrew thought to protest but knew that was useless. "The whole suicide thing."

"Yeah," Mike pipped up. "The whole suicide thing."

"In fact," The nurse finished reapplying a fresh bandage on his head. "I'm going to go get him now."

"I'm going to go call Daddy and let him know you're awake," Erin walked over and kissed her man on the head. "Also, I called the pastor. He said he is going to come visit you too. I really think you need the Lord right now."

"I better have a lab coat when you two come back," Mike ordered them. "And take your time. I want to have a quick word with Andy here."

The two women left the men alone. Mike calmly stood up and closed the door and locked it. Without a word, he walked over to his friend sitting up in the bed. The lack of emotion hid any intentions Mike had for his friend.

"Where is your burn?" Mike looked closer at the large bandage over the side of Andrew's head, and pointed to the spot where the burn mark was. "Right here?"

"Yeah," Andrew started to get a little nervous. "Right under the bandage."

A quick slap came across the side of his head, right on top of the wound. Then another, and another. Pap! Pap! Pap! Each hard slap against his head shot a lightning bolt of agony all over Andrew's body.

"You stupid mother fucker!" Mike continued to slap the side of Andrew's head even after the injured man tried to protect his vulnerability. "Do you have any idea the shit that went through my head when I thought I found your dead body? Any fucking clue? No, you don't cause you were knocked the fuck out. I thought your dog was having a snack on your god damn stupid brain, you dumb mother fucker!"

"I honestly don't know what came over me," Andrew finally got out when the slapping stopped. "Last thing I remember was thinking about jerking off and then bam!"

"You know what the worst part of this?" Mike glared at his closest friend. "I had to sit, in a room, with her, alone, no booze, for three days. You know what we talked about? For those three days? Your wedding plans, the names of your future children, and Jesus. The bitch tried to convert me for three whole days. So, you know what? Aside from the initial burst right there, I'm not too pissed at your dumb ass."

"Thanks." Was all Andrew was able to work out between the throbs in his skull.

"Oh no, I understood. I understood all too well. However, here is the thing. I learned how you deal with her. You drown her out and stare at her tits, or at least that is how I had to do it. So, while I'm staring at your future fun bags, I was able to think. Do you know what I thought about?" Mike got in his friend's face.

"Banging her?" Andrew joked.

Mike did not respond. Without looking, he reached into his pocket and pulled something out. A small metal object clinked on a table at the bedside as he opened his hand, palm down. Slowly, he moved his hand back and underneath was a small metal disk that almost looked like a metal flower, which save for a few black marks, the "stem" was untouched. After a second of looking at it, Andrew realized what it was. A spent bullet.

"The nurse didn't tell you the truth, because she didn't know the truth," Mike informed his friend. "There was a bullet in the gun. I found it jammed in the end. The bullet went off, something stopped it. What stopped that bullet, Andy?"

"What the...?" Andrew spun the bullet around in his fingers examining it.

"That's what I would like to know," Mike took the bullet from Andrew and put it back in his pocket. "How did you stop that bullet?"

A small knock came from the door. Mike turned and unlocked the door.

"You two done having a chat?" The doctor asked as Mike opened the door. "I can give you a few more minutes."

"You got my lab coat?" Mike asked unlocking the door.

"Right here," The doctor lifted a white coat. "You woke him, seems like a small price."

Mike took the lab coat, put it on and sat back in the chair. The doctor did many of the same things that the nurse did, but Andrew couldn't keep his mind on the physical tests. The throbbing pain of Mike smacking him in the wound was replaced by a surreal sense of curiosity. How did he survive? How did he stop that bullet? The projectile obviously hit the target, and there was nothing in the gun that could have stopped the bullet. How was he still alive?

"Well, Mr. Mullen," The doctor put his stethoscope around his neck in a very cliché fashion. "Physically, aside from the burn mark, you're fine. I'm going to leave you in here for the rest of the night and make sure that you are good to go, and in the morning we will move you over to the psyche ward."

"Thanks, Doc," Andrew shook the man's hand. "For all your help."

"Hey," Mike interrupted but was ignored, "who's wearing the lab coat?"

"Not a problem," The doctor started to head towards the door. "Hopefully the fine people over in there can help you move past whatever it is that put you in that dark place."

"Yeah," Andrew nodded. "I hope they can."

"You spaced out there," Mike pointed out after the doctor exited. "You good?"

"Yeah," Andrew leaned back. "Just a lot on my mind about all this. I need a drink."

"Even Jesus had a drink now and then," An older but jovial voice came into the room. It was the pastor that Andrew had been seeing to get ready for this wedding. "But it might mix poorly with any pain medication you are on."

No words were said. Andrew just nodded at Mike. Mike nodded back.

22

"Hey, Padre," Mike stood and walked up to the man of God, "Can I talk to you outside? I just want to go over a few things about seeing Andrew. Doctor's orders and all that."

"Sure." The pastor turned towards the door. As soon as he crossed the threshold Mike closed and locked the door.

"Thank you," Andrew smiled. "The last thing I need is to be read scripture, and being told how what I did was fucked up, and I'm going to Hell for it."

"Nope," Mike said and pulled a chair up next to the bed, and took the remote for the TV from the side table. "The only thing we need to hear about right now how two cartoon teenagers plan to score this week."

Mike held out his fist and Andrew tapped his fist to it, as the laughter of the two aforementioned teenagers filled the silence in the room.

<u>Chapter 5</u>

The psychiatric ward was not anywhere near as bad as Andrew had dreaded it to be. TV, three square meals a day, a bunch of board games with other people going through the same thing he was. Days were filled with sessions with the therapist, both group, and individual.

It was the individual sessions that were always a struggle. Andrew had no idea how to explain to the doctor that he had no idea why he did it. He did have the basic idea of what was wrong. However, he felt that the doctor thought he was just trying to say whatever he needed to get himself released. Andrew just kept explaining that he was tired of being boring and he that felt he was stuck in a hopelessness situation. He didn't want the path of a seemingly mundane suburban life. He also found no hope in barely surviving as he was. He just couldn't live with either of the paths placed in front of him.

It was in the group sessions that he felt he was able to start putting things together. He was able to look past the few paths that he had before him. He found that he wasn't as much of a loser as he thought. He found many people in awe at some of the adventurous stories that he told about himself and Mike. Bar fights, Mike tripping on too much acid while the two of them were running from the police. Even about the time that he had banged a woman at a concert in the portable toilet and the bout of gonorrhea that came with it. The individual sessions, however, those were the real killer.

"Do you love her?" The doctor scribbled hastily as he patiently waited for Andrew to answer him.

The doctor never made the patients go to his office for these discussions. They sat in Andrews small room. It was nicely furnished with a TV, a small writing desk, and a chair. The window let him look out into the courtyard where a beautiful garden of various flowers and plants grew. Andrew stood there now, at the window, with his arms crossed in the hospital scrubs they had given him. He wasn't sure if it was for comfort, safety or to identify him as a patient, but they did their job so he didn't really care.

"I do." Andrew stared out the window. His mind began to wander. "I mean, she seems like everything any guy could ever want."

"But is that what you want?" The doctor retorted. This was the question that always had Andrew lost.

"I'm not sure. I'm not sure what I want anymore," Andrew sat back down and buried his face in his hands. "She was great when we first met. She pulled into the garage, her car was broken and she needed help. I figured she looked good enough and she didn't have the cash on her to fix the car right there. I figured, I'd take care of her. Have a quick fuck for thanks. That would be the end of it."

"But that's not what happened is it?" The doctor set down his notes. It was almost as if this story had nothing to do with what was wrong with Andrew, or maybe it had everything to do with it. Andrew wasn't sure what the doctor was thinking but hoped talking it out would help him begin to put things into perspective.

"No," Andrew laughed. "Not at all. Took her out, she threw this Jesus crap at me. Asked me to go to church with her. One thing led to another, and I had a girlfriend. A girlfriend that would barely kiss me."

"That seems almost out of character based on the stories you told in the group." The doctor kept prodding. Andrew hoped that the doctor fully knew what he was doing, and that making him question his relationship was going to cure him.

25

"Yeah," Andrew got silent. "I mean it wasn't like I was really that faithful to her, or committed, at first, but the more I kept hearing those sermons and the more I kept seeing her, it was like all that wholesomeness just gobbled me up. Like I wanted to be good for her."

"Tell me, Andrew," The doctor picked his notebook back up. "You keep talking about all these things going on, and how they are for other people. But the question still remains. What do you want? You requested no visitors. You've been here, locking yourself away from friends and family. You've really had time to think about you. What is it you want? Do you still want to be that good person for her?"

"That just seems so boring," Andrew finally relented. "I got to admit, I miss the old days. Those days, doc, those days made me happy."

"The stories you tell the group certainly seem that way," The doctor took a few notes as he continued to listen. "So tell me, why are you doing what you're doing?"

"It's perfect," Andrew pondered to himself if that was the answer. "There is no risk, no real reward. Just a way to coast on through."

"You don't like that coasting, do you?" The doctor smiled, finally realizing his client had started to come to the point of understanding his problems.

"That's the crazy thing," Andrew chuckled to himself. "Part of me does. Part of me wants to just put life on autopilot. Feel like a bit of a big shot, and sit comfortably right there in the middle class. Then again, the other part of me put a gun to my head to stop all that."

"Hmm," the doctor closed his book and began to head to the door. "I see you have made quite a bit of progress. There is still more work to do. Then, it's all on you to figure out what you want. I think the talk therapy is helping. Maybe we can even release you soon and move on to clinical work."

"Sounds good," Andrew shook the doctor's hand as he left. "I kind of miss the outside world."

"I bet you do." The doctor took his leave at that.

Night time had slowly begun to overtake the day as Andrew reclined on the bed in his room and watched two drag queens fight it out on a talk show. They would be ripped apart from each other only to go back at each other swinging. He thought back to the bar fights he bragged about to the group. He hadn't had a good fight in a while. Andrew did also admit to himself that he missed the pride he felt in the morning having knocked some loud mouth frat boy's teeth out.

He fondly reminisced about the guessing game in the morning from some nights. Trying in vain to remember who was lying next to him, and why he hadn't called them a cab that night. He even found a soft spot in his heart for the little crabs he would occasionally have to shave and shampoo out of his crotch. He smiled at remembering how Mike would name them whenever he would start scratching in public.

Andrew realized that he could instead lead a very, very comfortable life. A luxurious life, with a wife, a house, his dog, and a cozy office job. No more fights, not more crotch critters. The cost was high, but he also felt he deserved that kind of life. No more struggling with bills, no more being so broke that it was either eat or go drinking, and then choosing both through dumpster diving. These thoughts filled his mind, as he slowly drifted off to sleep.

Chapter 6

Too loud! Andrew threw his hand at the TV in vain, as it was still attached to his arm. The television's volume that had been perfect for him to drift off to sleep, but had become way too loud to allow him to sleep.

He reached out, hoping some force of nature would respond and give him mental powers and turn the TV off without getting out of bed. To his shock, this time nature responded.

It was a slight tingle from up by his right shoulder. It wasn't pleasant; however, it wasn't painful. It was warm. Almost like the feeling of blood sliding down his arm to his hand. Andrew could make out a small object in the dim light cast by the TV. His concentration now on the odd, snake-like object that had made his way down to his fingers. It was obvious he had now stopped worrying about the television.

"What the fuck?" Andrew figured he would have freaked out more, had he been more awake, but the drunken half-sleep had dulled his sense of panic.

Sitting up in his bed, he gently reached over and touched the object. It was dry and slightly rough. What amazed him the most, was that he could feel his fingers touching it. He could feel what the tentacle, for lack of a better word, could feel. He followed

28

it up his shoulder and found that it was, in fact, attached to his shoulder. No, more like it had grown out of his shoulder.

Andrew stood up and slowly walked to turn on the light. The color was a sickly mix of brown and green. Not unlike, he noted, many of the poops he had taken in his life. The tentacle was, in fact, that length of his arm, but no wider than it. Sliding a hand under the new appendage, he found he could feel his own skin under it, and that it had caused no damage to his arm. Checking his shoulder would be the next best thing he thought.

Andrew gently took his scrub top off and watched as the tentacle quickly retreated back into his shoulder, and his skin closed as if nothing had been there. Thinking he frightened the tentacle, Andrew quickly threw his shirt back on and shut out the light. He repeated his actions from last time, he held out his arm and focused just on reaching. Sure enough, the tingling came first, then the sensation of the tentacle sliding down his arm and it was back.

Andrew's mind slowly began to put things together and realized he was controlling the growth. Naturally, he wondered if he could move it. This time, he focused not on reaching but on moving it to the left. His guess was right, the tentacle moved to the left. It felt not unlike moving a finger, or his arm. It moved as if it was a part of him like it had always been there. He then moved it right.

Now to deal with that damn TV. He reached out and the tentacle extended rapidly when Andrew focused on it growing. Then he forced it to slow down in the same manner as he made it approach the TV. He felt around with the tip, he was nowhere near accurate, but eventually found the power button. Just like moving a finger, he felt himself curl the tip and give the button a gentle push, and the TV went off.

He smiled as he learned he could curl it, and by the moonlight in the room, found a pen and picked it up. He retracted the tentacle and brought the pen to himself and placed it in the hand on the side of the tentacle.

Andrew had no idea what to think. He had no thoughts in his mind as this new appendage appeared on his body. The only thought he could manage was that he wanted to see if he could have two, and after repeating the action of the right arm on the left, he found that he could have two of the writhing things.

If there is one thing that man is good at, Andrew pondered if he was still, in fact, a man, is greed. As he learned to work them, he wanted more. Focusing, he found that he could grow more and more tentacles, with more and more concentration. Each new one coming from his shoulder areas, until his arms were hidden; they had been replaced with writhing squirming tentacles, each one independently controlled like it was just another finger. He also found that this had started to give him a headache. A small one at three tentacles, but as more appeared it grew worse and worse.

But a headache wasn't much to contend with the adrenaline that had begun flowing through his system at this point. Andrew's immature side decided to take over as he pulled back the arm tentacles and found that he could grow them on his chest and down his legs. Anywhere he had clothes on. He grinned as he felt one grow above his penis and he wiggled it around like he had an erection.

He retracted all the tentacles he had made, and the headache quickly subsided. He wasn't sure what they were. He wasn't sure where they came from, or what their purpose even was. Yet he was sure of one immensely important thing; Andrew Mullen was no longer boring.

Chapter 7

"Well," Mike's voice had a slight bit of cheer in it as he opened the door to his apartment. "Look what finally got out of the loony bin. Shithead! Look who's here."

A flurry of fur and barking came as the black lab rushed out the door and greeted his master. Doggy kisses and tail wags were enough to make Andrew drop to his knees and start returning the love to his old friend.

"He wasn't too much of a pain in the ass was he?" Andrew stepped into the doorway to Mike's place. The apartment was actually much more immaculate than one would imagine upon meeting Mike.

It was a one-bedroom apartment with an extremely comfortable sectional in the living room. It sat facing a huge TV with the latest 32-bit gaming console hooked up to it. Currently, a guy in a white gi was facing off with a one eye'd muay thai boxer, both paused mid punch.

"Nah," Mike walked out of the kitchen with two beers and motioned for Andrew to take a seat. "He's a good dog. Dumber than fuck, but a good dog."

"Cool," Andrew took one and downed it. "Dear god, I missed that shit."

"Got your mail too," Mike handed him the pile which Andrew just set on the table. "Erin's been up my ass trying to see if I can get her in that joint to see you."

"You tell her to fuck off?" Andrew leaned back in his seat.

"Told her to suck me off and then fuck off." Mike joked.

"Wasting your time," Andrew began to pet the dog that would not stop shoving himself closer and closer to his master. "Too degrading."

"So, they clean out that noggin of yours?" Mike finished off his beer.

"No," Andrew shook his head. "But gave me the tools to get it cleared out myself. Even then got to see a therapist."

"Cool," Mike stood to get more beer for the two of them. Andrew stood and followed behind him without him noticing. As Mike reached in the fridge, Andrew extended a tentacle and grabbed the bottle opener with it. Mike turned to reach for the bottle opener to be greeted by the tentacle trying to hand it to him. "Jesus Christ!"

Andrew had never felt pain like what he was experiencing now, before. He had been punched in the face and had had his nose broken. He had broken bones, slashed his leg open in a mosh pit on a broken beer bottle, and scrapped his knee falling off his bike. He had never in his years felt the searing pain of when Mike slammed a beer bottle on top of his tentacle and the tried to stab it with the broken end, repeatedly. Even as the bottle just kept breaking more and becoming sharper against the appendage, Mike continued to stab.

Andrew howled as he rolled on the floor clutching his tentacle, trying fruitlessly to protect it. Mike, looking to protect his friend, continued to attack. Climbing on top of Andrew, Mike had grabbed it and pinned it to the floor with his knee continuing to stab. When the bottle finally broke, Mike reached up and grabbed a butcher knife from the block on the table. This second of clarity was all Andrew needed to pull the tentacle back into his body.

"Where'd it go?" Mike started to look around the room, knife in hand.

"Back in me," Andrew screamed out, "You fucking asshole."

"Back in you?" Mike's eyebrow shot up in confusion. "The fuck you mean?"

"I grew it." After the tentacle receded the pain started to fade rather quickly with it.

"The fuck you mean?" Mike was still confused.

"That tentacle grew out of me." Andrew tried to explain.

"The fuck you mean?" Mike repeated as he helped his friend to his feet and began to clean up the beer and broken glass.

Andrew told the story of how he discovered the ability to grow the tentacles, and even began to show them off by grabbing two beers from the fridge and opened them. Andrew even showed that he was able to lift himself off the ground and use the ones coming from his legs as stilts and walk around the room. Mike sat there speechless.

"Can you fuck with them?" Mike finally spoke up.

"Is the only thing you think about your dick?" Andrew laughed.

"Dude," For the first time in Andrew's life, he waited as his friend tried to hunt for words. "Honestly, I'm a little in shock right now. Mother fucker I knew forever and a day just walked into my place and told me he can become a living hentai film. I tried to stab the shit out of it. I have no idea what that fucking thing is, but I know Japanese animated porn. So, that is exactly what my brain went with."

"It's cool," Andrew waved it off. "What I'm amazed by is the fact that you just beat the shit out of it and stabbed it with a broken beer bottle, and it didn't break the surface."

"I was going to use a knife," Mike informed him.

"Yeah," Andrew looked at his friend. They say that great minds think alike. Andrew didn't know if it was the adrenaline from the struggle or the beers he had downed while telling the story, but he had an idea. "Get that knife and a couple joints."

"You sure about this?" Mike asked his eyes beginning to go bloodshot after finishing the marijuana. Andrew slid one of his tentacles on the counter. Mike gripped the knife by both hands and poked the tip of the knife against the slab of living meat on the counter. The tentacle twitched a little bit, perhaps in anticipation.

Then Mike pulled the knife above his head and began to swing down.

"WAIT!" Andrew stopped him. "Get a towel. I don't know what's in this thing, but it might make a mess."

"Good thinking," Mike put a towel down and Andrew laid it on the towel. "One, two, three!"

Mike brought the knife down and pulled up a bent knife. He shrugged his shoulders and tossed the knife away. He checked to make sure Andrew was ok, who was so high he was just this side of passing out. Andrew nodded as he gritted his teeth. There was no damage to the tentacle. Mike left the room and came back with a hammer and proceeded to repeat the experiment. The hammer at least stayed together, but there was still no sign of damage to the appendage, just the look of dulled pain on Andrew's face.

"You said that you were able to only pull this thing out from anywhere your clothes touched, right?" Mike pondered. "That means basically anything on you that light isn't touching."

"Where are you going with this?" Andrew wondered.

"I got one more test I want to run." Mike left the kitchen and returned with a 9mm handgun.

"Aren't your neighbors going to call the cops if you start firing that thing?" Andrew started to get a little nervous at the firearm.

"Did you hear a gun go off?" Mike asked.

"Nope," Andrew sighed and braced himself. He then pulled the hood on his sweatshirt over his face, hiding it. "Go for it."

Mike took aim at the object on his table and pulled the trigger. The firearm clicked empty. Mike sighed and walked back out and returned with ammo. He loaded the gun and aimed one more time. With a loud crack, the weapon went off. Andrew's tentacle shot pain through it, but so did his face. Right by his left cheek.

"Dude," Mike stared at Andrew.

"What?" A muffled pained voice squeaked out of Andrew.

"That is creepy as fuck." Mike's voice betrayed the awe that he was trying to hide.

"What?" Andrew withdrew his third arm.

"Your face is all tentacle-y. Like covered with them. Like a mask of tentacles." Mike grabbed a nearby pan and used it as a mirror to show Andrew.

The face that looked back was so foreign, so alien, so eldritch. A writhing mass of small tentacles had erupted from his face. It looked as if worms had broken through his skin and covered the rest of his face. Even his eyes had disappeared into the mass as even smaller ones came from under his eyelids and left only small holes for his pupils. With but a thought, Andrew was able to retract them all with only minor irritation to his eyes. A small metal object bounced on the ground. Then after a moment of concentration, Andrew was able to extend them all again. He even found that he had just as much control over the ones on his face as the ones on the rest of his body.

"You thinking what I'm thinking?" Mike asked softly.

"Shoot me in the face." Andrew didn't even hesitate. He knew that this might be the answer to why he survived, and it was time to find out.

The sight of a gun barrel aiming at his face, and the sound of the weapon going off were two things in Andrew's life he was certain he was never ready for.

"Answers that question." Mike shrugged as he took the magazine from the firearm, walked into the living room and dropped the weapon on the table.

"I haven't got a clue how to feel about the fact that you didn't even hesitate." Andrew held a bag of ice to his face to help stem the pain where Mike didn't just fire once but instead emptied the magazine into Andrew's jaw.

"Eh," Mike shrugged. "Got to go to jail for something. Murder one seems as good as anything else. Besides, would you want anyone else to shoot you in the face to test your new superpower?"

"Come again?" Andrew cocked an eyebrow.

"Dude," Mike continued not even looking at Andrew. "You got magical, indestructible tentacles coming out of you. You have a mother fucking superpower. Like that Justice Hammer guy you cream yourself over or something."

"You're saying I can become a superhero?" Andrew's mind began running with images of him fighting off galactic threats, traveling afar with the team of superheroes known as The League. Dreams he had had since he was old enough to read.

"We both know you're too lazy for that, or not. The fuck do I know?" Mike popped open another drink and unpaused his game. "On the other side of the matter, you figure out what you are going to do about the Erin situation?"

"I think we need a break," Andrew shrugged. Being away from what he felt was making him the most boring person he had ever met, might do wonders for his life. "I just got to man up and tell her. Find a way to let her down gently."

"Do like I've always said. Have her suck your dick then as you are about to blow your load, tell her." Both chuckled at Mike's idea.

"You're an evil mother fucker," Andrew smiled. For the first time since being released from the mental asylum. He smiled, not the make-the-doctor-feel-better smile or even smiling because he felt he HAD to. He genuinely smiled. That man may not be blood, he thought, but that was his brother. "Got to be a little more tactful than that."

"Eh, you do you," Mike stood up after his friend. "Anyway, if you need a place to hide after she tries to stab you repeatedly." Mike gestured to the apartment.

"I dunno," Andrew headed to the door. "These tentacles seem pretty indestructible. Good way to test them."

Chapter 8

Even when Andrew first started dating Erin, he felt uncomfortable coming to the more affluent side of town. It always appeared sterile, and immaculate. Immaculate yards, kept up by hired lawn care services, surrounded by sterile houses where nothing ever goes wrong. All of it just how the home owner's association wanted it. To Andrew, it was always so unwelcoming.

The Hastings family did the best they could however to accommodate the love of their daughter's life. Inviting him to parties. Smoking cigars and drinking scotch out in the gazebo while talking about their latest stock options or other mundane topics. All topics Andrew had no idea about, and they only served to make him feel further out of place. He wasn't going to miss this one bit.

Andrew pulled his beat-up car along the curb behind an equally dilapidated car outside of one of the homes. Making his way up the lawn he tried to remember everything he was going to tell Erin. He had figured it out to the best of his ability on the ride over. He was going to tell her that he needed some time to figure himself out and that bringing her along for that ride wasn't fair to her. He didn't want to drag her along and then find that starting over without her wouldn't be right.

Adjusting the way he looked, Andrew rapped on the door. He could hear movement inside, so he knew the house was occupied, but no answer came to the door. So, he knocked his knuckles against the door a second time, much harder this time. This time he heard the footsteps come closer to the door. The door unlocked and a woman with blonde hair and blue eyes, like Erin would look in roughly 20 years, opened the door.

"Andrew!" Erin's mother greeted him warmly, with a light hug.

"Hi, Mrs. Hastings, is Erin home?" Andrew inquired feeling like he did looking for a girl when he was much younger.

"She is," the older woman looked away, "However, now is not a good time. We're kind of in the middle of a family meeting."

"Mom?" Erin's voice came up behind her. "Who's at the door? Andy!"

Andrew had to brace himself to stop being tackled as Erin threw her arms around him. Luckily, almost out of instinct two tentacles shot out the back of his pant legs and steadied him, then retreated when he could hold his balance on his own.

"Hey," Andrew tried to pry the young woman off him. "I just umm… stopped by to talk. Your mom says this is a bad time. So, I'll…"

"Nonsense," Andrew's fiancé grabbed him by the arm and drug him inside. "You're going to be part of this family, so you should be involved when there are problems. That way you can help be part of the solution."

Erin led Andrew into the living room where the both her father and another man were seated. Erin took a seat on the couch next to her father and forced Andrew to sit next to her filling the leather piece of furniture. The mother took off towards where Andrew remembered the kitchen was. Across from the three of them sat a man with his face in his hands.

"Andy," Erin began the introductions. "This is my Uncle Jeremy. He's my mom's brother."

"Erin," Uncle Jeremy spoke through his hands. "This is more of a family matter don't you think?"

"Uncle Jeremy," Erin's voice grew stern. "Andrew is going to be part of our family soon. He's my fiancé."

"Wait," the man lifted his head. "This is that Andrew? Andrew Mullen, right?"

"Yeah," Andrew confirmed. "I'm Andrew Mullen."

"No," Uncle Jeremy dropped his hands between his thighs and stood up. "You do need to stay. You are kind of involved in this."

"How is Andrew involved in this?" Erin's father asked, a ginger eyebrow raising above his glasses.

"Can we start from the beginning?" Andrew raised his hand calling attention to himself. "Uh, what am I involved in?"

"Gambling with the Martinano Family." Uncle Jeremy informed him.

"The Martinano Family?" Andrew questioned.

"A group of mafioso in the New Hancock area," Erin's dad, who couldn't have looked more like a rich guy cliché had he tried (sweater vest and all), stood up. "Jeremy here showed up to ask for money to pay off his debts to them."

"Look, Max," Jeremy held his hands out. "Just help me out of this one jam, and I won't do it again."

"Jeremy," Max shook his head. "You said that last time."

"Uhhh…" Andrew raised his hand again. "That's great and all, but how am I involved?"

"That's a very good question," Erin's father agreed. "How is Andrew involved?"

"Well, after last time," Jeremy leaned back in his chair. It was at this time Andrew noticed that Uncle Jeremy was missing both pinky fingers. "They wouldn't let me gamble on credit with them anymore. So, I told them that Andrew had said that he felt the bet was so secure that he would cover the bet."

"I never said that," Andrew defended himself. "I honestly never said that."

"We know Andy," Erin patted his thigh. "You have not even met my uncle until today."

"What did I even bet on?"

"That Simpson would be found guilty. It was such a sure thing." The uncle admitted.

"And they just took your word on that I back the bet? They didn't even try to verify that by meeting me or at least talking to me on the phone, or you know, something?" Andrew laughed at the notion of this whole story. "How much money do you owe them?"

"I had one of my friends there, pretending to be you," Jeremy hid his face with one hand this time. "And I owe them roughly 10 grand."

"Ten thousand dollars?" Andrew got in the old man's face. "I owe them ten thousand fucking dollars?!"

"Andy," Erin tried to calm him down. "temper."

"No," Andrew turned to her. "this is precisely the kind of shit I should get pissed and start swearing at."

"But the Lord, tells us…" Erin tried her normal go to calm him down.

"The Lord also whipped the shit out of a bunch of dudes in a temple," Andrew turned around to face her. Max stood up to get between them, but then backed down after he felt he knew Andrew was not going to hurt the man. "So, I don't think getting pissed at something like this is not out of the question."

"It was a sure thing." Jeremy tried to defend his actions.

"You need to go down to that place and tell them what you did." Andrew slapped the hand hiding Jeremy's face away.

"They'll kill me." Jeremy flinched back at the aggression.

"And if you don't they'll kill me, so an innocent life will be on your conscience. Sound like fun?" Andrew moved closer as if to force the man through the back of the couch cowering. "I asked you a question."

"No." Jeremy shook his head.

"Good," Andrew slammed his hand to the back of the chair, his palm whizzing past the gambler's ear. "So, what are we going to do?"

"I'll make the call," Jeremy let out a nervous fart. "We'll go talk to them."

"Great," Andrew snorted, "now sounds like a great time to clear this up."

Chapter 9

Andrew had spent the rest of the evening at the Hastings house. Erin's mother had made a rather large meal for all of them. However, few had the desire to handle any of it. Erin had tried to talk Andrew out of his actions as much as she could, and Max had attempted to give Andrew the money to make this all go away. Neither of them could budge Andrew nor the desire he had to make sure Jeremy paid for putting Andrew's life in danger. The whole family stayed up until it was time to leave for the meeting.

The car ride was quiet the entire trip. Andrew drove Jeremy's car to the meeting place hidden in the docks of New Hancock. He steeled every bit of his nerves that he could to grab the door handle and open the car door to the smell of fresh water and hear the gently rolling waves. Andrew had had people threaten to kill him before with empty words, but now he was about to stare down the people who were more than willing to make good on those promises.

Andrew looked around. It was much earlier in the morning than he wanted to stay up. Normally at this hour, he would have already had to kick the dog out of the bed for kicking him in its sleep. Instead, he was about to go try and talk some sense into the mob and try and get his name cleared. Andrew opened the door and stepped out of the car. He heard the passenger door open. The silence of the area was the worst part of it all. No idea if anything was coming for him, or where it was coming from. Luckily for Andrew, the silence was quickly broken by the sound of footsteps running away from the passenger side of the car.

"Hey!" Andrew called out. "Get your ass back here." There was no response. Jeremy had bolted to whatever safety he could find, and then kept running. He was soon out of sight.

Sighing, Andrew began to walk toward the address that Jeremy had written on a slip of paper and handed him. Andrew threw the hood on his sweatshirt on and made sure it covered as much of his face as possible. Being in this place that the current time was not something Andrew wanted to be associated with.

It only took a short while for Andrew to find where he was instructed to go. The warehouse was completely dark. Andrew could only imagine what the room he was walking into was like. He could see it perfectly in his mind's eye. The room would be completely dark, aside from a single lamp that shown down on a single wooden chair. A table with all sorts of nasty implements would be sitting next to him. Andrew banged on the door, hoping to roust whoever was inside.

"You Mullen?" A small door slid open as the voice asked.

"Yeah," Andrew responded as he was instructed, hands open and at shoulder height.

"Where's that Jeremy guy?"

"Took off running like a bitch."

"Sounds like Jeremy." The voice let out a chuckle. Andrew wasn't sure if that made him more comfortable, or if the joke was meant to make him feel that way in order to make him drop his defenses a bit.

"Wouldn't know." Andrew shrugged. The door opened and a man in a black suit, white shirt with a black tie motioned for Andrew to come in.

"Wouldn't know?" The man led Andrew into the middle of the warehouse. The place was dark, pitch dark aside from a wooden chair in the middle of a spotlight. Andrew rolled his eyes at how well he called it. "Why don't you have a seat and we'll discuss that."

"I'd rather stand." Andrew shook his head and folded his arms.

"Not a request." The man told him. Three other men who looked strikingly similar to each other emerged from the shadows. Each one pulled a gun from a shoulder holster inside their suit jackets and aimed it at Andrew.

"A seat sounds wonderful." Andrew raised his hands showing that he had nothing in them and sat down.

"Sounds like you don't know Jeremy." The man who spoke before stood in front of Andrew and leaned on the table with many unpleasant objects.

"Just met him a few hours ago," Andrew explained. "When I heard this crazy scheme of his."

"Really?" The man motioned for the others to move. Andrew could hear each one move surround him and then stop.

"Yeah," Andrew leaned back in the chair and made himself comfortable, trying desperately to hide how nervous he was. "And as soon as I found out, I dragged his sorry ass down here. Took everything not to slap the shit out of him. I'm sure you guys have had the same feelings about him."

"We did," The man nodded. "Had to even take a few fingers."

"You know what gets me?" Andrew sat back up and leaned his hand on this thigh. "Why the hell would he deal with you guys when the next town over legalized gambling, what, five years ago?"

"Who knows," The man moved closer to Andrew. "But you know what I do know?"

"That store brand spaghetti sauce is shit compared to what mamma made?" Andrew smiled at his own little joke. Got to keep that air of cool under pressure.

"Actually," The man nodded. "You'd be amazed how close some of them can get. That's not it though. I know that you didn't meet Jeremy until a few hours ago."

"Really?" Andrew got confused. "Great, so we can get this all cleared up and go on our ways. I'm sure you have to go hunting for him. So, I'll just be hitting the old dusty…"

"Not so fast, Mr. Mullen," The man shook his head. "You see, while I know that, my bosses, however, don't know that and I don't think they'd care too much. All they want is a picture of your corpse. To send a little message to our good friend Jeremy, about things to come for him."

"Wait," Andrew protested. "But I'm just an innocent guy. Had nothing to do with this."

"And my heart goes out to you and your loved ones. Wrong place, wrong time though," The man pulled his gun back out and lifted it to Andrew's chest. Andrew didn't even have time to let out a gasp when all the men pulled their triggers.

"Take his wallet," one of the other men called out to another after the firing stopped, and Andrew's body slumped to the ground. "Maybe we can send some of our low level guys to find some good shit."

"I ain't grabbing it," Another voice shot back. "Probably covered in blood and shit."

"Just fucking turn around and grab it," the leader of the pack yelled back. "I've got a hard-on from killing that guy, and I got to have a bitch take care of it."

The Martinano soldier shrugged, sighed and turned around. Then he screamed.

An abomination now towered over him where Andrew's body should have laid. A beast covered in writhing tentacles stared back at him with eyes that appeared solid black in the lighting. Six long tentacles coming out of its back, making almost makeshift wings, each moving to their own accord. The creature in the clothing that Andrew wore, looked to stand 8 feet tall. The man didn't get much of a look though, due to the fact that the creature made a backhand motion with a thick tentacle coming where its arm once was. The tentacle slamming against the man's skull made a meaty thud as it crashed against the attempted killer's head. His now limp body went end over end past the other three and skid across the floor, motionless.

His compatriots wasted no time in opening fire at the monstrous attacker. With each shot, they could see its body twitch, jump, and contort but not slow its pace. The beast made a sweeping motion with the tentacles on its back and they coiled themselves around an unlucky member of the crew that the leader shoved into the monster's grasp.

"Did you shit yourself?" Andrew's muffled voice came from a hole where the tentacles spread apart with each word. He brought the frightened man eye to squirming eye with himself, as his body twitched from the bullets attempting to free the captured man. The mafia member nodded slightly. Andrew set him down. A finger-like tentacle pointed in the distance. "God damn, that stinks. You might want to go hide. I think you've learned your lesson."

A leg tentacle whipped out and grabbed the other non-leader gunman and began slamming him against the concrete floor like a rag doll while the monstrosity moved towards the leader. The man kept firing as Andrew slid closer and closer, his leg tentacles slithering along the ground.

Much to the disbelief of the leader of the mob squad, the gun clicked empty. The man threw the gun at Andrew who ducked the discarded weapon. Andrew grabbed the man by the throat with an arm tentacle and lifted him off his feet. The two began to slither outside of the building. The man clawed and fought with everything he had to try and free himself from Andrew's grasp until his fingernails had begun to peel off and bleed, but it was to no avail. The adrenaline running through Andrew's veins had shrugged off the sting of all the bullets hitting him. This man's flailing attempts to save his own life were like a gnat trying to harm a rock.

"Let me ask you something." Andrew pulled the man closer who began kicking at Andrew's body. "You know what I know? I know that you have made a huge mistake. Don't you think?" The man nodded his head; it was a struggle, but the man nodded his head. Using every ounce of strength Andrew could muster he launched the man as far as he could into the cold dark waters surrounding the place.

"Guess that really doesn't matter now." Andrew spat to himself as he heard the man yell as he flew a lot farther than Andrew had meant to throw him.

Andrew quickly shed his tentacle form when he reached the old beat up car. The bullets he had stopped in between the tentacles shielding his body dropped to the ground with several tinks against the pavement. He reached into his pocket and found the keys that Jeremy had given him; a stray bullet had hit the car key and taken off half of it.

With a sigh, Andrew lurched to a payphone lit up by a telephone pole close to another warehouse building. As he moved, the pain of the fight began to overtake him. Each step hurt like he had been stung by a very large bee repeatedly, and then punched by a heavyweight boxer. Soon his whole body felt this agony. With a groan and a yelp, Andrew reached in his pocket hoping to find some change. To compound his luck, Andrew found he didn't have enough. Andrew picked up the receiver anyway.

"Hello?" Mike answered the phone next to his bed, with a groan as he found his morning starting much earlier than he had intended.

"This is a billable call from PickMeUpAtWarehouses. Do you accept the charges?" An electronic operator recited.

"No," Mike hung up the phone and rolled back over. Andrew could walk home, he thought. Then another thought entered his mind. "It's way too early for this shit. Whatever you managed to get yourself into, Andy, it has got to be good."

Mike got dressed and started his car and sped down the empty urban streets. Mike found Andrew collapsed at the payphone with the receiver hanging off the end. His clothing riddled with bullet holes. He lugged his body in the passenger side of the car and bucked him into the seat belt.

As he did a man in a suit came rushing out of the building. A distinct smell followed him as he came closer to Mike. He quickly reached in his pocket and pulled out a wad of cash.

"You got to help me, man," the man shoved the crinkled money at Mike, who gladly accepted it. "You got to get me out of here. Look, I'm a member of the Martinano family, you get me out of here I'll make sure you're a made man. You just got to get me out of here. There is a fucking monster loose. Killed my friends. Huge fucking monster."

"Whoa buddy," Mike stuffed the money in his pocket. "Monster? And why do you smell like shit?"

"Just get me…" Tears began to roll down the man's face. The tears of relief from rescue turned to a face of sheer terror when he saw Andrew passed out in the passenger seat. "Holy fuck!"

"You know what, Andy?" Mike chuckled to himself as he watched the man run in the opposite direction, fleeing for his life. "Yeah, this was worth getting out of bed."

Chapter 10

"Rise and shine, fuck face," Mike's voice stirred Andrew from his sleep. "Coffee and pot. Best hangover cure on this plane of existence."

Andrew tried to sit up, but the soreness that shot through every muscle of his being only worked to hold him down to the couch. He then slid a few tentacles from underneath him in an attempt to use those to move, only to find the same muscles that wouldn't let him move wouldn't let those move him as well. Finally, after watching his friend struggle just to right himself, Mike came to the rescue and slid Andrew into a sitting position.

Slowly, Andrew reached for the cup of coffee. Mike had left it black with a bit of sugar and cream on the side. After a quick sip, Andrew added what he felt it needed and started to feel his stiffness give way to movement. Next, he picked up the joint carefully rolled on the table next to it, lit it and inhaled deeply.

The coughing fit that came afterward was most definitely not what Andrew needed now. Each cough sent a shock of pain through his body that threw him back down on the couch and Mike to his side, patting his back to help him through the fit.

"How ya' feeling?" Mike asked after the coughing subsided.

"Like I got hit by a truck. Repeatedly," Andrew informed his friend. "Then again, I guess fighting four mobsters wouldn't feel like a soft, warm dream."

"I don't imagine it would," Mike took the joint off Andrew and took a hit. "So, care to tell me why you were fighting four mobsters in the middle of a bunch of warehouses?"

"They were trying to kill me," Andrew sipped his coffee again. His body had started to feel much, much better. "Erin's uncle made some bets using me as a fall guy. So, we went to go straighten everything out, and they tried to shoot me."

"I think they succeeded," Mike joked. "But they weren't expecting a fucking monster's wet dream to come and fuck their shit up."

"I'm not a monster." Andrew coughed. The idea of being thought of as no longer human rubbed him in a way much worse than he expected. He knew he wouldn't have looked human when he donned his tentacle form, but still, there was a man underneath.

"Sorry man," Mike apologized. "I know, but that mobster you let live came to me for rescue. When he saw you in the car I think he shit his pants."

"Would have been the second time he did it." Andrew gave a slight chuckle.

"That was shit I was smelling when he came running out of his warehouse." Mike confirmed.

"Yeah, I grabbed him with some of my tentacles I had coming out of my back," Andrew recounted. "And he promptly vacated his bowels. Figured I'd let him live. Someone's got to tell the boss what happened and not to fuck with me. Besides, him doing it with poop in his britches is just much funnier in my mind."

"Wouldn't disagree with you there," Mike laughed as the idea of the lone member of the Martinano family talking to the Don and everyone in the room looking at him like he's crazy while sniffing the air. "So, tell me, how do they work? You know in a situation like that?"

"It was weird," Andrew admitted. "When they initially opened fire, the tentacles shot out almost like a reflex and blocked my body. The impact knocked the wind out of me. So, as I was lying on the floor I just thought of how I wanted to look when I came back up, and BAM! There I was. A thing born right out of their nightmares. Everything just moved so… naturally. It was like I was using just another limb. Just like moving my arm or my leg. Only, there were like a hundred or them or something. I'll tell you, man, it was wild."

"Dude," Mike sat back. "They lost three members, and you sent one back crying. I think it's going to be a while before you hear from them again."

"Lost?" Andrew questioned. "What do you mean lost?"

"Andy," Mike leaned back on the couch. "You killed three of their guys. I didn't see it, but that's what the survivor told me."

"Jesus," Andrew had never even thought of that. He didn't realize the strength that he had with these new appendages. All he knew was that he had a power. A power that he defended himself with. Killing a man with it was something that never even crossed his mind. He wasn't sure how he felt about what he had done. It didn't feel good, he knew that. At the same time, these men had tried to kill him. Better them than me, is what he finally decided on for the moment. "Eh, fuck 'em. Better them than me."

"Amen, to that," Mike said into his cup of coffee. "Down for food?"

"Nah, I should be getting to Erin's. I got to pick up the car," Andrew waved the idea off and tried to stand. His body did not like that idea and forced him back on the couch. "On second thought, what did you have in mind?"

It was a few hours before Andrew was able to finally pull himself off the couch and remain standing. Mike gave his sore friend a ride back into the suburbs where Andrew had left his car.

"Want me to come in?" Mike asked as he pulled the car behind Andrew's car parked along the curb.

"No," Andrew leaned in the open passenger window after he slowly climbed out of the car. "I'm pretty sure I can get home from here. Shouldn't be too hard of a trip. Besides, I think I should let them know what went down with the meeting. Keep Erin informed of how great of a person her Uncle is."

"Nice," Mike nodded. "See if you can get me a picture of her face when you tell her he left you for dead, and when you turned into a giant squid monster."

50

"Think I'm going to leave that part out," Andrew said and patted the top of the car signaling Mike to drive off. Slowly, he began to make his way to the front door. "Definitely going to leave that part out."

Andrew wasn't a few feet from the door when it burst open wide and Erin rushed out. As soon as she got to him she threw her arms around him and smothered his face with quick kisses. Andrew tried to hide the fact that he was wincing as she squeezed him. Eventually, Andrew was able to push her back and steady himself.

"Andy!" Erin smiled. "You ok? Got a bit of a hangover from last night."

"Yeah," Andrew nodded. "I'm ok. Your uncle here?"

"No," Erin shook her head and began to pull Andrew towards the house. "He stopped by earlier, said he worked something out with those guys."

"Did he say where I was?" Andrew questioned the story. "Being as I wasn't there with him?"

"He said the two of you had a few drinks, to celebrate, and that he dropped you off at home. Since you couldn't drive." Erin opened the door.

"No," Andrew followed her inside. It appeared that they were the only two in the house. "We didn't go out for drinks."

"It's ok, Andy." Erin waved what she thought was a defensive move off and walked into the kitchen. "You can have a few drinks to celebrate the end to that fiasco. Tea?"

"No, thanks," Andrew shook his head. "And no, we didn't have drinks because he left me at a warehouse with four of those gangsters."

Without a word, Erin dropped the box of tea bags. She turned towards Andrew with a look of disbelief.

"He said," Erin bent down to begin to pick up the bags off the ground. Andrew slowly got up from his seat to help her. "He said you guys all worked it out."

"The only thing that got worked out," Andrew informed her. "Were his legs as he bolted. That and their punching skills on me."

"My uncle wouldn't lie to me, Andrew." Erin's voice began to get angry. "Family doesn't lie to each other."

"Really?" Andrew laughed and took off the shirt Michel had lent them before they left. Exposing all the bruises on his chest and arms. "Does this look like we all just 'worked something out'?"

"I don't know how you got those bruises," Erin slammed the box down on the table. "Family doesn't lie to each other."

"Ok," Andrew got confused. He wondered how she thought he had gotten those bruises, or why she was defending her uncle this hard. "But you don't believe me? Why would I lie about something like that?"

"I don't know why you would make those things up about my uncle, Andrew, but if you are going to lie to me about what happened, then I think you need to leave." Erin stormed off into the hallway and grabbed Andrew's key's from a hanger. She returned to the kitchen and handed them to Andrew.

"I am so confused right now." Andrew raised an eyebrow.

"Especially if you think that my own blood would lie to me," Erin glared at him. "And then you would tell me, that a man who fought off someone who tried to hurt me and shown me the light of the lord, would lie to me. Then yes, you are very confused. You need to leave, Andrew."

"Erin," Andrew stopped at the door as she led him to it. "What did Jeremy tell you? How did we work things out?"

"Leave." Erin shook her head and pointed to the door.

"Erin," Andrew looked her in the eye as he put the shirt back on. "This might be important. If he said they worked something out, did he say how?"

"Leave," Erin repeated the word.

"Erin, I love you," Andrew looked her in the eye, he still wasn't sure if that was a lie or not. "I need you to tell me how it got worked out because I'm not sure if your uncle is still in danger or not. Those men hurt me, badly. They're not going to stop until they get their money. They could take it out on him, or me again, or heaven forbid you. If he's willing to sell out strangers, he might be willing to sell you out as well."

"First," Tears of anger began to roll down Erin's face. "You come in here and claim that my uncle lied to me. Then you claim that he left you to get hurt. Finally, you stand here and tell me that he could have sold me out to the mafia? How dare you? How dare

52

you stand there and say these things, you... you... asshole! Do you want to know? Fine, he said they worked out a payment plan. That's it. He said he explained the situation, apologized and they told him he could make payments to them. Happy now?"

"One more question," Andrew stepped outside, and the door was slammed in his face. "HOW DID HE LOSE HIS FINGERS?"

"In a farming accident a few years ago!" Erin yelled back.

Andrew stood at the door for a second. He ran his tongue over his teeth, as he pondered how on earth that woman believed what she was told. He shrugged and realized that it hopefully wasn't his problem anymore and that he sent the Martinano family a strong enough message.

Andrew opened the door to his beater car and slowly sat down on the brown upholstered seat. He gripped the leather steering wheel and took one more look at the house. He was sure that Erin would calm down and call him later to talk things out. As he shoved his keys in the ignition, he smiled to himself thinking, he probably wasn't going to answer.

Chapter 11

Andrew pulled up to the apartment building that he lived in and made his way to the front door. A glass panel in the front door had been broken and cleared out, obviously for someone to gain access to the building that wasn't supposed to have it. Andrew thought nothing of it, he didn't live in the best neighborhood in New Hancock, and sadly, this was not a rare occurrence.

Andrew checked his mail in the lobby. Just bills and junk mail. Andrew dropped the pile of mail, bills and all, in a close by trash and began to head up the stairs towards his apartment. Each floor he checked the door jambs to see who the unlucky victim of that night's break-in was. Each door and each floor he checked the jokes in his head about his apartment being broken into would become truer and truer in his head.

Until he reached his door. The short trip to check the five other doors in his building to his small little studio apartment did not give him enough time to ready himself. His door had settled in a slightly open position. Not enough to see in, not enough to be closed. Just open enough to make Andrew not want to open it.

Andrew slid a thick tentacle down his right arm. Andrew tensed it until it was as stiff as a board. A pointy board that could do a lot of damage swung or stabbed at someone's throat. Andrew pulled it back as if to throw a haymaker punch, and used his right foot to kick the door in.

Nothing was touched. The apartment was a wreck just like Andrew had left it. He listened for the sounds of an intruder and found nothing. He walked into his bedroom and found his bed as unkempt as he left it. He walked over to his dresser drawer and opened it up. A small cigar box sat off to the side. Using his left-hand, Andrew opened the box and pulled out a wad of cash that he had stashed in there. He counted it and found nothing was missing. The bathroom was untouched as well. Strangely enough, Andrew noted that the bathtub was cleaner than he had left it.

Andrew scratched his head, as he walked back into the living room. He whistled quickly in hopes that his dog would come. Nothing. Shithead was normally a very shy dog, and Andrew thought he must have still been hiding from whoever was here.. He let the tentacle slide back up his arm and made his way back into the bedroom. He walked over to the closet that he left open a crack in case Shithead had gotten scared and could hide. No dog.

With a shrug, Andrew figured the dog had taken off in the ruckus and was probably in one of his neighbor's apartments. It had happened before when there was an attempted break in. Andrew was grateful that his neighbors were such good friends with his dog. They usually were ambivalent towards Andrew. Shithead? They loved Shithead almost as much as he did.

Andrew figured he would check after he made sure that he could get the door fixed so that the dog had somewhere safe to stay and not run up and down the hallways. Andrew went to the phone to call his landlord when he noticed the answering machine blinking. He reached down and pressed the button.

"Good evening, Mr. Mullen." An unknown voice greeted him.

"Hello, strange voice on my answering machine," Andrew replied simply to amuse himself.

"As you can see you had a visitor this evening. After a rather unbelievable tale by one of my subordinates, we found it appropriate to take matters into our own hands in dealing with the now astronomical debt you owe us.

"I'm sure by now you are wondering how we found you. You see, your friend Jeremy decided to talk quite a bit after we paid him a little visit this morning. Unfortunately, he was unable to inform us how you managed to kill three of my soldiers, but he was able to inform us as to where you lived."

"Where the hell'd he get that information?" Andrew asked himself.

"Lucky for him, we were able to find a solid middle ground and find a solution to pay off his debt that his little bet caused, but we'll discuss that later.

"You see, we understand that this was a scam by him. The sole survivor made that conclusion after meeting you. Had Jeremy walked into the building we would have been more than reasonable and let you go. In fact, had we killed you that evening we would have gladly heavily reimbursed any remaining family members. We're businessmen, Mr. Mullen, not killers. Having that reputation would not do us a bit of good.

"Sadly, now I must pay off three families. This causes me quite a bit of a problem. As a businessman, I would much rather not have to pay these families. So, I added that as your debt along with the money that Jeremy owes us.

"But why did we break into your apartment, and not take anything? That is probably your question right now. We could have robbed you and used that money to pay off your debt. Well, upon inspection we determined you did not have enough assets to cover the cost you incurred. So, we will be coming for you, Mr. Mullen. We will be expecting your full hospitality. However, we noticed that there was not enough food for all of us, should we come calling. So, Mr. Mullen, we took the liberty to make sure your freezer was stocked, as a reminder that we are coming for you and expect a warm welcome.

"As for how your gambling friend will be paying….." The tape ended.

Andrew wanted to think of a quip about the machine running out of tape, but he couldn't come up with one. His thoughts were frozen. Andrew walked slowly to his fridge. He hadn't bought groceries in a while and did not have much food in there. Andrew opened the door.

The horror show that had become his fridge was enough to knock him to the ground. Blood covered the walls where various slabs of meat and organs had been haphazardly thrown about. A large intestine sat on the five remaining beers for the six-pack he had in there. In the center of this nightmare sat a silver-plated tray with a silver dome on top of it.

Andrew knew he didn't want to open the dome, but something inside him had to see. He had to confirm what he was fearing as he choked back the vomit. He felt the weight of the tray as he used two tentacles to slide it out of the mess that it sat in. Red blood spilled out of the side as he tried to steady it in front of himself. With a free hand, Andrew lifted the dome. When Shithead's cold unmoving eyes stared back at him blankly, Andrew dropped the tray with a loud clang.

Scrambling as fast as he could Andrew reached to the phone and pounded out the seven digits he needed as fast as he could. He stumbled on the numbers and had to redial several times, until…

"This is Mike." Mike's voice answered

"I need you to get over here," Andrew stammered. "As fast as you can. This is a fucking emergency."

"Andy," Mike's voice grew concerned. "What's going on?"

"They fucking killed him," Andrew began to cry, "They fucking killed Shithead!"

"Who?" Mike shouted. "Never mind, I'm on my way."

True to his word Mike appeared at the apartment in no time. Andrew sat on the curb, doing everything he could to hold his composure out in public but losing horribly.

"They fucking killed him, man," Andrew wiped tears from his face. "The killed and butchered him."

"Who, Andrew?" Mike sat down with him. "Who is the dead mother fucker that killed that dog."

"The Martinanos," Andrew stared at the ground. "Said it was revenge for the guys I killed. So they broke in and killed my fucking dog. Said they're coming for me soon."

"Andy," Mike put his arm around his tearful friend's shoulder. "I'm going to up there and clean your fridge. You want a new one, just say the word. When I get done, I'm coming down here and we're leaving. They can come back for you, but they ain't gonna to find you. We're going to find that son of a bitch that run out on you, find where these people are, and we are going to give them a fucking horror show that would make any gore hound cum blood. Do you hear me?"

Andrew nodded. "I hear you."

"I fucking love you, brother," Mike told him. "And tonight, we are going to become the fucking most horrific thing Erin's uncle has ever seen, and these fucking shit stains have ever seen. Do you understand me? Now, while I go up there and take care of Shithead, I need you to sit here. Cry if you need to, fucking yell, do whatever. I don't give a shit. There is only one thing I want you to think about, the only fucking thing. I want you to think of a name that you are going to call yourself when you kick in their front door and start leaving a god damn body count so high that every nightly news is going to be killing each other to get the first picture. Do you feel me?"

"Yeah." Andrew nodded.

"Good." Mike stood up and walked into the apartment building, leaving Andrew to his own devices.

Chapter 12

Sometimes inspiration hits in the strangest places. Luckily, for Andrew Mullen, over the past few days since he left the mental hospital, his life has been nothing but a strange place. Trying to dump his fiancé has left him now in a battle with the local mafia, the blood of three lives on his hands, and now one of his two best friends had to be scraped out of his refrigerator. A strange place indeed, considering how opposite it was from the life he had tried to leave.

Andrew sat in the bar in a quiet booth with his other best friend. That much was normal. That was very normal, and the kind of normal that he welcomed very much. Just one drink after another. Enough, he felt, to begin to clean out his now scarred mind.

"You sure you don't want to do this tonight?" Mike sat across the table from Andrew.

"Too stupid," Andrew said after he put down the glass of beer he had just finished. "Everyone is expecting us. Jeremy has probably gone into hiding. The Martinanos are probably on such a high alert that I would catch big fucking bullets if not bombs to the face as soon as I walk in there, and I don't know if I can handle that. Go in too hot-headed, make too many mistakes."

"Fair point," Mike agreed. "You think of a name yet? If you're going to go do superhero shit, you need a superhero name and a costume. Got to have a costume."

"I'm not going to go do superhero shit. I'm going to go get these assholes off my back, and then move on with my life." Andrew admitted. "I have a feeling that if I were to start living that life, this would all keep happening over and over and over. I really don't want to end up having to scrape everyone out of my fridge."

"Dude," Mike leaned in and pointed at his friend. "That's why you get a costume and a name. No one knows who you are."

"The Martinanos know who I am." Andrew pointed out.

"Actually," Mike remembered the message Andrew had played for him after he had cleaned out the apartment. "They don't. They didn't believe that guy that shit himself."

"So," Andrew scratched his chin. The beard that had started to come in from not shaving for a handful of days was starting to get itchy. "They're going to just think I'm some different giant monster coming after them for no reason when I break down their door."

"No," Mike leaned back. "Because you're not going to leave a mother fucker alive. No one is going to believe the ones you miss. Just a mass of broken and destroyed bodies. News and police will chalk it up to a gangland battle, you walk away the big fucking hero."

"I'm not going to kill anyone," Andrew shook his head. "No more killing. None. I'm done. May have happened in the heat of the moment, but it shouldn't have happened. That's how I got into this mess."

"Ok," Mike folded his arms. "How do you plan on handling this problem then? Tie them all up? Leave them for the cops? Watch them pay their way out of it then come back for more. This is a fucking war. It isn't going to stop until one of you are dead. Hate to say it."

Andrew thought for a moment. Is that what he wanted? To be locked in an endless war with the Martinano family? To be watching his back for the rest of his life when they finally make the connection as to who he is? He knew that killing wasn't something

60

he wanted, but he also knew that living in fear was not something he wanted either.

"You're right," Andrew admitted. "But still, if I can avoid it, I'm going to. We still have one hurdle to get over before we confront them, though."

"What's that?" Mike asked.

"We have to find out where they are," Andrew informed his friend. "And the only way we are going to do that is to talk to Jeremy."

Both sat there in quiet. Neither one knew how to get a hold of Jeremy, but they knew who did and neither of them wanted to go and talk to his niece. Andrew especially didn't after what happened last time. Hell, he thought, she probably wouldn't even talk to him.

That was when it hit Andrew while being lost in thought. Looking over to the boxing match on the bar T.V., one boxer was on his way to the ring draped in a long robe. His face obscured from the cameras. The bright cloth dangled from his arms, covering his gloves. Visions of the covers of books Andrew had read came to mind. Horror novels with figures draped in the same style robe. Faces obscured, arms and legs hidden. It was perfect.

"Mike," Andrew pointed at the TV. "I think we just found my costume."

"All you need is a name." Mike agreed, thinking the exact same thing.

"All I need is a name." Andrew parroted.

Chapter 13

Darkness fell on the city of New Hancock as Mike's car sped down the road. It had been days since they two had sat in the bar discussing Andrew's costume. Along with Andrew beginning physical training, the two had formulated a plan for Andrew to break into the house and start demanding answers disguised as the tentacle monster. It seemed like a solid plan and would give Andrew some practice of using his tentacles for mobility.

The clock on the car had just turned to midnight as Andrew stared out the window. He didn't want to go talk to this woman. He didn't want to face her after the way she blew up at him. Mike had told him that no one would know who he was. No one would be expecting a nine-foot tall, eldritch horror to barge into their house demanding answers.

The car pulled up to the curb about a block down the road. Mike made sure to find a spot without a street light showing over it. Mike killed the engine and Andrew got out of the car. Wearing a hoodie that he knew Erin had never seen, he threw the hood over his head and began growing out the fleshy tendrils and becoming the living freak show he was starting to feel like.

"Hold up," Mike hit a button by his left foot and the trunk popped. "Before you start making every Japanese school girl in the area wetter than a rain storm, I got a little something for you."

Mike pulled a mini flashlight out of the glove box and walked to the back of the car. Andrew stood over him, waiting; the two leaned down and Mike began to dig around in the back. Out of curiosity, Mike shined the flashlight at his friend, wanting to see the full figure for himself. He quickly dropped the electric torch out of shock at the face that stared back at him.

It had looked like Andrew's face was melting into a pile of long strands that had started to rot. Tentacles had firmly attached to his eyes, turning them into an almost pure black mess. They writhed and moved as Andrew's irises would have expanded and contracted. What was originally a mouth and upper lip, now looked alien as a latticework of tentacles obscured it. Mike knew Andrew was still underneath but couldn't help but be frightened.

"Do me a favor," Mike instructed Andrew. "Never to do that again. Anyway, I thought that shit hid when the light touched it."

"Only when it touches the… spawning point?" Andrew had no idea what to call where the tentacles were coming from, as he had honestly never seen it himself.

"Cool," Mike added trying to avoid seeing the monstrosity before him. Mike pulled out a small box and handed it to Andrew. Andrew pulled back his guise and opened the package. It was a long robe, very similar to a boxer's robe. The bright red, white, and blue sequined colors still showed up in the darkness. On the back, in big stylized letters, read "Squid Boy."

"Squid Boy?" Andrew laughed.

"Well, you hadn't picked out a name yet," Mike scratched his head. "Besides, it's only a prototype. Obviously, it's not long enough and all that. We'll see how it goes and then we'll see about getting you a big boy costume."

"Alright," Andrew took the hooded sweatshirt off and tossed it in the car. He threw the robe over himself and resent out his tentacles. "How's it look?"

"If I wasn't already afraid of clowns," Mike couldn't help but stare. "I sure as shit would be now."

"So extra terrifying," Andrew's muffled voice let out a laugh. "Excellent."

"Might want to change the voice," Mike pointed out. "Still sounds like you."

"How's this?" Andrew tried a much deeper voice.

"No." Mike shook his head.

"Like," Andrew went completely valley girl. "Oh my god, I'm coming for you!"

"Yes," Mike nodded. "That one, that very one."

"How about this?" A whispery, raspy voice as if it was only to be carried on the wind came out.

"Actually, that's perfect," Mike nodded. "Go get 'em, kid."

Andrew began to use his tentacles to slide along the ground by moving his leg tentacles in a slithering motion. He made sure to avoid any form of light on his way to the house. As Andrew moved into a backyard to the house next door, he was hoping completely undetected. A dog tried to come out of its dog house and defend its property, however, a quick glance in its direction sent him back with his tail between his legs

After a quick slide around the pool and using his tentacles to jump a fence, Andrew found himself in the Hastings backyard. He extended his leg tentacles up to give him a boost to the window that he knew to be Erin's. There was no light on and it was pitch black. Andrew created a few tiny tentacles in between the holes in the screen and was able to dislodge the pins holding it in. Luckily for Andrew, the window was open, and he was able to use his tentacles to guide himself into the house.

Andrew's eyes quickly adjusted to the darkness, and he realized that his wish had actually come true. Andrew was alone in the room. Checking the memory book in his mind, he knew Erin very rarely stayed up this late. Even when the two were on dates, she had to be home by at least 11.

"This is the second night Erin hasn't been home." Andrew heard Erin's father say. Andrew lowered his height and slid into the hallway.

"I don't know where she could be." Mrs. Hastings responded. The two were downstairs in the living room. Knowing that he could hear everything they were saying, Andrew stayed put where he was hidden.

"We should call the police." Mr. Hastings recommended.

"Look," Mrs. Hastings tried to calm herself down and tried to reason with her panicked husband. "She told me she was going out with Jeremy. I tried calling him and just left a message on his machine. If we don't hear back from him soon, we'll call the police."

"We've got to do something," Erin's father slammed something down on the arm of the chair. "What's your brother's address? I'm going over there."

"…He lives on Randolph St. 414, I think," Mrs. Hastings told him. "Look, don't do anything hasty. Give him a few hours, they could be out on a camping trip or something…"

Andrew didn't even hear the end of the conversation. He quickly made his way back out of the house and back to Mike's car, with no regard for being seen or not.

"414 Randolph," Andrew told Mike who stood by the car smoking a cigarette. "We need to move now. Something happened to Erin."

"The fuck you mean?" Mike tossed the smoke and jumped in as Andrew dropped the tentacles and jumped in the passenger seat. "What happened?"

"I don't know," Andrew slammed on his seat belt. "Jeremy is involved. I overheard her parents saying she went with him a few days ago, and that she hasn't checked in since then."

"Must be having fun," Mike added as two sped off into the night.

"Not like her, especially in that area," Andrew rubbed his chin stubble. "I couldn't get her to even stay out past 11. There is no way something hasn't happened."

There were rough areas of New Hancock, like where Andrew lived. Then there were the bad neighborhoods. Andrew had a hard time imagining anywhere on Randolph street he had wanted to be, especially at this time at night. The religiously named barber shops and every other storefront had bars on the windows confirmed this.

"Drop me off on the corner and keep moving," Andrew told Mike as he climbed out of the car. He threw the cloak's hood up. "Give me ten minutes then come to the address. If I'm not there, make another ten-minute drive."

Andrew marched down the street confidently. That was when it hit him, he's moving in to save a girl he doesn't know if he loves. He was afraid of facing her after an argument when normally he would have just told her to fuck off. Maybe the wedding was still on.

His train of thought came to a crash when a revolver was leveled at his face.

"Give me your wallet and you get to keep walking," A man dressed in black baggy pants with a red bandana ordered him. "Give me any lip and you get lead. You got it?"

Andrew didn't even break stride as a tentacle reached out, grabbed the weapon and slapped the man across the face with it. Another tentacle shot out, and with the two of them, Andrew destroyed the gun. He tossed it back at the man.

"Go and rethink your life," Andrew called back as he kept moving. "Idiot."

Andrew reached the address and brought all the appendages out to play. The old dilapidated door didn't stand much of a chance to the force of six tendrils slamming against it, smashing it off the hinges.

"Jeremy!" Andrew called out. "Come on out!"

Andrew's voice was responded to with a shotgun blast that knocked him off his leg tentacles. Then in a smooth movement, Andrew rose back up before Jeremy could reload the double barrel. Two tentacles shot out and grabbed the man's arms and began to pull.

"You talk, or I will rip them off," Andrew got up in the face of the man. A warm liquid could be felt landing on a lower tentacle. "Erin Hastings, where is she?"

"Jesus fucking Christ!" Jeremy screamed, "What the fuck are you?"

"I'm the demon that Hell sent to wipe shit stains like you off the face of the Earth," Andrew applied outward pressure and heard the distinctive pop of a shoulder joint leaving the socket. "Now fucking talk!"

"I don't know what you're talking about," Jeremy screamed in pain, the other shoulder popped. "Ok, I sold her. I sold her to the Martinano family. Fuckfuckfuck…"

66

"You sold her?!" Andrew used more tentacles to make himself bigger. "You fucking sold your fucking niece?! Where, you waste of life. Tell me where she's at before I rip your tongue from your face."

"The slave auctions," The distinctive smell of shit filled the air as Jeremy cried. "They said virgin pussy would fetch a high enough price to pay my debts."

"Where is she?!" Small tentacles slowly reached out from Andrew's eyes and wrapped themselves around Jeremy's teeth and dug into his gums and began to pull out one of his molars.

"FUCK!" Jeremy screamed, "Ender's strip joint. That's all I know. Please god, please. Let me live." Jeremy begged as blood began to run down his mouth. Andrew dropped the sniveling man to the ground.

"Get on the phone and call the police. Confess to what you did. If you don't, I will come back. I will end your miserable life you sniveling, little fuck. Do you understand me?" Andrew began to leave. "And if you're lying to me, not even prison will keep you safe."

"You ok?" Mike found Andrew standing outside using his sleeve to wipe his eyes vigorously.

"Blood in my eyes," Andrew was back to normal. "I started pulling his teeth with my eyes. Really bad move, really bad."

"Better hope your ass doesn't have hepatitis now." Mike ran back to the car and pulled out a bottle of water from under the seat. He held Andrew's head back and flushed his eyes as best he could.

"Fuck," Andrew swore. "It would be the least of my problems tonight. Found where she is, hopefully."

"Where?" Mike used Andrew's discarded sweatshirt to dry his face.

"Ender's Gentlemen's club." Andrew made his way back to the car.

"That place has been closed for a few years," Mike informed him.

"The Martinano's must own it," Andrew was slowly getting his vision back. "Turned it into a sex slave auction house."

"Jesus," Mike slowly made the connection. "He sold her into sex slavery. Ex or not, we got to fucking move."

67

The tires squealed as the car blasted into the night.

Chapter 14

Many of the buildings in the area were abandoned. This meant that not only would no one call the cops should massive gunfire erupt, it also gave Mike a spot to sit in the car, safe and sound, unnoticed. A viaduct about a block away from the club was a perfect spot to give Mike just that. Andrew climbed out of the car and took a few deep breaths.

It had been one hell of a night. Hell, his entire life had been one hell of a night since he put that gun to his head and pulled the trigger. He put his arms on the roof of the car and did his best to ready himself. He had fought a few wasps in the warehouse a few nights ago and still remembered the sting. Now, his whole game plan was to just walk in the front door of the nest, kick it a few times, and swat down anything that came out. Not a good plan by any stretch of the word, but with the limited time that he had to come up with one it would have to do.

"You good?" Mike rolled down the window on Andrew's side and spoke to him from inside the car.

"Nope," Andrew chuckled. "I'm about as far from good as I can be right now. Chest hurts like a mother fucker where that asshole shot me."

"Eh," Mike shrugged. "Stop being a baby about it. People get shot every day, you don't hear them complain about it."

"Usually," Andrew smiled at his friend's attempt at a joke. "Those people die from getting shot."

"And you don't," Mike lit another cigarette. A small tentacle reached in grabbed the tobacco and brought it to Andrew's lips, then returned it to its owner. "So, stop whining and get in there. You've got asses to kick and a hero to be. Who knows, maybe she'll actually fuck you after this."

"Yeah," Andrew threw up his hood and changed forms. "Time to go be one of those superheroes, huh? Live my childhood fantasy. Fuck it, here we go."

Andrew strode off and left Mike to himself. The man finished off the cigarette and tossed it out into the night. He leaned back in his seat. His best friend, no, his brother, was about to march off and maybe die for a girl that he didn't even love anymore. Mike leaned back up and hit the button to open the trunk again.

Digging through the back, Mike pulled up the carpet that hid what would normally be a spare tire and pulled out his pistol. Mike stuffed a few extra magazines in his pockets, made sure there was a bullet in the chamber, and closed the trunk. Sure, his friend was about to march off to his death, but Mike would be god damned if he was going to do it alone.

Andrew found a solid looking door that at one time seemed to the be the entrance to the old strip joint. He noticed a sliding door at about eye level to a normal person. Figuring someone would open the slot as soon as he knocked, he slid a tentacle right underneath and banged on the door. Sure enough, the little window slid open.

"Passwor…urk!" A voice was caught by surprise as the tentacle wrapped itself around the man's throat and pulled him in to the door head first, knocking him unconscious. Then, with several dexterous movements after feeling around, Andrew unlocked the heavy steel door.

Two guards must have seen what was going on as Andrew stepped inside as one took off running, probably to warn the others of incoming danger. Over the thumping bass sounds that a woman

70

was probably being forced to dance to, Andrew really couldn't tell what was being yelled.

"Holy shit," The second guard stood frozen in shock of what he saw. "Mikey was right. Muthafucka was right."

"And if you heard his stories," Andrew leaned in, "You might want to use this opportunity to run."

The man did not have to be told twice. He bolted out the door Andrew had just come in. However, his escape did not last long. He turned the corner to run towards the back of the building to meet Mike who didn't hesitate to slam his weapon against the man's temple. Mike grabbed the small machine gun the man had strapped to him and inspected it. Made sure it was loaded, and then checked the man for any sort of keys, which he luckily found. He then began to make his way towards the back of the building.

Andrew followed the sound of the bass, hoping it would lead him to the center of this mess. A man tried to jump him from around the corner with a knife, but a tentacle shot out, grabbed the man's wrist and threw him across the room and into a glass booth with merchandise. A small pool of blood began to form under the man as he began to moan in pain. Andrew slid over and noticed the man had fallen on his knife and was slowly bleeding out. With a sigh, two tentacles reached down and twisted the man's head 180 degrees with a very distinctive snap, and the man moved no more. Andrew didn't want to kill and told himself that this was for mercy. That cherry had been popped, however, and he felt that by the end of the night, that man wasn't going to be the only one.

A hallway across from where Andrew entered the entrance area, seemed to be headed to where the thumps were coming from. Behind a curtain in front of him, Andrew could see the flashing lights and hear the sound that was once just bass become actual music. 80's pop rock. Not his favorite, but he could get down with a man singing about getting sugar poured on him. Andrew took a deep breath.

Mike peeked around the corner. Two guards stood by the back door and were discussing what the commotion was inside the building. One guard nodded and headed inside. Mike stood there in silence and quickly formulated a plan.

71

The lone guard pointed his gun at the bald man that came his way.

"You need to turn around right now." The man with the weapon told the staggering man headed his way. Mike popped his hands up showing he wasn't there to cause any trouble.

"Sorry," Michael slurred his words. "I'm looking for the bathroom. Maybe at least a bush. Say, there ain't anyone around here. Can I take a piss over there?"

"No," The guard shook his head. "Only thing you can do is go back the other way."

"Look," Mike turned to the building and opened his zipper. "See? Not hurting anyone."

The guard came up behind him and grabbed him by the shoulder. Mike threw his heel back and landed it straight into the guard's groin. The man yelled out in pain and turned around. Mike wrapped his arm around the man's neck and shoved him face first to the ground. The applied pressure from the chokehold and a few quick punches to the back of the guard's head meant he wasn't going to be moving for a while.

Mike stood up and zipped up his pants. He checked the man for anything useful, found some more ammo, and went inside the building.

The back door opened right to a hallway. Three doors were in front of Mike. One was for the dancers, one was for the DJ booth, and one to the main office. The sound of a door slamming open and a few gunshots could be heard coming from the other side of the wall. Two people were in the office, arguing numbers. One was an older gentleman, and the other voice was an electronic voice.

Not having a choice, Mike made his way to the dancer room. There were two girls tied to chairs, and each one blindfolded. Each one of the girls was dressed in something revealing that was probably taken from the dancers closet. One was silent and just shaking her head in disbelief. The other was praying every prayer she could probably think of.

"I bet of all the prayers you just said," Mike lifted the blindfold off Erin, "you weren't expecting me to answer."

Erin was speechless. Mike quickly undid the ropes tying the two to the chairs. The girl shaking her head bolted to the door and

72

out the back door. Mike grabbed Erin's hand and headed to the door. He listened for any sounds and found nothing.

"Where's Andy?" Erin finally choked out.

"I'm taking you to him." Mike led Erin away from the back door and towards the DJ booth.

Mike quietly opened the door. To his surprise, a DJ was controlling the booth and making sure the music was going as planned. He stopped as soon as he saw the automatic firearm was aimed his way.

"Don't shoot!" The man with headphones stammered. "I just spin the records."

"Yeah, yeah," Mike waved him off. "I get that. Get going."

The man began to take off.

"Wait," Mike called out. "How do I work the announcing thing?"

A grin came over Mike's face as the man showed him which button to press.

"Ladies and gentlemen," A voice came over the intercom a familiar voice, it was Mike. "I'd like to welcome you all to Ender's Gentlemen's club. I hope you all had a fun time watching Candy, up on this stage. Unfortunately for all of you, your chance to buy her tonight is over. However, we do have a very special treat for you. Making his way from the front entrance, we have the one you all have been warned about. The one who is long, and strong, and about to get his murder on! The one, the only, I give you all the beast from 10th Street, the muthafuckin' Flayer!"

"Flayer?" Andrew questioned what Mike had just called him. He hadn't heard it too well over the music. Sounded better than Squid Boy he guessed. That was when Andrew realized there was no time like the present. The sound screeched off, time to walk through the curtain.

The room was silent as the 9-foot monster slid out from behind the curtain to the main room. Andrew's heart beat like a drum. He looked around the room and couldn't count how many men were there. Most were well dressed and looked like your everyday business types. The Martinanos were certainly easy to

73

discern, as they were all aiming their weapons at Andrew. Ok, Andrew time to be cool.

Andrew slid forward, which apparently was the signal for the gangsters to open fire. Mike ducked down under the DJ set up in the booth. Using his arm, he held Erin's head down, as the bullets continued to fly and occasionally ricochet off the stand.

A man flew up and into the DJ booth. Without hesitating, Mike slammed his foot against the man's temple until he stopped moving. He then peered over the edge and popped off a few shots. The guards he had fired at were unhurt until a pair or tentacles grabbed them by the necks lifted them in the air and slammed their heads together until they cracked open.

Andrew had allowed the "customers" to leave. They weren't going to bother him too much. One had tried to run past him but tripped over his own feet. Which saved Andrew a bit of effort as he was planning on doing the same thing. Instead of reloading, one of the guards, who Andrew guessed probably hadn't taken any logic classes, tried to rush Andrew and punch him. With a long tentacled hand, Andrew caught the fist and began to spread his and elongate his appendages over the attacker's arm. The man screamed in horror as they continued to move up his arm, and then in one swift motion he was lifted in the air and thrown at another guard. The guard was already mid fire couldn't stop his gun and watched his friends back eat a few rounds.

As more shots erupted from the DJ booth, this time one striking a guard in the leg, a couple of the guards turned and opened fire at their flank attacker. This allowed Andrew to move up behind them, and as a stray bullet took out one of the guards, a tentacle grabbed the other by the belt and with all his might, Andrew threw him towards a pillar in the room. The man hit the pillar with a meaty thud and then hit the ground unmoving.

A guard made a hand signal and the guards retreated. The fighting stopped. The remaining guards both took their eyes off Andrew and looked towards the stage curtain. A slim figure appeared from behind it and walked on stage. The figure stood just short of six feet tall. Andrew guessed that had to be due to the combat boots it was wearing. The figure's face was obscured by a mask that had the appearance of a shattered porcelain doll, with

74

black streaks under the eyes, and lips painted the same color. The stranger's hair was hidden behind a nun's habit.

As Andrew looked and studied the figure now coming towards him, he could see that it was a woman. A solid black corset added some decoration to the black spandex was she wearing. Andrew also admitted to himself, that from what he could see, she was not too bad to look at.

The woman reached the end of the pole stage and stood at Andrew's eye level. Neither moved. Andrew worked an unseen tentacle into his pocket and pulled out a couple of loose dollars and tossed them on the stage. Andrew wasn't sure what the effect of his taunting her would be as the woman watched the money hit the ground. However, once they touched the hardwood floor, Andrew got his answer.

The woman tilted her head. She then turned and took the pole in both hands, and with an effortless motion she ripped it from the ceiling to slam against Andrew's head like a baseball bat. The blow shot the tentacle monster off his feet and through one of the pillars that he had previously thrown a guard against. Then in the blink of an eye, the woman was standing over him.

"Funny," An electronic voice emotionlessly crackled at him. "Squid Boy."

"Look, I didn't have a name…" Andrew couldn't finish his sentence when the woman landed one of her combat boots against Andrew's side, lifting him from the ground and into a nearby wall. Normally, Andrew's tentacles could absorb all the impact from the attacks. The cracking he heard and the difficulty that he was having breathing told him that this woman was hitting hard enough to break through it.

As the woman approached Andrew knew he had to think fast. Feigning further injury to lure the woman in closer, Andrew shot a tentacle around her ankles and pulled her off her feet. Without letting go, Andrew lifted the woman in the air and used a tentacle to punch her square in the stomach and throw her away from him. To Andrew's surprise, as the woman flew she was able to right herself. Andrew was sure that he felt more pain from hitting her than she felt from him throwing her. It was as if Andrew had just shooed a bug away from a picnic that it was desperately trying to get to. It moved her, but obviously not hurt her.

"I killed a man with a shot that hard," Andrew told himself, genuinely amazed.

The woman gave no response just kept moving towards her target.

"Look, we can do this all night," Andrew decided if violence wasn't going to solve the problem, maybe reason would. "But here's the thing. I'm only here to get my fiancé and leave. You let us go, and we'll walk right out that door. No harm, no foul."

Andrew's answer was a boot to what would be his outer ankle, if it had not been made completely of tentacles. While it wasn't his flesh getting kicked, the pain he felt could have fooled him. The woman began to tower over Andrew as he went down to one knee to ease his weight off the injured ankle and struggled to maintain standing from that shot.

Much to either fighter's surprise, a pair of feet coming out of nowhere, slammed against the side of the woman, knocking her to the ground. Mike climbed back to his feet after his attack landed and raised his weapon and began to fire. The woman nimbly dodged from where she was lying but twisted right into a pair of tentacles reaching for her throat.

The woman struggled with all her might as she felt the tentacles tightening in, trying to stop her breathing. Andrew heard a strange electronic pop as he continued to put pressure on the trapped woman. The woman slapped and punched violently at the tentacles. Andrew did everything in his power to maintain his grasp, but he knew he was losing. It was only a matter of time before she was freed if she hadn't run out of air by then.

"That's enough!" An older voice shouted. The woman instantly stopped struggling. "Let Sister Slaughter go, she'll be a good girl, you have my word."

"Sister Slaughter? That was the best you could come up with?" Andrew raised a tentacled eyebrow at the woman as he let her go.

The woman hit her knees gasping for air and shot a middle finger in Andrew's direction as she climbed to her feet.

"Better than Squid Boy." A female voice coughed back. The popping must have been the voice synthesizer she was using.

"If you had been listening," Mike leaned down, staring at the unblinking doll face. "It's Flayer, Named him after my favorite metal band."

"I said enough, you three. Slaughter, get out of here." An older man with a cane walked on stage in the center of the room as the woman got to her feet and staggered off, still coughing. Andrew finally recognized the voice as the man on the answering machine. "So, I guess we pissed you off pretty bad huh? Hacking up your dog really lit a fire under your ass."

"Buying my fiancé didn't help much either," Andrew informed the old man.

"Sure," The old man nodded. "That would have set me off too."

"Any of these fuckers the one that hacked up my dog?" Andrew slid closer to the man.

"I think it was one of those that you smashed their brains out," The old man walked around the stage looking for something. His cane clicked with each step. "Do an old man a favor, get me a chair."

The two grunts quickly pulled one of the lounge chairs on stage. The old man struck them both with his care and pointed to Andrew.

"I want him to get me a seat," Andrew obliged to the request and used a few tentacles to bring a bar stool with a back up to the stage. The old man had a seat. "Water." Andrew turned around and headed to the bar. He heard the guns get back into position, but nothing happened. Andrew slid back with a glass of water and a tentacle handed it to the old man. The old man took a slip and motioned to his subordinates to leave.

"Come closer," The old man beckoned the monstrosity closer. "I'm 82-years old, and I've seen a lot of shit in my life. I have not seen anything like you. I want to get a good look at you."

"Alright." Andrew slid closer to the old man when he stopped a few feet off, the man motioned for him to move closer. Andrew stopped when he stood right next to the old man.

"My god," The old man reached out and touched the mass of tentacles protecting Andrew's face. "You're an ugly looking son of a bitch, aren't you?"

"I've seen uglier," Andrew told him. "I met a man who sold women like cattle and ordered the death of an innocent man and his dog."

"Ha," The old man let out a solid belly laugh. "You know who I am I take it?"

"The leader of this ragtag of wannabes." Andrew scowled.

"Yeah," The old man sighed and sat back in his chair. "Ragtag wannabes. Vincent Martinano. I led this group. We used to not be so haggard mind you. Used to run this whole town, gambling, whores, backdoor booze."

"Used to?" Andrew asked, his curiosity peeked as to why the old man stopped the fight.

"Yeah," The old man nodded. "Until your type came along."

"Us types?"

"Why are you still wearing that mask? I already know who you are, Mullen. I knew as soon as you mentioned that woman we had in back," Vincent pointed to the back.

"She's up there!" Mike pointed out.

"Andrew?!" Erin called out. Erin stood up and looked down at the scene below. Andrew looked up at her and dropped the tentacles covering his face.

"That's better," Vincent pulled a handkerchief out of his pocket coughed into it, folded it back up and stuffed it back in his pocket. "You see, Andrew, everyone in this little group made fun of Micky, and laughed him out of the gang. I believed him. I've tangoed with your types before. That's why I hired the little woman who just kicked your ass. It's because of you types I had to get into trafficking, I had to sell hard drugs. I don't want to do that, hurts too many innocent people. Hurts the kids. But how can I compete with you guys running around? All you super-powered freaks. We set up, one of you comes in and shuts us down, and the cycle continues. How long you been at this?"

"A few days or so," Andrew confessed. "Not entirely sure. The days have kind of been a blur."

78

"Ha," Vincent laughed again. A solitary tear rolled down his face. "We used to be the biggest threat that you all had to face. Now, we're not even a threat to a day one rookie. Oh, how the mighty have fallen."

"I would have just left you alone..." Andrew began.

"I'm going to stop you right there," Vincent leaned forward. "No, we would have been doing this dance over and over again. I still have an image to maintain, I had to stand up to you or my men lose faith in me. This is the ending that had to happen. I just have one request."

"Huh?" Andrew towered over the man. He did not see Erin and Mike walk up behind him.

"You!" Vincent pointed at Mike. "You the guy shooting from the booth?"

"Yeah," Mike confirmed proud of himself.

"He's a good man," Vincent turned back to Andrew. "Got to keep good friends close. Back to what I was saying though. Andrew, I'm the last person to lead this family. My kids and grandkids wrote me off years ago and want nothing to do with all this nonsense. I want you to end the era. Put an end to it."

"I'm sorry?" Andrew questioned what the man was saying.

"Look, kid," Vincent coughed again, this time just into his hand. "I've survived two bouts with cancer. I've fought in a war to stop a madman nearly take over the world. I'm not a world-threatening power. I'm not even worth a blip on your radar. Give this old man one last request, I spent my whole life doing my best to lead an exciting life. I'm not able to keep this up anymore. Please, don't let my death be boring."

Andrew never thought it would end like this with the Martinano family. He looked at the old man sitting in the chair. He envied him. This man did what Andrew had wanted more than anything. This old man had lived a life worth telling about. This man accomplished something that took a suicide attempt to change in Andrew. This man was not perfect, but he certainly was not boring.

Andrew thought for a moment then looked the man in the eyes. Vincent sat back in his chair. His elderly eyes begged Andrew for the rest. A rest from the race that his kind had lost a long time ago and prison just seemed a sad way for a man like this to go. Andrew nodded.

A tentacle slid out from Andrew's arm and slowly pressed a point against the old man's chest. Vincent took it in his hand and aimed it directly at his heart. The old man licked his lips and nodded. In a quick sharp motion, the tentacle shot right through the spot the old man indicated. Probably a spot he knew too well from executing men in the past. The old man's body didn't jump, didn't struggle. It just slid down and bled when Andrew removed the tentacle.

Andrew stopped and stared at the motionless man. He realized he just ended a chapter in New Hancock's book and wasn't too sure how he felt about that. Andrew turned and faced his friends. He retracted all his tentacles and moved closer to them.

"Hi Erin," Andrew waved softly. "You ok?"

"What the fuck?" Erin stepped back. "Who are you?"

"It's me," Andrew smiled. "It Andy. Look, it's kind of a long story. I got superpowers. I'm still Andrew though."

"No," Erin shook her head and recoiled as he tried to move closer. "No, Andrew. I don't care about that. I'd love you no matter what you look like, but you've changed. The Andrew I knew and loved wouldn't have done what you did. He wouldn't have killed."

Andrew stopped.

"But I saved you." Andrew protested.

"No, Andy," Erin shook her head. "Mike saved me. You walked into a place and just started killing people. You're not a hero, you're a monster. Superheroes don't kill, Andy. Look, please do me a favor. Don't ever contact me again."

Andrew almost went after her as Erin bolted towards the door. Mike put his hand out and stopped his friend. Andrew looked over at Mike who just shook his head.

"Real world," Mike put his hand on his friend's shoulder. "This isn't a comic book. You have changed, and she doesn't like what you changed into. I think deep down you don't either."

"But I saved her." Andrew let out softly.

"No," Mike confirmed. "I saved her, you walked in the front door and started kicking ass. Now, come on. Before the cops start to show up. I'm sure those guys Vincent let out already called them. I'll go buy you a beer."

"What do I do now?" Andrew asked. "It feels like there is nowhere to go from here. I've been running around for this whole time with a goal and it's over."

"Andy," Mike hoisted the gun on his shoulder. "You missed what Vincent said. He's seen so much in life. He's seen a ton of 'your type.' He's competed against them, you just got your ass wrecked by one. I'm guessing some are good and some are bad. So, you thinking what I'm thinking?"

"I don't know, Mike," Andrew sighed as he took everything in. "I don't know."

"I don't know about you, friend." Mike patted Andrew on the back. "It's not a perfect life, but I sure as shit don't think it's gonna be boring."

The Flayer:
Ongoing Vol. 1

Issue 1

Andrew Mullen had gotten his wish. All he wanted was a way out of a future he found to be too boring and stagnate. A great job, a beautiful fiancé, a perfect dog, and a future full of white picket fences and upper-middle-class life were all his for the taking. To him though, it felt more like a life of day in, day out ennui and sitting around waiting to die. Andrew changed all that two months ago when he put a gun to his head and pulled the trigger.

Since then, he had gained the ability to grow tentacles from anywhere on his body if light did not touch where they extruded from. He had fought off one of New Hancock's most notorious organized crime rings when he went to go rescue his now ex-fiancé. He'd lost his dog and that upper-middle-class life had gone out the door. In other words, he was no longer boring; but as they say, be careful what you wish for.

"You're doing that thing again," Mike sat next to his friend who was more like his brother, at the bar as they were both having a drink. Andrew, who had barely touched his, had joined just to get out of the apartment for something other than work. "That thing with your brain."

"Huh?" Andrew snapped out of his thoughts and looked over at his friend who was so drunk he could topple over at any minute. "Sorry, just a lot going on upstairs."

"Andy," Mike wrapped a tattooed arm around his friend. "If I can shoot at the mafia for you, I can shoot those thinky thoughts too. Bam!"

Mike wasn't wrong. Andrew's fiancé had been sold by her uncle to pay off a gambling debt to the Martinano family. He had made a high dollar bet in both his and Andrew's name that didn't pan out. This led Andrew off on his first big superhero adventure to save her. Unfortunately for him though, Mike had saved the girl, while Andrew let a taste for vengeance take over and just began fighting, and in his blindness; killing.

"You know what happened the last time you took me drinking to deal with my problems." Andrew laughed slightly as he made a gun with this finger and thumb and pointed it at the side of his head.

"You're right," Mike snatched the beer in front of Andrew, downed it and put it back in front of him. "No more beer for you. Although, it did give you superpowers, so maybe more beer equals more superpowers. Drink up, fucker." Mike passed his half drank beer in front of Andrew. The man welcomed the gesture, took a sip, and smiled.

Andrew looked up at the TV in the bar. The 11 o'clock news had come on. Each time the news had come on for the past few months, at least one blurb of his whole story was being played. Very, very few were positive. Many of the stories told their own version of the events and continued to try and instill fear in people to get them to continue to watch. Most of them were focused on trying to find out who or what he was. During all the stories, enough footage was aired to let Andrew relive the entire event. It showed everything the police recovered from the tapes. From Andrew entering the building to him driving a tentacle through the chest of the head of the organization, Vincent Martinano. It even showed Erin running out the door from him.

The only person that could be identified in the entire footage, that was still alive, was Andrew's ex, Erin Hastings. Andrew felt sorry for the girl. The most horrible night of her life and these news vultures were doing everything in their power to make her relive it. Most of the time she would just walk away from the cameras without saying a word, and sometimes she would break down in tears begging to just be left alone. Not once though, much to Andrew's relief, did she say that she knew who either of her rescuers was.

The police were still baffled though. Thanks to the call from Jeremy, Erin's uncle confessing to his crimes, the police had shown up shortly after Andrew and Mike had left the building. A handful of the gangsters had survived the encounter with medical attention, but every single one of them was too frightened to explain what they had seen. Jeremy, who also had an encounter with the creature had ended up in the mental ward for post-traumatic stress disorder after he claimed that he was horribly tortured by the creature.

"Hey," Mike yelled to the barkeepers. "I need two more beers and for you to turn that shit off. My boy, Flayer there, is a fucking hero. Fucking news, talking all that shit."

"He's a freak!" A patron shouted back.

"You're a fucking freak!" Mike attempted to shoot up out of his seat, but an unseen tentacle held him down across his lap like a seat belt.

"That's right," The patron shot back, "Just sit there next to your boyfriend."

"You're not my boyfriend." Mike looked at Andrew.

"I know," Andrew continued to drink his beer. "Let me handle this."

"You gonna do something?" The man came up behind the two friends drinking at the bar. On the darkened floor of the bar, no one could see a tentacle slide behind the man's ankle, just as no one could see that the tentacle came from Andrew's pant leg.

"No," Andrew told the man without turning around. "We're not going to do anything but sit here and have a cold beer. Here, I'll buy you a round."

"Listen," The man slapped the back of Andrew's head. "I don't want nothing from no faggots."

"You're right," Andrew smiled as he pulled the tentacle forward fast, hooking the man's leg and tripping him. "You have had enough to drink."

86

The bouncer and a male bartender picked the man up and escorted him out of the bar. The female bartender walked up and changed the channel from the news to some poor quality late night movie.

"Thanks," Mike smiled at her and raised Andrew's half full glass to her and downed it. "Two more please."

"I'm with you," The bartender brought the beers. Attractive was too minor of a word for Andrew to have used to describe her. Tattoos, tight leather skirt, and a low-cut top. Andrew wasn't sure if that was just what he was choosing to notice, or it had been so long that that was all he cared about. "Rumor is that he knew it was sex ring, and that he had come to rescue that Erin girl. Any man that would go up against the mob is a man I would love to meet. I mean she just bailed on him. I would have ridden that guy till he broke. To think of what he could do with those tentacles."

"I know him." Mike smiled at the girl and leaned in on the bar counter.

"Sure, you do." The woman nodded laughing, "Uh-huh."

"I do," Mike took a sip of his drink and slapped his drunk hand on the bar. "I've known the guy for years."

"Really?" The woman leaned in on the counter closer to Mike. Andrew got a good view of the pair of tits hiding as he looked her up and down, and then cursed himself for feeling like he was objectifying the woman. "Really thinking about cutting you off for the night."

"Look," Mike's drunk brain quickly deceived a plan. "How's about this. You give me your number, and I'll pass it along to him."

"So, I give some barfly my number, and deal with him calling me, pretending to be this tentacle guy all the time," the woman began to summarize what she figured Mike's plan was. "Can't get rid of him and lose not one but two of the regulars here. Mike, do you really think I'm that crazy?"

"Tell you what," Mike leaned in. "Don't give it to me. My boy, Andrew here knows the guy too. Andy here is queerer than a 3-dollar bill…"

"No, I'm not," Andrew protested. "I'm really not."

"Shut up, Andy," Mike didn't even turn to his friend. "He passes that number along and I've never even seen it."

"Didn't Andrew have a fiancé a few months ago?" The bartender punched a hole right through Mike's plan. Mike's drunk brain had to think quickly to patch it. Lucky for Mike, having alcohol shut off the filter in his brain usually wielded an answer with some sort of results.

"Why do you think they broke up?" Mike fired back at the woman. "What do you think he did? Walked into a strip club and killed a bunch of people?"

"Ok, fine, but you don't get to see it." The young bartender relented. Andrew could not believe that the barmaid bought all that. He figured that it was more than likely that she just wanted to shut Mike up.

"Fair enough." Mike closed his eyes as the woman wrote her name and phone number on a scrap of paper and handed it to Andrew who folded it and stuffed it in his pocket. He then showed the woman his open, empty hands before he tapped Mike to re-open his eyes.

"See?" Mike smiled, "Was that so hard?"

"I get bothered by either of you two," The woman pointed at them before going back to cleaning a glass. Legs this time; Andrew thought while devouring the view of the slender skin trapped in fishnets from behind. It had been a while since he had a nice no-strings-attached hookup, and she was not a bad candidate. The only downside is it would either involve letting out his secret, or it would make their favorite watering hole an awkward experience. "I make sure Bruno kicks both your asses at the door whenever you guys come by. Got it?"

"No problem, Kristin," Mike finished off his drink. "I think we're going to call it a night anyway. What do we owe you?"

The woman ran some numbers, on the computer behind her, and returned Mike a slip of paper. A large "0.00" sat on the bottom.

"Boss heard about Andrew losing the fiancé bit," Kristin told them, "And figured things were bad since no one here had seen you two for a month. So, he told me your next beers here were on the house."

88

"Mitch," Mike pulled out his wallet anyway and made a motion for Andrew to put his away. Mike pulled out a fifty-dollar bill and put it on the bar. "Is always a good guy. In that case, though, this is yours. Don't stop being a sweetheart, Kristin."

Both men stood up and headed to the door while throwing on their coats.

"Andrew," The barmaid called out as they left. "Remember, no matter your life choices, you're always welcome here."

"It's who he is," Mike called back. "Not a choice."

"I really wish you hadn't told her that," Andrew said under his breath to Mike as he threw up a hand to wave goodbye as he exited.

Issue 2

Both men's boots crunched in the snow as more gently came down around them. New Hancock was never known for terrible winters like in the Midwest. Snow would usually fall at night and stay throughout the winter but would never be too much of a hassle for anyone. The cold stung and was even worse when the wind would kick up. Luckily, tonight was not one of those nights.

The alcohol had begun to work itself out of their systems as Andrew pulled the collar of his grey trench coat up over his neck. Andrew still felt that he was as plain and boring as the snow beneath him. Five-foot-eleven, brown hair, brown eyes; just plain. Not much he could do about that. He also trimmed down the bread that had grown roughly two months ago, into a tasteful goatee.

Mike stood as almost a polar opposite to his almost corporate looking friend. Tattooed heavily from his toes to his neck, bald as a cue ball, and ornamented with multiple piercings. Many that Andrew could easily see, and a few he really wished he had never seen.

"Hold up," Mike dipped down an alley and stood behind a dumpster. "Got to drain the lizard."

"Cool." Andrew lit a cigarette and leaned on the wall on the other side. He hadn't been much of a smoker his whole life, but he found that it helped immensely with dealing with the changes he had been going through since October.

"So," Mike's voice covered the sound of rented beer hitting a small pile of snow. "You gonna call he?."

"Nah," Andrew let out a puff. "Would make things awkward there. Besides, then she would know."

Both men had a rule. Never piss where you drink. For a small bar like Zero's, most of the customers were regulars. People Mike and Andrew had known and had been drinking with since both were able to get a hold of fake IDs. Taking one of them home, then never wanting anything to do with them would just make coming back to the bar four times a week too awkward. Something neither man wanted. The only exception being first timers there.

"So fucking what?" Mike zipped up and walked back over to his friend. "I've talked to her a few times. She's going to New Hancock U. Leaving come the fall, you get your dick wet, have a little fun. You send her on her way. No harm, no foul."

"Till she starts bragging about banging a superhero," Andrew shrugged. "Then everyone knows that I'm that dude on TV, and everyone come looking for me. I don't want to face the public I don't even have a name yet."

"Sure you do," Mike smiled. "You're *The Flayer*. The hero that would make Lovecraft get hard."

"Besides," Andrew lamented. "She wants Flayer, not Andrew Mullen. Not really what I want to deal with."

"She's thinking about tonight," Mike pointed out. "You need to as well. It's been too long, Andy. You need to let loose and have a little fun. You need to find a little super girl. You know those weird ones that wear a mask or too much makeup, to hide their identity. The kind of girl that would give a coulrophobic an awkward boner."

"What on Earth are you talking…?" Andrew began but was suddenly cut off.

"Get the fuck off me!" A woman screamed from further down the alley. "Help! I said get the fuck back!"

"This little fillies got some fight," A male voice laughed. "Hey, Hernandez, you ever heard of a rodeo fuck?"

"The fuck is that?" Mike didn't need to ask twice. When he turned back around to face Andrew, he found a tentacled monstrosity wearing the long grey trench coat his friend once was. Smaller tentacles had covered his head. Every orifice was enclosed with a cage of writhing tentacles, pulsating and moving as a pile of worms trying to find a comfortable position on hard bed. Andrew's eyes became pulsating, dark black rings, matching the rest of the tentacles on his face.

A mass of tentacles replaced his legs in a massive pile that almost resembled a tree trunk covered in writhing snakes. Long tendrils came down his arms covering them and making long whips where fingers and arms used to be.

The tentacles came out of Andrew's body where ever light did not touch. He could call on a tentacle of any width, and any length, and used them to make a suit of armor underneath his clothes.

"This way." Andrew shot off with a slither in the direction of the scream and could only hope he could make it in time. Mike reached in the dumpster that he had been urinating on and found an old curtain rod. Without hesitation, he continued after his friend.

Andrew blessed the fact that he had been training in his horrific form, especially when he found the three men and the cornered woman. Without making a sound Andrew took a quick survey of the attackers. Three men, a white guy, a black guy, and a Latino. All about the same age and build, neither of them armed with anything more than a knife.

The black man and the Latino both held the young woman down by her arms. Andrew figured that wearing a short skirt like that, and kicking as she did, it was only going to be a matter of time before her underwear was off and she was going to be used then possibly murdered.

Another fact that Andrew loved about his tentacled form, was that he didn't need to walk. During his time playing with his tentacles in the mental hospital where he discovered them, Andrew taught himself how to slither along the ground in a similar fashion to a snake. Much to his enjoyment and the dismay of the would-be rapists, slithering was practically silent.

So, when Andrew shot a tentacle around the throat of the white attacker and lifted him from the ground, it took all four of the people involved in the attack completely by surprise. With a snap of the appendages, Andrew tossed the would-be attacker down the alley. The man's body crashed into some trash cans. The sound of a metal rod striking something told Andrew the goon was out of the fight.

"Holy shit," The black man exclaimed, "That's that freak from the news. Holy fuck, that thing is real."

The thing you will find about must rapists is that their prey is usually never stronger than them. To them it's not about sex, it's about having that power over a helpless victim that makes them feel more like the big, tough guys they want to feel like. When you compare a five-foot-five woman to a nine-foot-tall monster that has been seen having no problem killing, the option of having power over it is long gone. As quick as the attackers came to that conclusion, they too were gone.

Mike popped out from behind a dumpster just as the Latino attacker tried to duck behind it. A solid crack with the curtain rod knocked him off his feet, the second one knocked him out, the third one straight to his crotch was just because Mike found the man's actions that detestable.

Andrew shot down the alley behind the black man. Much to Andrew's dislike, the man was not just armed with a knife. The man pulled a gun from his front waistband and began to shoot over his shoulder at Andrew. Andrew, knowing the pain of bullets all too well, chose not to change his course and continued chasing after the man only taking one bullet to the chest that stung then dropped to the ground after penetrating his shirt but not the tentacles guarding Andrew's body.

Out of nowhere a bright light shown straight at Andrew. The light seemed more intense than any flashlight and burned his eyes just too look at it. Throwing a tentacle up to block the light from blinding him felt to be his undoing, as a concussive force threw Andrew off his feet, and into the snow. A small explosion had also sapped the oxygen from the area taking Andrew's breath away for a second.

Between the burning in his eyes and the immense pain in his arm, Andrew could not find his feet after he finally caught his breath. He tried to stand almost completely blind, slipped and then noticed something that truly frightened him. When Andrew fell, he reached out like he normally would to catch himself and expected a tentacle to catch and right him, no such luck. He fell harder than before and felt his fingers drop into the snow.

"Fingers?" Andrew questioned. The change in physiology must have messed with his brain as he acted like his legs were exposed when trying to get up, only to find the tentacles on his legs were still intact. With a slip and a slide, Andrew landed face first in the snow.

"Hold still, friend." A new voice filled Andrew's ears and a strong arm helped to right Andrew into at least a sitting position once he retracted his leg tentacles.

"Get off my friend, you costumed asshole!" Mike's voice came to Andrew this time as his vision started to come back. Before looking up, Andrew continued to look at a writhing piece of something on the ground. As his vision cleared up, he noticed that the writhing had stopped and on the ground before him was one of his tentacles severed from his body.

"My friend," The first voice responded to Mike. "It was a case for accidental friendly fire. My sincerest apologies!"

"That armor looking suit ain't gonna do shit when I'm done with you!" Mike's yelling was followed by the sound of the curtain rod swinging and only hitting air, was quickly followed by the sound of two grunts coming from Mike.

"My sidekick is attending to his wound," The older voice informed Mike. "Now, if you promise to behave, I'll get my knee out of your back and we can talk about this."

Andrew attempted to pick up the now lifeless tentacle from the ground only to find that his arm did nothing but shoot blinding pain through his entire body. A pair of hands gently pushed him back against a brick wall.

"Hold still," A new, much younger man smiled down at Andrew. His face hidden behind a white bandit's mask, and his body adorned in white robes. His white boots crunched in the snow as he adjusted position to look at Andrew. "Your arm looks pretty bad, let me have a look at it."

"You're Choir Boy," Andrew let his normal voice escape from the tentacled cage that covered his mouth. Andrew wasn't sure why he hadn't disguised his voice. It had to be either the pain or the fact that this was the sidekick of a hero of The League that was treating his wounds. "You're fucking Choir Boy."

"Yes," The young man got a chuckle, as he looked at the redness covering Andrew's arm. Taking snow around him, as clean as he could find, and placing it on Andrew's arm seemed to begin to kill the burning sensation. "Usually everyone seems to be more excited for my partner over there. It's kind of nice to be the first one recognized. You're that guy from the news, right?"

"Yeah," Andrew quickly searched for things to say. "The Flayer, I guess."

"You guess?" The older voice had come closer to Andrew. Andrew looked up to see a man in a white suit of armor with a gold crucifix emblazoned on it. The man wore a helmet hiding any features that Andrew could have used to guess the man's identity. Though, being a huge fan of the world of superheroes and of The League, Andrew did not need anything more to know who the man was.

"The Holy Frijole..." Andrew's voice seemed to trail off.

"That would be me, my friend," The man nodded. "How is he Choir Boy?"

"Pretty bad burns," the young man began had pulled a roll of gauze out of a satchel at his side and began to wrap Andrew's arm. "Flayer, what are your known weaknesses?"

"I have no idea," Andrew had not taken his eyes off The Holy Frijole. For only the second time in his life, Andrew felt in awe just because of someone's presence. "I didn't think I had any."

"Taking on crime without knowing your weaknesses?" The Holy Frijole laughed. "You're either very brave or very stupid. Then again, the same could be said of all of us costumed heroes, huh?"

"All set," Choir Boy told Andrew as he helped him to his feet, "You should be good in a few days. That is if your body's healing abilities are anything like the rest of us. I would give you something for the pain, but from the alcohol on your breath, I don't want anything that strong to mix with it and have an adverse reaction. Though, in the morning you are definitely going to want to take something."

"Thank you." Andrew used a tentacle to wrap around his body and brush the snow off. His arm had already begun to feel better. What pain was there, was quickly ignored as Andrew looked at the two heroes in front of him.

"Who the fuck is this?" Mike joined his friend's side.

"Mike," Andrew gestured to the two. "This is the Holy Frijole and his sidekick Choir Boy."

"Who the fuck is that?" Mike raised an eyebrow. "What the fuck kind of name is that?"

"The name was given to me by the children I regularly see on mission trips. I am a sitting member of The League," The Frijole reached a hand out to Mike to shake, which Mike ignored. "I take it you are Mr. Flayer's sidekick. What do they call you?"

"I ain't nobody's sidekick," Mike snickered. "Ain't that right, Andy?"

"You two are so at ease with using your names when out on patrol?" Choir Boy questioned.

"Actually," Andrew used a tentacle to absently scratch the top of his covered head. "We're not actual superheroes. We were just at the bar having drinks and heard trouble."

"With the way you shot into battle to save that woman," The Frijole laughed. "You could have fooled me. Speaking of Choir Boy, have you taken a look at her?"

"She took off during the battle," Choir Boy then left the other three. "I will have a look at the other wounded though."

"You're not normally from New Hancock," Andrew pointed out. "What brings you into town?"

"Two reasons actually," The Holy Frijole began to fumble with his helmet, and eventually took it off. Revealing an older man in his early fifties, with very distantly Mexican features, and a mustache that would make porn-stars jealous. "Since the one of you with superpowers has not attacked me, I feel it is safe to take off that stifling thing."

96

In a gesture of solidarity, Andrew retracted all his tentacles, revealing himself too, and shot out a hand to the man. Who took it in his strong grip.

"Father Eduardo Vasquez." The superhero smiled.

"Andrew Mullen." Andrew had not felt his heart jump this high since his first kiss.

"The pleasure is all mine," Eduardo quickly turned to try to shake Mike's again who reluctantly accepted this time. "Sorry about the mishap there. The reason I'm in town is that the news has been showing two superpowered beings in combat and I was sent by The League to investigate. In a town this big, I'm surprised to have just run into one of them."

"More like shot," Mike quipped. He then felt a job to his ribs, he wasn't sure if it was an elbow or a tentacle, and frankly, he didn't care. "Don't jab me, fucker."

"It was an accident," Andrew informed his friend. "We were both after the same target. It happens. So, you found me, who else are you looking for?"

"A slender person," The Frijole began to describe the person he was after. "The one you fought at the strip club on that night."

"Sister Slaughter," Andrew gave the Frijole a name. "That's all I heard her called."

"You all need new names," Mike added. "Everything is just so terrible."

"You named me," Andrew looked at his friend.

"Except yours," Mike backtracked. "Your's is awesome."

"An evildoer taking the name, and visage, of the faith," Eduardo rubbed his forehead. "Is Catholicism that sinister looking?"

"It is kind of creep," Mike shrugged. "You all worship a dead dude nailed to a two by four."

"Shut up, Mike," Andrew added another bump to the ribs.

"Do that one more time, fucker," Mike pointed a finger at his friend's face. "Not like he's a priest or something... Aw shit, Father Eduardo..."

"Haha," The older man laughed. "No offense taken. I understand that it can look a bit odd to... outsiders?"

97

"Yeah," Mike nodded. "Atheist."

"Ah," Eduardo smiled, "Well, you are always welcome to come to my…"

"Save it." Mike put a hand up to stop him.

"Fair enough," The Father nodded to acknowledge the choice Mike made. "You Andrew?"

"I'm kind of between a lot of things right now," Andrew admitted.

"Well," The Father continued, "There are many like us at my church feel free to stop by, even just for fellowship with your fellow heroes. I'm not from too far away."

"I might do that." Andrew liked the idea more and more that there were others like him out there. Meeting them might be a good chance to find out more about what was going on with him. As with the now-canceled wedding, Andrew felt that maybe a bit of support might help him feel better about this change in his life too.

"Excellent," Eduardo smiled at the idea of adding another to his flock. "Anyway, have either of you had any contact with this Sister Slaughter?"

"Other than that night," Andrew informed Father Vasquez. "No, haven't heard anything. Vincent Martinano told us to stop fighting and she kind of stormed off."

"Hmm," Eduardo rubbed his chin. "She sounds like a henchman. I must be on the move. It was good meeting both of you. Choir Boy, how are the others?"

"Good, Father," The sidekick shouted back. "Knocked out, but the paramedics will be able to take them just fine. I already called into the New Hancock Police, so they should be on their way soon."

"As I said," The Father shook both of their hands again. "Thank you for your help. We really should be going before the police show up. They might drag you two in for questioning, or other things. Since neither of you two are registered."

"Sorry, we couldn't be more help," Andrew apologized. "We'll take your advice and get out of here."

"You two have been a great help, actually," Eduardo gave them a little bump to their egos. "Helped stop a rape, helped me solve half my mission, and gave me a lot to go on with the whole Sister Slaughter thing. Ah yes, I almost forgot."

Father Eduardo pulled out a card and gave it to Andrew. The name of the church and Father Eduardo's name and number were on it.

"Thanks, Father," Andrew put it in his pocket. "I wish I had something to give you."

"No need," The father waved his hand. "We'll be in touch. Now hurry, go."

The two began to put snow behind them as the sound of sirens started to come closer in the background. Andrew stuffed his hands in his pockets and fumbled with the business card that The Holy Frijole had given him.

"Couldn't be much help?" Mike scowled. "We did all the damn work. Hell, you decided to go all starstruck and totally forgot about..."

"I know," Andrew beamed with excitement. "I totally just got shot by the Holy Frijole."

Issue 3

Seven in the morning came early for Andrew. Sleeping on just a mattress with nothing else on the floor did not help much either. Andrew looked over at the alarm clock on the floor next to him and threw the comforter off the bed when he noticed that it was not seven A.M. but was eight in the morning.

Andrew rushed to his dresser and pulled out a dirty old t-shirt and a pair of beat-up jeans. He had no time to change his underwear or take a shower. So, smelling like a brewery would have to do for the day. He figured that Mike could stay up in the front while he stayed in the back and worked on the cars.

Luckily for Andrew, the studio apartment was even smaller than the name suggested. A kitchen in the same room as the living room only had a two-burner stove, and a small, but brand new, fridge. Dishes had to be done in the bathtub, which was a blessing and a curse for Andrew. Needing to shower made sure Andrew hardly ever ran out of a dish, and laziness meant that sometimes he would be cleaning himself having pots in the same tub.

The living room held a few bookshelves. Mostly horror and comedy novels that Andrew had bought, put up there, and never thought about again. These included a compilation of stories by H.P. Lovecraft that Andrew had glued the pages together and hollowed out. This book was where Andrew had once kept a 9mm pistol, but now only holds whatever marijuana that he could scrounge together.

A couch sat on its lonesome, across from an old medium sized TV, with a VHS and the "King Chilla" monster movie series in the cabinet underneath. Next to that, an old 8-bit video game system sat nearly untouched for two years.

In the kitchen, Andrew leaned down to grab a dog food bowl from the floor. Absentmindedly, Andrew reached in the cupboard over the stove pulled out a can of dog food. Before he opened the can he stopped himself. His dog, Shithead, had been butchered by the mafia gang he had gone to battle against two months ago. Andrew tossed the empty dog food bowl back on the ground with a sigh. It had been this long and he still was going through the same old routine.

Andrew grabbed a set of keys that hung on a hook on the wall next to the door and bolted out the door. Almost jumping flights of stairs he made it down to the first floor of the old apartment complex he lived in and rushed to his old beat up car. His old beat up car that had a new parking ticket in the windshield.

Andrew unlocked the car and tossed the parking ticket on the passenger side floor and attempted to the start the car. Unfortunately, much like it's owner, the car hated the winter. It decided that not working today was going to be its best option.

"Come on, you piece of shit," Andrew slammed his hand against the dashboard. What normally encouraged the car to get its act together and work, failed this time, and failed miserably. This time Andrew slammed hard with both hands on the dashboard. Although instead of worrying about the car, Andrew's mind shot elsewhere. His arm no longer hurt.

Andrew rushed back into the building and back inside. He threw off his coat and hooded sweatshirt and stared down at his arm. His perfectly normal arm. Andrew took a deep breath waiting for the pain to come from finally paying attention to it. The pain never came. Then, mustering what he could and bracing for more pain, Andrew attempted to summon a tentacle out of his arm. Nothing came. Pain did not come, but neither did the tentacle that he attempted to summon. However, Andrew did feel a small wiggling up his shirt sleeve. Andrew reached inside with his other arm, careful not to let any light in and felt a small tentacle wiggling in the darkness.

"At least you're starting to work again." Andrew took solace in the idea

Andrew stopped and looked at the time. His car wouldn't start, and he was already late. Andrew decided he really should just call into work. Andrew picked up the phone and called the mechanics shop. Mike always understood and if there wasn't much work would to do, he would tell him to just chill for the day. If there was work to be done, he would probably come out and get him.

This time there was no answer. Something in Andrew's stomach sank. Despite Mike's carefree attitude towards many things in life, he loved owning and working in that shop. He always told Andrew it was quiet there. With all the pneumatics running to the occasional sound of one of the two of them dropping something, he found it peaceful and quiet. Mike loved it so much, he never even took days off aside from the days when he decided to randomly close the store. Even then he would show up sometimes and work on his own. The shop was his baby.

Andrew got a hold of himself. Nothing probably happened to Mike. It's not like when Erin went missing for two days and was sold into sex slavery. Andrew tried to call Mike's home phone. Again, nothing. This was weird. Andrew had no idea what to do, or where Mike had been. Had he been at the shop and was working, or was he being sodomized by a rich businessman who intended to kill him after he got done torture fucking him? Andrew tried the home phone one more time.

"This better be a big, fat transvestite who intends to blow me," Mike groggily answered the phone. "If not, I'm coming over there anyway and making you choke on my cock."

"Thank fucking God," Andrew gave a sigh of relief. Andrew didn't even question the tone of voice or the greeting on the phone. Mike hated to be woken up no matter the circumstance. "You are alive."

"Fuck, Andy?" Mike groaned. "You ok, dude?"

"Yeah," Andrew got himself together. "When you didn't answer the shop phone I figured something was up."

"Sorry," Mike coughed a bit. Andrew could hear his friend light a cigarette and groan as he sat up in bed. "Last time when you did that superhero shit, you're out for a few days. Between getting my own ass kicked last night, and this fucking hangover, I didn't go in, or bother calling you. Besides, it's the 25th and no one is coming to the shop today. The rest of the world takes the day off, so we might as well too. You ok? You don't worry usually."

"Yeah," Andrew admitted. "I guess still a bit jumpy. Shit changes and usually something bad happens. I get shot, my girlfriend gets kidnapped, you know the usual shit."

"That's cool, brother," Mike took a drag. "I was headed over there later anyway, the bitch below you has been complaining about the heat in her place. I turned off her radiator since she couldn't pay her rent, figured I'd go turn it back on so she thinks I fucking did something. Want to catch some lunch afterwards?"

"Sounds like a plan." Andrew agreed.

"Cool," Mike groaned as he laid back down. "I'm going back to sleep. I'll be over later."

Andrew sat the phone on the receiver after the distinctive click from Mike's side. Andrew turned on the TV and found the channel that told him what was on the other channels at that time. It was, in fact, December 25th. Andrew sighed, got up, and left the building.

Old habits die hard Andrew told himself as he made his way down the block. A small brick church lived nestled into between many homes in the area. Attending a church service was not something Andrew did regularly, but he felt that at least showing up said something for himself, even if it was much later than after the pastor ended the sermon.

Andrew pulled the heavy wooden door open and stepped through the door. The church was so small that there was no main lobby. A little bulletin board sat next to the entrance which was the extent of the community outreach for the place. Several pews lined up in pairs made a little walkway leading straight up to the podium where the pastor would usually give his sermon.

"Whoever it is," A voice called from the back. "You already missed the sermon."

"Sorry, Pastor Dink," Andrew called back, "Kind of a crazy night."

"Andrew!" An elderly, well-dressed man stepped from behind an open door to the right of the stage and offered a hug to Andrew, who warmly accepted. "Haven't seen you in a few months. Figured you gave up the faith after what happened to Erin. She called and said the wedding was off. Are you still with her?"

"No," Andrew looked down at the floor as he gave his answer, "We split shortly afterwards. She said she needed some time to herself."

Andrew knew that lying was wrong and wondered if lying to a preacher got him a special place in Hell. Then again, just being in the building and the two years of attending a church, already made him question a lot of what he previously thought about God and the nature of the universe. As with all the answers you think you have though, the universe has a funny way of changing the questions. To Andrew, he felt this was going to be an endless cycle for the rest of his life.

"Ah," The pastor nodded understandingly, "the Lord does work in ways we cannot possibly comprehend. Maybe he has someone better in store for you, or maybe you'll be stronger together when she has time."

"Yeah." Andrew took a seat in the pew next to where the two were standing and Pastor Dink took a seat next to him. Andrew wondered what other things were in store for him, and if maybe, there was a light at the end of this tunnel. Maybe there was some special reason he was given this "gift".

"Anyway," The pastor leaned back and folded his arms on his portly stomach. "What brings you over here? Its Christmas, shouldn't you be with your family?"

"Don't really have one aside from a really close friend, and he still hasn't got out of bed yet." Andrew chuckled.

"Too much eggnog last night?" The pastor shared in the joke. "You look like you did too."

"Just a touch," Andrew nodded with a slight smile. "Really just have a lot going on lately. Been working a lot with my therapist. Still feels like a lot to handle."

"They say the Lord never gives us more than we can handle," The pastor began. "Most people tend to think that means you can do anything on your own."

"I don't know," Andrew interrupted. "I have had way too much on my plate lately."

"I know," The pastor nodded. "You see Andy, I believe that what is meant by that is, that "we" doesn't just mean you or I. "We" means us; the human race. Look at all the evils in the world that could have never been cast off by one man. If "we" could, then I would be out of a job, huh?"

"Guess you're right." Andrew cracked a smile at the pastor's joke.

"We're all in this together," The pastor reminded him. "Whenever there is a lot, you don't have to face it alone. You need to remember that. Did you go drinking alone last night?"

"No," Andrew shook his head. "Mike was there. Guy even tried to hook me up with the bartender. I just don't want to have to keep relying on people to help me through these things."

"It's better than the alternative," Pastor Dink rubbed Andrew's shoulder in support. "Suffering alone leads to a very dark place."

"Or in the case of what I did," Andrew shook his head looking down, "A very permanent one."

"I wasn't going to bring that up," Dink added flatly.

"Do you think he forgives me for it?" Andrew looked up at Jesus crucified on the cross hanging on the stage.

"Have you prayed for him too?" Dink asked, hoping to remind Andrew that there was someone else who had a say in it.

"No." Andrew shook his head.

"Why don't we pray for that forgiveness together?" Pastor Dink took Andrew's hands in his.

The two sat there silently. Andrew wished he could gather his thoughts to say a prayer. His thoughts ran too fast too focus though. He hoped that maybe whoever was listening, was listening more to the Pastor than to him. Oddly enough, Andrew found just this moment of trying to catch a calming thought. Eventually, one by one, he found he could catch onto something. The remains of the anxiety he felt about not being able to contact Mike seemed to float away. The feelings of frustration about his car were next. Finally, the depressive thoughts about losing so much so quickly were going as well. The small bit of quiet that came after was enough to get Andrew going again.

Andrew silently raised his head to see the Pastor watching him. The man still had a grip on Andrew's clasped hands in solidarity. That too helped Andrew to feel calm and really stick to the point that he was not alone in this.

"Thanks." Andrew finally spoke and stood up. The Pastor followed suit.

"If you need some more time to talk one on one with the Lord, I don't mind stepping back into my office." The Pastor patted Andrew on the shoulder.

"No, thank you though," Andrew let out a slight smile. "I think he heard me very clearly."

The two began to walk towards the door together. Andrew stuffed his hands in his pockets and felt a reminder of last night.

"A quick question," Andrew began as they reached the door. "I ran into a Father Eduardo Vasquez last night. I was wondering if you knew anything about him."

"Hmm…" The preacher began to search his memory banks. "I do believe I've heard a few talks by him. Can't really remember where. I think it was about mission work. Guy really seemed to be into it. I had dinner with him once to talk about some of his trips and to organize one. Why do you ask? Thinking about switching teams?"

"No, though the idea of actual wine is tempting," Andrew joked. "I was just poking around, seeing what I could find out about the guy."

"Sorry," Dink shrugged. "Seemed like a good enough guy when I saw him. Little odd though. Always had a younger guy with him. Dillon, I think his name was. Medical student. That's right! Dillon Tyler. Anything else I can help you with?"

"Just one more question," Andrew thought back to the night before and the dispute in the bar with the patron. "You watch the news lately? What do you think of those guys that broke up the sex ring?"

106

"Well," The pastor smiled. "between the three of us here, while I don't condone killing, I think it's good that someone is starting to clean up New Hancock. Seems like the old heroes just kind of left this town to rot. Sure, they make a fly by every now and then but this guy though. He looked like he had something to prove. To make himself known. Plus, he saved your Erin. Seems like a good guy to me."

"Thanks," Andrew smiled. "I'm sure I've taken up enough of your time. I think I'll be going."

"You know you're always welcome here, Andrew." The two hugged and Andrew took his leave.

Andrew felt a little lighter as he left the tiny church. He couldn't say for sure if he had been heard, but it felt like it. He had been skeptical at first about accepting Eduardo's offer. Now though, having someone vouch for the good Father, Andrew felt a little better about possibly heading to the superhero's support group.

Andrew checked his watch. With the walk back to his apartment, Andrew could probably make a cup of coffee and maybe look at his car before Mike came over. The pastor was right. Today was Christmas and a day to spend with family.

Issue 4

"So, it took a shit finally?" Mike walked up behind Andrew as his friend peered under the hood. Andrew jolted up in surprise and before his head could bang on the hood a mask of tentacles protected him from the impact. "Dude, you are still creepy as shit when you look like that."

"Lot of good it did," Andrew retracted the tentacles and rubbed his head. "Still felt it like there was nothing there. "But yeah, piece of shit wouldn't start this morning."

"Well," Mike peered in. "I see your problem, we don't have some food or booze in us. This doesn't look like a job we can do sober. We'll come back out in a bit. I'm freezing my nuts off out here, and there is a ton of metal in them, so that is just making it worse."

"Sounds like a plan," Andrew liked the idea of at least getting food. Sure, he also liked the idea of getting high, he just didn't like the idea as much as Mike did. As much as the world around Andrew started to suck, in his mind, he had been allowing the feeling of being sober and experiencing life to become more and more present. "I think the Christmas parade is about to start."

"Really," Mike raised an eyebrow. "The Christmas Parade. Hoping to see Santa? Did he bring you a nice football?"

"Fuck you," Andrew laughed, following Mike inside. "You're going to do like every year. Get high, get teary-eyed when you see that one giant balloon and start crying about how awesome your childhood was. I mean, it's a fucking masked turtle."

"Hey," Mike stopped as he got to Andrew's door, pulled out a key, and unlocked the door. "You leave the turtle out of this. They're all just teenagers."

When the two entered the studio apartment, Mike quickly found his favorite spot on Andrew's couch, then with a little untying and a kick, tossed his shoes towards the door. He picked up the remote for the television and turned it on.

Andrew walked into the kitchen and pulled a Chinese food menu out of a drawer where he kept all his odds and ends. He called, placed an order and sat down next to his friend.

"What are you waiting for?" Mike got on Andrew's case as soon as he sat down. "Break that shit out. Bet it'll do wonders for that burn mark on your arm."

"Actually," Andrew pulled up his sleeve. "Look. No pain, no redness, and the tentacles are starting to come back."

"Dude," Mike pulled down Andrew's arm for a better look and gestured for him to bring them out. Andrew complied and found that they were coming out completely. "Holy shit, you're completely healed. Come to think of it, your head wound, and those broken ribs healed fast too. Looks like you got a little more than some tentacles."

"Yeah," Andrew was amazed. Just a few hours ago, they were barely coming out, now it was as if there was no problem at all with them. "Completely healed up."

"I have got to get me some of these superpowers." Mike wished under his breath.

"Too bad, I got rid of the tool." Andrew laughed as he got up out of his seat and pulled out the hollowed-out Lovecraft book.

"We regret to inform you," a female news anchor on T.V. addressed the viewing population. "That the New Hancock

Christmas Day Parade has been postponed, due to an ongoing emergency downtown."

"The fuck is this?" Mike turned up the volume as Andrew sat back down.

"As you can see behind us," the news anchor continued. "The First Hancock Bank building is currently under siege. Police tell us that SWAT has been held back by a barrage of gunfire coming from the building, and that law enforcement has made a call out to the National Guard."

The sound of gunfire could be heard erupting from the building. The camera panned up the side of the building to catch what was making the racket or even hoping to catch a glimpse of the perpetrators.

"Are they really stupid enough to try and rob a bank on a holiday?" Andrew questioned with his eyes glued to the story.

"Looks like it," Mike had even set the drugs to the side and focus on the story, enthralled. "Wait did you see that?"

Andrew caught a glimpse of a familiar face inside the building. A pale visage stared out the window surveying the situation below. The nun's habit with the broken porcelain doll face was all Andrew needed to see.

"Seriously?" Andrew rubbed his chin. "That's got to be that Sister Slaughter chick, from the Martinano family."

"I thought they were done," Mike added. "At least that is what the leader told you before you stabbed him."

"Yeah," Andrew stood up and walked into his bedroom. He opened the closet and swung through some shirts until he found a red, white, and blue sequined robe. He threw it over his body and tied the belt while making his way back to the living room. "Let's go."

"Go where?" Mike continued to sit on the couch.

"Fuckers are screwing with our parade," Andrew pointed out the obvious. "After the car wouldn't start, my day has been shot. All I want to do is sit on my ass, maybe smoke pot, watch you cry over a floating turtle and eat Chinese food. They are messing with that. I am not letting this whole day go to complete shit. You coming or what?"

110

"Not like I got anything else to do," Mike reached for a package that he had brought with him. Andrew had not noticed it before as he was spending most of his earlier focus on his only means of transportation. "But since you put it that way. Here. Merry Christmas."

Mike handed the package to his friend who took it and quickly opened it. Inside was a much sturdier, thicker and longer hooded robe. The material on the outside looked and felt almost like black burlap, while the inside was much softer and much more comfortable. The weight told him there had to be more in between the layers than met the eye.

Andrew did not hesitate. He took off the boxer's robe and threw on his new one. He shot out his tentacles into full form and looked in the mirror. When he first imagined what he would look like attacking the Martinano compound this, this was what his mind's eye was seeing. He was glad that with the mask up, no one could see him grinning like an idiot underneath.

"I take it you like it," Mike smiled, knowing too well the answer. "Took me a bit to get it made for you. Kind of had to guess on the sizes. Can't just tell the guy making it that you don't know what size my friend with tentacles is going to be."

"Yeah, thanks, man," Andrew turned towards his friend. "I feel bad, didn't really get you anything."

"Oh no," Mike grabbed his coat. "You're going to get my turtle balloon back. That's more than enough."

Andrew retracted his tentacles as the two made their way out of the door. The two got in Mike's car and headed towards downtown.

Issue 5

Downtown was a panic. Luckily, this gave Mike a chance to park a bit away from the action but still within earshot of the police. The boys in blue were still trying to clear away news reporters and spectators from what was hopefully not going to be a hail of bullets.

Andrew climbed out of the car first and threw up his living armor and began to slither towards the action. He stopped when he realized there were no footsteps behind him.

"Aren't you coming?" Andrew turned and asked his friend.

"And how do you suppose I do that?" Mike shrugged leaning on the car. "Place is surrounded by cops and reporters. They'll be all over me in a second. You, on the other hand, ain't got to say shit and can move right on through with no one knowing who you are. Go be the hero this time, dude, I'll be your getaway driver."

"You sure?" Andrew asked even though he knew his friend was right. He didn't want to admit it, but he was scared. He wasn't going in there to save someone he knew. He wasn't going in there to avenge a dead loved one. He was going in there for the sole purpose of being a hero. He was putting his life on the line for absolutely nothing. He was putting it up against someone that had already given him a run for his money, where his only saving grace was a lucky shot and some help from a friend.

"Go," Mike waved his friend off. "Go be the hero and get me my damned turtle balloon."

Andrew nodded and slithered off in the direction of the bank.

To the surrounding police, it was almost as if Andrew had appeared out of nowhere. A few staggered back at the sight of the horror. A few changed their aim from the bank building and trained their guns on the ten-foot creature now before them. All of them waiting for whatever it was behind the robe to do something.

"What's the situation?" Andrew asked a cop in his best raspy whisper.

"You're that guy from the news." A cop finally spoke.

"Yes," Andrew affirmed the acknowledgment. "I'm here to help with the situation. I saw what I'm guessing is the leader on the news report. I've dealt with her before. So, I'm here to lend a hand."

"You ain't getting anywhere near that bank unless you're bulletproof," The second cop informed him. "We already had one of our boys sent to St. Pats for treatment."

"I am," Andrew informed them, keeping his voice monotone to help try to maintain an air of mystery about himself. He honestly couldn't tell if it was working or not. "So, who do I talk to about the situation?"

The second cop pointed him in the direction of a much more decorated looking officer barking orders to anyone that would listen while shoving microphones out of his face. Andrew slid his way over to who he guessed was the chief. The man looked up at Andrew and stopped, the same as all the cameras around him.

"Holy hell," the chief huffed, looking at the mass of tentacles before him. Another man dressed in a suit, who Andrew recognized as the Mayor, could not find the words to even talk to the monstrosity. "You're that thing from the strip club. I don't know what you are, but you aren't shooting at us so I'm guessing you're on our side."

"That would be correct," Andrew nodded. "How can I get into the building?"

"You're going to stop them?" The chief raised an eyebrow. "Alone?"

"Yes." Andrew decided it would be best to give quick answers. He was still trying to learn his new persona, and this was just as good of a place as any to learn.

"Well," The chief shrugged. "Be my guest. SWAT told me the best entrance was through the back. There is a loading dock. Could be where their getaway car is stashed too. If we take control of that, they are trapped in there like rats."

"Hostages?" Andrew asked eyeing the building.

"Just the skeleton crew of security," the chief informed him. "Don't know how many bad guys are up there."

"Then one more thing," Andrew started down at the leader of the police. "I want fire rescue on the sides of the building ready to catch anyone that falls from the building."

"Why?" The officer shrugged.

"We're here to save people, not kill them," Andrew informed him. "And I find killing too distasteful. So if a few of them happen to attempt to learn to fly I want to make sure they survive."

"Alright," The chief agreed after some thought. The chief got on his radio and called in the order. "But don't be afraid to put them down if you have too, and don't get in the way of my guys if they have to pull the trigger."

"Fine." Andrew began to slide off in the direction of the loading dock.

Andrew could feel all the news cameras on him. He added a foot to his height as he moved by. Maybe it made himself more imposing to any villains watching the news, but honestly to him that wasn't why. Andrew knew that somewhere in New Hancock a child was watching afraid for his parent on that skeleton crew and was waiting for someone to save the day. That child wanted his parent to come home and enjoy Christmas. They wanted a superhero to come and right now, Andrew was ready to be that superhero.

"Hey," The chief gave him a shout. "What's your name?"

"I'm the Flayer." The Flayer said back without breaking his determined stride.

114

"Who put him in charge?" The man in the suit asked.

"Mr. Mayor," The chief looked at his boss. "You didn't see the video that we uncovered from that place. Between what happened that night and right now, I think the heroes are starting to return to New Hancock."

The back of the building was generally unguarded. The police presence kept the bad guys inside, and the bad guy's presence kept the good guys outside. A few SWAT members stood by the door. They had been informed of Andrew coming and were ready to take the lower level; hopefully with Andrew's help.

"We're ready when you are, Mr. Flayer." One of the members nodded at The Flayer as they stacked up on the door.

"No need," The Flayer waved them off. "Open the door and fall back. It's Christmas and I would much rather go alone than have some children not have their parents today."

"Not going to happen, sir." A female SWAT member informed him. "We'd rather have a safer city for them. Even if we have to sacrifice ourselves to do it."

The Flayer looked around him. Police ready to take a bullet for the city they live in. Not just the SWAT members, but the beat cops, the desk jockeys, the fire crews and the EMTs. Even the Mayor stood next to the chief ready to protect his city. Originally, The Flayer made himself look tough in front of the cameras to give kids at home a hero to look up to. He wanted to let them know that someone could be counted on in these situations. He realized he was wrong. There already was someone protecting them, and now it was his turn to protect their protectors. For the first time since moving to New Hancock, Andrew Mullen felt like this was his town, these were his people, and it was up to him to protect them.

"Alright," The Flayer nodded in agreement towards the woman. "Then let's begin."

The SWAT members were already lined up outside of the overhead door to the lower level parking garage. The Flayer took point and stood in the center of the door. He could feel his heart beating a mile a minute, and he was starting to love it. This time, compared to two months ago, well, the feelings were different. Last time was vengeance. This time, he felt pride; he felt the adrenaline; he felt like a fucking *hero*.

However, after a three-count from the SWAT team, the door swung open and all The Flayer felt was bullets. Lots and lots of bullets. He couldn't tell the caliber, but what The Flayer could tell was that they were bigger and hit harder than he had started to get used to. These hurt more. These hurt a hell of a lot more.

The bullets stopped and soon The Flayer's eyes began to adjust to the darkness around him. Still standing, thanks to his tentacles steadying him, Andrew slid forward and could see the men with rifles aimed at him. No one moved. The Flayer could see in their eyes a mixed sense of emotions. Most of them held one look, that was the second easiest to read behind their military flak vests and balaclavas; confusion. Deep down The Flayer couldn't help but smile, because now he got to give them the one emotion he found he excelled at giving people: pants-shitting terror.

The Flayer slid forward. A tentacle that appeared to shoot out of nowhere slapped the gun out of the hand of the man right in front of the monster. A second quickly followed up and slammed him against their getaway van, taking him out of the fight. Two more watching the door itself tried to sneak up on Andrew, who in turn wrapped a pair of tentacles around their legs. The Flayer lifted them in the air and threw them against another pair of goons, one after the other.

By this time, the remaining member of the lower level guards tried to reload his weapon. His hands began to shake as he watched the monster come closer and closer to him. It didn't seem stoppable after it had swatted down his friends like they were mere fruit flies. He dropped the magazine and watched as a fleshy brown appendage wrapped itself around the magazine and hold it up to him.

"You want to try that again?" The Flayer hissed at the enemy a few inches from his face. The familiar smell of feces in someone's pants at the sheer sight of the creature had become an all too familiar smell, and this guy was no exception. "No? Drop your weapon, put your hands above your head, and lay on the ground. You will have my word that your life will be spared." The man quickly did so.

116

The SWAT team finally entered the room. None of them were too sure what had stopped them from coming in after the gunfire ended. What they all did know was it had to have something to do with watching this creature that they had seen only on video in action, and just being glad that he was on their side.

An older woman sat watching a monitor in a large metallic looking room. Her elbows rested upon a metal rounded table with five other people. Each person was dressed in a colorful suit of stretch material with plates of armor covering vulnerable spots. No one said a word as they slowly watched the gunfire die on the second floor of the bank. Occasionally someone would fall out a window and the fire crew below would catch them, and the police make an arrest.

"That him, Vasquez?" The woman said not even turning to the knight in white next to her.

"That's him, Ms. Claremont," Father Eduardo Vasquez confirmed. "His name is Andrew Mullen, said he goes by The Flayer."

"What kind of a name is that?" Ms. Claremont asked under her breath.

"I think his sidekick gave it to him." Vasquez continued.

"He's good," A middle-aged woman in a tight purple dress noted. "Quick and efficient. Whoever trained him really knew what they were doing."

"I don't think anyone has trained him, Mary," Vasquez looked to her. "I've seen him in action. A very smash mouth style of taking any shot thrown at him then picking up the leftovers."

"It doesn't matter," Ms. Claremont waved the discussion off. "I want to make sure he feels our presence. I want one of you to go and say hello. Not you Vasquez, you've done enough."

"I'll go." A large black man in a green bodysuit with a red hammer on the chest.

"Be friendly, Hammer," Ms. Claremont instructed. "Congratulate him if he wins, pick him up if he falls. No need to get into anything special. I think I'll be paying Mr. Mullen a visit soon enough."

The Flayer needed a breather. A bathroom stall seemed like a great place. He had not had this much exercise since the bar fights Mike and himself used to start after way too many shots of liquid courage. Even the Strip club had not had this many guys trying to kill him. He needed to start some sort of workout.

Being alone for the first time since the battle began, The Flayer also found it to be a great time to relieve himself. Using a few tentacles to hold up his robe, The Flayer undid his pants and the tentacles blocking his groin slid back to expose himself, and the let the rain begin.

A guard happened to be walking by, on high alert based on the commotion that he had been hearing on the lower levels. When The Flayer let out a groan of relief the guard knew someone that wasn't supposed to be was in the restroom.

"Who's in here?" The guard kicked open the bathroom door and quickly found the stall with feet under it.

"Give me second," The Flayer told the guard. "I'm taking a leak here."

The guard gave no response but realizing that the voice was not a compatriot, opened fire on the stall. The gunfire stopped however when four tentacles whipped out from underneath and above the door and held each of the man's limbs tight suspending him in the air. The guard dropped the gun under the pressure of the restraints and felt the two around his legs release. The upper two holding his arms pulled him into the stall and slammed him head first into the toilet. The force of the blow knocked the attacker out cold.

"No manners on these guys." The Flayer zipped himself up, accidentally caught a tentacle in the zipper, reversed and finished. The Flayer stopped and thought about the flushing the toilet the guard now rested his head in, but he decided against it. Had the guard let him finish, then maybe he would have been a bit nicer.

The Flayer made his way to the fourth floor and as soon as he got there, he noticed something odd. Normally on every other floor, the sound of walkie-talkies crackling permeated, warning others of the impending monster taking down the guards. This floor had none of it.

"This has got to be where she is," The Flayer whispered to himself. "Now if I was a villainess with the flair for the cliché, where would I be?"

The Flayer made his way down the halls, looking for the room his mind was telling him to find. The entire floor was dark. The city had cut the power earlier the hero guessed, to make it harder for the bad guys to see and much easier to get snipers to pick them off from the windows. However, the bank robbers were just as smart, closing the blinds where ever they could without being seen.

Finally stopping by a room with large glass windows, The Flayer found the room he was looking for. A faint glow came from looked like a TV in the room, which illuminated the large glass table and all the chairs around it. Andrew slid past the door to look at the chair that sat at the head of the table. The chair was spun around facing the television which showed the news reports of the bank robbery. Whoever was at the TV's controls flipped through channels until they found the cartoon station.

Expecting a trap, a tentacle slid across the door handle and gave it a gentle juggle. It was unlocked. Keeping his distance from the door he found there to be a slight gap under the door and slid one underneath. No trip wires were found, no pressure plates. The door was simply unguarded. Time to make a grand entrance.

The Flayer gently opened the door and slid inside. With a jolt, the chair at the front of the room bounced a little and spun around. The figure covered in black stretching fabric, a tight black corset, a faux leather mini-skirt and matching combat boots spun around. In the spin of haste and surprise, the Nun's habit fell off the woman's head and revealed a mass of wavy brunette hair. The broken porcelain doll masked figure scrambled to pick it back up and save a little face.

"You can turn it back on," The Flayer hissed. "I love watching that chihuahua slap that cat around."

"If it isn't Squid Boy," An electronic voice came back at him, while a gloved hand motioned to a chair at the end of the table. "Why don't you have a seat?"

119

"I'd really rather not, Sister Slaughter," The Flayer looked down at the seat, and shook his head. "Truthfully, I haven't figured out how to sit down and get back up in this thing yet."

"Too bad," The masked woman shrugged. "Normally, I would have jumped over this table and thrown you out that window by now, but you're too late. There is no need now."

"I am?" The Flayer pondered. Had he missed the whole point of that attack on the bank? Was there something he was missing?

"My men have already loaded the van with everything the vault had," The voice tried its best menacing laugh. The Flayer found it more fitting of a Saturday morning cartoon. "They're about to pull away any minute now, and with as armored as that van is it can't be stopped. All I have to do is wait for my extraction. Without your little friend, I highly doubt you can stop me."

"You mean the red van with the bank's name on it?" The Flayer tried to get information from her. "The one that the SWAT team and I took control of a little bit ago?"

"What?" The electronic voice was so deadpan that The Flayer couldn't help but force himself to stifle a laugh.

"Yeah," The Flayer moved over to the window and lifted the blinds to look out. "See?"

Sister Slaughter got up from her seat and looked to where the tentacle was pointing to see the red van she described sitting surrounded by police. She put her hand on her forehead and just shook her head. Also, much to The Flayer's surprise as he felt a sharp pain in his left shoulder, his guess about the snipers being there was right.

"Jesus." Sister Slaughter jumped back from the window and back to the safety of the blinds, in a shock.

"Yeah," The Flayer tried to hide the pain in his voice completely dropping the whispered hiss. "Good thing for you, New Hancock's finest are horrible shots."

"Then I guess I'm not getting an extraction." The woman's electronic voice sighed.

"You can give up," The Flayer knew that wasn't going to happen, but he felt he had to try anyway. "I'm sure those nice men down there will be happy to give you extraction."

"Or," Sister Slaughter walked back to her spot at the head of the table. She leaned on the table with both hands on the edge. "I fight my way out."

Sister Slaughter gave an almost effortless flip to the table, to bring it end over end at the tentacled beast. However, the table was longer than the room was high and got stuck between the ceiling and the floor, came back down and broke into a plain of little stardust pieces.

"I'm sure that looked cooler in your head." The Flayer quipped.

The snide remark wasn't met with one from Sister Slaughter. However, it was met with a fist square in his solar plexus from her. The Flayer had forgotten how fast the woman was, and how hard she hit. As he did everything he could to maintain his balance and breath as more fists came his way, The Flayer had a thought. Where Mike's balloons really worth getting his ass kicked for?

Thinking quickly, The Flayer threw up a mass of tentacles in front of him in an attempt to stop the barrage. Bunched together, the tentacles turned into a makeshift shield. Sure, he felt the blows where ever they were from, but there was no sound of cracking bones nor was there a loss of breath.

Then, as one kick came at the mass, it opened at the last second and engulfed Sister Slaughter's leg. With a strong swing, Andrew lifted the woman off her feet and threw her against a wall. With a heavy thud, the villainess was on the ground but quickly sprang up and launched herself at her prey, effortlessly taking him off his feet. She rammed him through not only the glass wall of the boardroom but also a section of drywall beyond it.

The Flayer seized this opportunity while headed for a third wall to wrap his lower tentacles around her legs. The two came to a crashing halt on the floor with Sister Slaughter on top. As she regained her composure, and postured herself up to a seated potion on the "chest" of the fledgling hero and began raining blows down directed at his head. Without even thinking, this time the tentacle shield came up, directing the pain to his arms and avoiding the shots to the head. Using a few leg tentacles, the creature was able to lift a copier up from a nearby cubicle and bring it crashing into Sister Slaughter's back, throwing her off him.

Both combatants shook off the fatigue they were starting to feel and came running at each other. This time, however, it was Slaughter that decided against just punching blindly, and dropped to her back as The Flayer slid at top speed towards her. The Flayer didn't know what happened, only that he was flying through the air and soon felt open air on his back. Four stories up and being thrown out a window was not going to feel good. So, The Flayer thought, the bitch might as well feel the pain too.

Sister Slaughter had just climbed to her feet and tried to catch her breath just as a lone tentacle reached out and pulled her out the window. Within seconds, she was face to face with the horrific mass that was The Flayer's face. If Andrew's mask could have smiled at her it would have as he maneuvered both of their bodies in the air to trade places as the two came crashing down to the concrete.

The Flayer wasn't sure how much damage had been done to his enemy, but he knew that most likely he was not going to even attempt to get out of bed in the morning. He shut his eyes for a second trying to regain his composure. However, a gloved pair of hands helped him up and off his feet, and he was once again in the air. This time his body was headed straight to a brick wall of a nearby building.

Landing head first did not do much good for The Flayer's vision as he tried to pry himself from the building he had crashed into. The brick, concrete, and rebar had stopped him from going completely through the wall and had ensnared him. With great effort, The Flayer was able to pry himself free. To make matters worse, a now habit-less Sister Slaughter was coming at him fast with a police car held above her head.

With every ounce of strength that Sister Slaughter could muster, she threw the car like a dart at her opponent. Her fatal mistake caught up to her as she turned around thinking the battle was over. The Flayer caught the car in the air with a mass of tentacles. He didn't have time to marvel at his own strength as he used the car like a baseball bat and struck the woman.

Sister Slaughter's body did not give though. The woman held her ground. Which was exactly what The Flayer had wanted. A large gathering of tentacles grabbed the trunk of the car as well as the hood and pulled the car around Sister Slaughter, pinning her arms to her sides. Hearing her struggle to get free along with the sounds of the car giving in to the woman's unrelenting body was The Flayer's cue. He lifted the car and turned it upside down, slamming the top of the car, and the head of Sister Slaughter, into the middle of the road; not once, not twice, but three times.

The car was half buried by that point in the street and there was no way that that woman was getting out of that. A pair of combat boots kicked wildly trying and failed to get free. The Flayer took a deep breath, slid over to the car, and sat down feeling like he wanted to collapse.

A break was not in the cards for the hero of the day as a huge cheer and a chant erupted from the crowd. News reporters, police and spectators rushed over to Andrew in a mass of camera flashes and hands helping him to his feet. It took a few seconds for Andrew to understand what the crowd was chanting through the questions being rapid fired at him from reporters. It was his name.

Using this to motivate him, The Flayer stood tall over the crowd and tried to think of the best superhero pose to give them a picture of. Unfortunately, he had still had not regained his full mental capacity and it only came out as a gentle wave, then a thumb up gesture. Which the crowd didn't mind and erupted in a larger cheer.

Police surrounded the victor and started to escort him through the crowd, pushing aside cameras and news reporters. The commotion was almost too much for The Flayer to take. That's when it all changed. A deafening hush fell over the crowd, followed by murmurs of "who is that?" and "Is that!?"

The Flayer couldn't see who everyone was talking about, nor was he able to even hear who. However, the crowd parted was and revealed a strong looking man in a green spandex costume with red boots and a red hammer on his chest. The Flayer did everything he could to contain his excitement. It was his childhood hero. The man that he had looked up to and made him buy every comic book that he could get his hands on; It was the Justice Hammer.

The Justice Hammer made his way through the crowd and was coming straight towards the man of the hour. The Flayer was unsure if his suit showed whether he was trembling from excitement or not. He prayed heavily that it could not as the superhero stood in front of monstrous hero, sizing him up. Without a word, the black man shot a hand out at Andrew, who, not thinking put a tentacle in it, and the two shook. This was more than the high five Andrew had received when he was a child. He couldn't even smile under his armor, just be slack-jawed and stare.

"I heard there was a pretty nasty bank robbery here in New Hancock," The Justice Hammer's voice boomed to make sure he was heard by the crowd. "Come to find out its already been stopped by The Flayer here. Congratulations."

"Thank you." Was all The Flayer could squeak out.

"Maybe with some more practice," The Hammer boomed again. "You can get that nasty villain off the streets and we can all start cleaning up this city!"

The crowd broke out into a cheer again. That was when The Flayer caught what the Hammer had said. He quickly looked to the car where Sister Slaughter was pinned and noticed no boots were kicking, just lying there, flopped to the side and empty. The Flayer wanted to curse, but there was no time for that as the Hammer hovered up to raise The Flayer's tentacled arm in victory for the crowd.

124

Issue 6

"Take a look at that," Mike held a newspaper up. "Right there on the front page. Andrew "The Flayer" Mullen having his arm raised in victory by The Justice Hammer himself."

"Ugh," Andrew groaned as he stirred on his couch. When he made it home he didn't even make it to bed. The pain and fatigue overtook him and he passed out on the couch. He didn't even remember how he had gotten home. "Good morning to you too."

"I'm not done," Mike turned the paper around to show an unhappy stick figure standing by a poorly drawn car over top the comics on the back page. "And all the way over here is Mike, left standing by his car for fucking hours waiting for your ass so you two can leave and eat Chinese food and get high. And this guy over there with the slanty eyes is the delivery driver. He got forgot about."

"I didn't have a choice," Andrew slowly pulled himself up on the couch to a seated position. "What was I going to do? Have the news media follow me back to your car and blow my whole identity?"

"Fair point," Mike conceded. "I do have a pager though."

"Dude," Andrew looked on the coffee table and saw a bottle of aspirin. He opened the bottle, poured out a small handful and dry swallowed them all. After a coughing hack and a quick glass of water from his friend, he continued. "I got back and just passed out. See? I'm still wearing the damn robe like a blanket."

"Fuck it," Mike shrugged and took a spot on the couch next to Andrew. "I'll just chalk up some of that ass beating you got to being from me too."

"Deal," Andrew rubbed his head in his hands. Everything hurt as it moved. Andrew looked down at his forearms from where he was making tentacle shields from and noted the giant black and blue marks all over them. He knew his body probably had the same marks all over, but he really did not feel the need to check. "Were we going to open the shop today?"

"Nope," Mike slapped his friend on the back sending a jolt of pain through his body, sending his friend back down to the couch. "You owe me Chinese food and relaxing. So that's our plan today."

"Good," Andrew righted himself after the pain subsided. "I was going to call in any way. I feel like I got hit by a damn wrecking ball."

"According to the news reports," Mike tossed the newspaper on the table. "You were used as a wrecking ball a few times. I'm surprised either of you two were able to move after that."

"Yeah," Andrew nodded. "That was not fun. As soon as I saw that woman, every fiber in my body just told me to walk away. Walk away, Andrew, don't get shoved through a bunch of walls. That might hurt a little."

"I can only imagine how Sister Slaughter feels this morning," Mike pondered as he leaned back. "Turned out you slammed her so hard you broke into the sewer. From what they recovered, it looked like she tore off her costume and got herself in there."

"I bet she'll think twice about doing that again." Andrew lit a cigarette and tossed the pack on the table.

"This is a no smoking building, fuck face." Mike snatched the cigarette from Andrew and put it out.

"You just said you wanted to smoke pot in here." Andrew pointed out.

"I wanted to smoke pot," Mike smiled. "I technically own the joint, so I can do what I want."

Andrew ignored his friend and turned on the television. Quickly, he found the twenty-four-hour news station and left it on for nothing more than background noise. Slowly and gingerly he got up off the couch and made his way to his bedroom, with a grunt and a groan.

Andrew took off the robe he had worn all night and inspected it. Small tear marks, and pieces of drywall, concrete, and broken glass laced the back of it, but in the big picture of it, the robe withstood the beating it took very well. Andrew noted that there was not even one single bullet hole.

"Andy," Mike called out from the living room. "Come quick."

Andrew rushed out to see himself towering over a cameraman as he made his way into the building. Suddenly it stopped, and a headline came up over the tentacle mask's face. "Have Heroes Returned?" was what it read. Andrew sat down and gawked at the TV. He was national news.

"Over the past twenty years," The news anchor started. "The city of New Hancock has been, and other large cities around that nation have been asking one question as crime rates begin spiking to a new high. Where have all the heroes gone?

"In times past, a quick look up at the sky could have easily seen a man, or woman flying high above making sure that citizens were safe. Then one day, as if they had never been there, the heroes were gone. Super criminals and gangs had begun running the streets of major cities in numbers, and with skills that the police could not deal with.

"Yesterday, it appears that has begun to change. This footage used with permission from a local news source has shown one new face ready to take up the mantle of hero. A being calling itself 'The Flayer' assaulted a bank that was at the time being robbed by a super criminal that we were told was referred to as Sister Slaughter, and the following battle arose."

The video showed, though rather shaky, the fight between Andrew and Sister Slaughter as they tumbled to the streets below.

Then it recapped the woman's defeat. Followed by Justice Hammer raising Andrew's tentacle in victory.

"Not only does this video show an obvious battle between two superpowered beings," The news anchor continued. "but it shows that the heroes of old are still alive as we see Justice Hammer arrive on the scene. So, aside from seeing a new face take over protecting the city, this begs the question 'Where have all the heroes gone?' We go now to our panel…"

Mike changed the channel to something more mindless before he took a rip from a glass bong and handed it to Andrew. Andrew sat there with the smoking device in his hand staring blankly at the television now showing an old woman on a game show guessing the price on something. Andrew looked down at the bong and handed it back to Mike.

"I can't," Andrew just shook his head. "Something about this doesn't feel right."

"The fuck you mean?" Mike took another huge rip and attempted to hand it back to Andrew, who shook it off.

"I dunno," Andrew leaned forward and put his chin in between his thumb and forefingers on his hands. "I mean, it's weird. I just saw that hailing me as a hero. I can just imagine little kids starting to look up to me…"

"Of course," Mike agreed, "you're like ten feet tall when you're about to get your whoop ass on. Everyone has to look up to you."

"Not what I mean, dipshit," Andrew laughed a little. "I mean, as a role model or something. Maybe I should clean up my act a little."

"Ok," Mike sat the bong down and looked at his friend. "Let me explain something to you. You are Andrew fucking Mullen. Ain't nothing changed. Oooo… you got superpowers and did something to help the city. Big fucking deal. Cops do that shit. Firefighters do that shit. Nothing has changed, except for the fact that you got these dicks coming out of you now. Let 'The Flayer' be the role model, cause to me, you're still Andrew Fucking Mullen and no amount of dick arms and superhero shit is going to change that. You're my best friend, my brother, but I'm still pretty sure you're functionally retarded. You get what I'm saying?"

"You really kind of rambled on there," Andrew pointed out. "But yeah, nothing has really changed."

Andrew wasn't sure at first what it was going to feel like being a hero. Mike had pointed out to him the one thing that he had never thought of. Nothing had changed, and the only thing different was that he was being hailed as a hero. He could start this whenever he wanted. He could stop this whenever he wanted. This wasn't a change in his life. This was a hobby.

Andrew's train of thought derailed when the doorbell went off.

"Did you already order food?" Andrew questioned his friend.

"Nah," Mike got up to open windows and started to try and fan the smoke out of the room. "Maybe someone figured out who you were and has come to question you."

"Doubt that," Andrew said as stuck he his head out that window to see who was out there. A woman stood by the front door waiting patiently for a response. "Looks like some woman in a suit is just standing out there."

"Here," Mike pushed his friend aside. "I'll get rid of her. Hey! You out there! You selling blowjobs?"

"No." The woman called back. Andrew could see the confused look on her face.

"Then go away," Mike yelled back at her. "We don't want whatever your selling."

"I'm actually here to see Mr. Mullen," The woman responded. "I have a check for him."

"We already got one," Mike looked back at Andrew and gave him a thumbs up. "Yeah, got a whole book of them. Wait… did you say you had money for him?"

Andrew rushed over and buzzed the woman up. Both men scrambled to at least clean the place up a little and Andrew threw his robe in the closet in hopes to hide it. Before the men knew it there was a knock at the door and Andrew rushed to open it.

"Good morning," An older woman easily in her mid to late 50's stuck her hand out. "I'm looking for Andrew Mullen."

"That would be me," Andrew shook her hand and stood out of the way of the woman as she practically marched inside. "Would you like a cup of coffee miss...?"

"Claremont, Jeanie Claremont. Just call me Ms. Claremont if you will." The woman walked past the seating area and straight to the kitchen where she began to hunt for the things to make the coffee.

"I can do that," Andrew informed her. "Why don't you have a seat?"

"I've very particular about two things, Mr. Mullen," The woman shot Andrew a smile. The black- haired woman did everything she could to try to make it not seem forced but failed miserably. "My men and my coffee. So, if you don't mind I would prefer to make it myself."

"Fair enough." Andrew sat down on the couch that he had spent the night in earlier.

"The line is," Mike interrupted from the busted looking recliner to the side of the couch. "Ground up and in my freezer. I like my men like I like my coffee."

"I don't believe I asked you," The woman didn't even turn to acknowledge him. "You're the sidekick I take it?"

"I ain't anyone's sidekick." Mike laughed off the insinuation.

"The one from the video," The woman continued to scour through the cupboards. "Where is the percolator?"

"The fuck's a percolator?" Mike asked Andrew under his breath. Andrew shrugged not knowing the answer.

"Don't have one," Andrew informed her. If he didn't know what one was he probably didn't have one, he figured. "I just make instant to get my morning started and we have a coffee maker at the shop."

"No coffee then," The woman hurried back to the couch. "So you're not the sidekick? Then who are you?"

"I'm Mike," Mike informed her.

"Yeah," Andrew added "he's Mike.

"I wasn't asking you, Mr. Mullen," The woman seemed to scold Andrew who decided it was best to keep his mouth shut from that point on. "Well, we don't need just a Mike in this conversation so please leave."

"Yeah," Mike leaned back and put his feet up on the coffee table. "See, that's not happening. I've been through a lot with my buddy here, and I really don't plan on just up and leaving."

"Anything you have to say to me," Andrew continued on not listening to his own earlier advice. "You can say in front of Mike."

"Your friend," Ms. Claremont turned her attention to Mike, "is a superhero that can apparently grow tentacles out of his body."

"Yeah," Mike nodded. "I was in the video you mentioned earlier. I even named the big guy."

"Could have done a better job," Ms. Claremont stared down Mike. "A little forethought on the subject would have been nice. At least Andrew here came up with The Flayer. Squid Boy seems rather easy don't you think?"

"Look, I got two questions," Mike leaned in. "Number one: Fuck you. I named him Flayer. Number two: How the hell do you know that Andrew is this Flayer guy? And how the hell did you find us?"

"That was a statement and a couple of questions." The woman pointed out trying her best not to get agitated by Mike.

"Still two questions." Andrew pointed out and was silenced by a finger in his direction.

"I found out who you were from speaking with a Father Vasquez. From what he told me, you opened your secret identity like an open book to him," Ms. Claremont checked her watch absently "From there it was just a matter of finding a New Hancock phone book. You really should hide yourself a little better, Mr. Mullen. Lord knows, who else will be able to look at the white pages."

"Fair enough." Andrew nodded feeling like a child being embarrassed for a silly act.

"Now," Ms. Claremont finally turned her attention to Andrew. "You and I have some business to discuss. As I stated before my name is Jeanie Claremont. I am the Lead Coordinator for The League. I act as the head of the group and as a liaison

131

between the Normals, everyday people, and the Supers. That would be those with 'superpowers.'

"Due to recent actions on your part by you. We at The League have taken notice of your abilities. As I'm sure you can recall, we sent the Justice Hammer to you yesterday to greet you into our ilk."

"Wait," Andrew interrupted. "You want me in The League?"

"Please don't interrupt me, Mr. Mullen," Ms. Claremont sighed. "I've done this for quite a long time. The faster I get through this the faster we can all get on with our days, and the faster I can answer your questions. No, Mr. Mullen, you are not being granted formal membership into The League. The League is a group of the best of the best. The elite. You are what we would prefer to call 'Street-level.' Nothing you have shown can be used to handle a national or even apocalyptic threat. However, who knows what you will be capable of with training."

"So why are you here?" Mike asked.

"Will you please let me talk?" The woman rolled her eyes at Mike. "Though you are not a member of The League. We at The League have found quite a need for guys like yourself, Mr. Mullen. You see, there are various levels of threats to life as we know it. The range is from street-level, to world, to cosmic, to apocalyptic. To keep our higher-level heroes available to handle these threats we rely on various superheroes at various levels to handle them for us. Saving our top heroes for the big problems.

"In order to encourage the street-level guys to handle the small stuff, we at The League have authorized a stipend to be paid based on performance. This here," Ms. Claremont opened up a briefcase she must have placed on the table when she walked in and pulled out a small envelope. "Is the check for the rescue of Miss Erin Hastings and Miss Adriana Barker in October. Our accounting department is still working on your check for last night."

"I'm getting paid to be a superhero?" Andrew questioned as he took the envelope, opened it and pulled out the important part.

"Dude," Mike marveled over his shoulder. "Look at all those zeros."

"Two," Andrew pointed out. "There are two zeroes. The check is only for three hundred dollars. Was saving Erin really only worth three hundred dollars?"

"No," Ms. Claremont shook her head. "There were two girls and they were worth a lot more. However, you incurred several penalties during your heroic action. We, at The League, do not condone killing. Therefore each death that occurs directly by your hand incurs a penalty to be assessed."

"All that's well and good," Mike sat back down in his chair. "But how is Andy supposed to even cash that check without giving out his identity."

"As you can see on the check a fictional name is added," Ms. Claremont pointed out. "This name corresponds to a bank account that has been set up with a bank that we own and operate. You walk in, you hand them the check, and they hand you cash. Plain and simple. In fact, due to the high level of security we use to mask the identities of our heroes, you will not have any taxes, social security or any of the sort removed from your check.

"At the same time the bank, offers many of the same options as a traditional bank. Savings, checking, money markets, investment options, the whole nine yards. Again, not even the employees know your true name, or even that you are using a fake name. So, in the case of an emergency, we will have no one to contact.

"We also provide you, Mr. Mullen, with a legal identification card, that has your new name on it. Any government official can run your identification card and it will come up in their system."

"So," Andrew cocked an eyebrow at the woman. "The government knows who I am?"

"The government knew exactly who you were," Ms. Claremont got a laugh at the question. "as soon as you took your mask off to kill that gangster. What matters, Mr. Mullen, is that the government doesn't care. We're a necessary wild card, and as such you are a necessary wild card. So the government has basically washed its hands of your superhero self and put you in our care, so to speak. You step out of line, the government doesn't deal with you, we do."

"And someone collects the check for it," Andrew added it all up in his head.

"Exactly," Ms. Claremont reached back in her briefcase and handed Andrew a stack of papers. "These are the more precise rules and regulations, along with a contact form, and a basic information form. You are to fill them all out and send them to me at this P.O. Box. That is of course, should you decide to continue your exploits. No matter what you choose, that check and the next one are yours. However, I do recommend that you refrain from any heroic activity until you are processed within our system. After this point, any heroic activity you make is not representative of The League and will not be added to your payments. Any questions?"

"No," Andrew stopped for a second. "This is a lot to take in. Do you have any way I can contact you if I do?"

"No," The woman informed him. "Not directly anyway, in fact, unless you end up being a member of The League, you may never see or hear of or from me again. So now is the time to ask."

"I got one," Mike piped up. "Since last night, the news has been asking one question. Where have all the heroes gone? Growing up, people used to tell me you could occasionally see them, making sure everything was good, wholesome, and all that shit. Now, they're nowhere to be found. So where did they go?"

"That is a difficult question," Ms. Claremont crossed her pant-suited legs and licked her lips in thought. She looked down and checked her wristwatch and stood up. "Unfortunately, not one that I have time to answer. I bid you both a good day, and Andrew, I hope to have those papers on my desk soon, and I do encourage you to take Father Vasquez up on his offer. The networking alone is worth it."

Andrew stood up and showed Ms. Claremont to the front door which was only a few feet next to her the whole time anyway. He then walked back to the couch sat down and began looking at the papers, realized it was a bit much to handle right now, and set them back down.

"Lot of shit." Andrew sighed as he looked down at the papers on the table and the check sitting next to them.

"Could be a lot of other shit too," Mike informed him. "Money, fame, pussy, and the opportunity to really cement the one thing in stone that you wanted more than anything. This is your chance to get out of a boring rut. Cause face it, up, work, home, and bed is just as boring as the other shit you were going to have to go through with Erin. Besides, you start collecting those checks you can actually start paying me the god damn rent on this place."

A laugh came over the two men.

"You're right," Andrew leaned back. "But not with this check. I say since there is no superhero shit going to come from me until I decide to fill this out. We use this check to party. It's almost New Years. We go out, we get fucked up, and if there is money left over we do it again the next night."

"See?" Mike began digging the bong back out from where he hid it and placed it in front of Andrew. "There is the old Andy I used to know."

Andrew smiled, grabbed the lighter and took the biggest hit he had taken in a very, very long time.

Ms. Claremont climbed into the back seat of a black luxury car. Father Vasquez was already seated in the seat next to her. He took her briefcase and set it on the floor between the two of them. Ms. Claremont took out a small container of perfume from a bag by Father Vasquez's feet and spritzed herself.

"That place reeked of weed and despair," Ms. Claremont scoffed. "I don't like the look of those two. Two idiots. One with powers and no mind of his own. The other has the will and no powers. Looks like a dangerous combination to me. I want them followed, Vasquez. Make sure they're on the level."

"I'll have Choir Boy take care of it, ma'am." Father Vasquez nodded.

"Excellent," Ms. Claremont turned her attention to the driver. "And find me a decent cup of coffee, please. All they had was instant. What kind of barbarian drinks instant coffee?"

Issue 7

"I haven't seen him in this good of a mood in years," The bartender at Zero's, Andrew and Mike's favorite watering hole, pointed out. "I guess losing that hundred and twenty pounds did wonders for him, huh?"

The clock hasn't struck midnight yet in the City of New Hancock, elsewhere on the east coast it had. The TV played a New Year's Eve special hosted by a man that had already started to look past his time, and silently played music that made Mike feel past his prime as he sat at the bar nursing his beer watching his friend have the time of his life.

Andrew had moved the pool table with the help of a few people and made a makeshift dance floor to do the worst possible drunk dancing he could manage. Whether the poor dancing was intentional or not was a matter up for debate. To Andrew though, it didn't matter. Any woman he could grab became his partner and any song the old jukebox could spin became the greatest dance song ever. Including, much to Mike's surprise, anything metal that it happened to play.

The bar usually was dead, and New Year's Eve proved to be no different in the number of patrons. Andrew was lucky enough to get some of the old bar flies out of their seats and busting a move

136

with him. The women in their fifties may not have been able to keep up with the young guy, but they gave it their all.

"Yeah," Mike addressed the bartender. "Mitch, that guy's had a lot going on in his life. I think the weight of it all finally came off his back. It's good to see him cut loose."

"Hey," Andrew took a break to take a seat next to his friend. A beer sat at the bar waiting for him. With a slight stagger, Andrew hopped up on the stool and wrapped his arm around his best friend. "Dude, man, dude."

"Yeah?" Mike was forced to pay attention to his friend.

"Ok," Andrew continued. His speech had easily begun to show how many beers he had put inside of himself. "Ok, ok, I got this realllly great idea."

"Alright," Mike started to get a chuckle out of his obviously drunk friend. "What's your great idea?"

"Ok," Andrew pulled his friend in closer, and pointed to a booth occupied by two girls. One with raven black hair, the other a brunette. "See over there in the booth? The goth one and the one that looks like she can't choose between a metal look or grunge, with her feet up on the seat?"

"Yeah." Mike tried to steady his friend to make the pointing not so obvious.

"What's say," Andrew grinned big. "What's say let's go over there and try and pick them up. I haven't picked up a woman in so long."

"Andy," Mike smiled at his friend. "I'll tell you what. Why don't you go over there and see if you can get them in that three-way you always wanted?"

"Oh... my... god..." Andrew hadn't even given that a bit of thought. "That has got to be the greatest idea ever. Imma go over there right now."

"Ok," Mike encouraged his friend. "Go get 'em, tiger."

"Ok," Andrew tried to stand up, and he almost fell. He caught himself on the bar but righted himself. "Here I go."

Andrew staggered over to the booth were two women, roughly his age, sat having a drink. As Andrew approached he quickly about-faced and returned to his friend.

137

"I totally forgot how to do this…" Andrew admitted to Mike, his eyes wide with nerves. Both Mike and the bartender shared a laugh.

"You go over there and talk to them," Mike told him when he could catch a breath from the laughter. "That's it. It's been a while, but you got this."

"I totally got this." Andrew finished the beer that he had left on the counter.

"I'll have another one waiting for you when you strike out." The bartender joked.

"Hey," Andrew pointed at what he thought was the bartender but seemed more like he was pointing at the cash register. "If the Flayer can stop a bank robbery, I can talk to women."

"You got a point there." Mike smiled at his friend. Even drunk, Andrew was able to keep his mouth shut about his new hobby.

"Ok," Andrew steadied himself. "Here I go."

Andrew staggered over to the table with the two women. Unsure who to address first Andrew said nothing while the two girls just stared at him.

"Hi," Andrew finally got out. "Hi."

"No," The raven haired girl dressed like it was Halloween responded while her friend just glared at him. "Just no."

"Fair enough." Andrew began to walk away when the other girl in the band t-shirt and old leather jacket stopped him.

"And tell your friend no too," Her eyes felt as if they would tear out his soul if either of them tried to approach the table again. "I've had a rough week, just want to have a few drinks in peace, and would love an excuse to kick someone's ass. Got me?"

"No problem, ma'am." Andrew shot the ladies a thumbs up while backing up. The brunette squinted her eyes at him. Andrew wasn't sure if she what thinking, trying to look tougher than she did, or was working out a fart. Either way, he decided that if it was in his best option to leave. Especially if the woman was working out a good beer fart.

Andrew staggered over to the two at the bar. True to his word the bartender had three shots of whiskey waiting at the bar.

"They said no," Andrew informed the two men. "They also said to tell Mikey here no too."

"Eh," The bartender smiled took one glass, slid one to Mike and one to Andrew. "I've seen you work miracles in my bar for too long. You'll get it back. Been out of the game too long."

"But Andrew is back, baby!" Andrew declared as all three clinked the shot glasses and downed their drinks.

The night remained uneventful from that point. Slowly, after the clock had hit midnight, the bar began to drain the drunks out into the streets. Some people had found others to take home for the night. Others, like Andrew, found themselves to be not so lucky. Eventually, the lights went on and last call was announced. At this time, only the two friends, and the two young women remained.

Eventually, the girl dressed in all black left her brunette friend and stepped outside. Andrew excused himself to use the restroom one more time. The brunette approached the bartender and asked for her tab. The bartender turned away and began counting it up for her.

"Hey," Mike turned to her sipping on what was left of his drink. "Sorry about my friend. It's been a little crazy, so he's had a bit too much to drink."

"Don't worry about it," The woman didn't even turn to face him. Her voice slurred showing that she too had had a bit too much. The woman pulled a wallet out of her leather jacket and pulled out some cash. "We told him no, and he left us alone. No harm, no foul. Nice little bar."

"Cool," Mike smiled thinking to himself that had Andrew waited a little longer he might have had a chance. The more she drank the friendlier she got was what Mike figured. "Yeah, it's a great place to get away. Nice and quiet, and the college students tend to go for the trendier bars, so not too much trouble."

"Bitchin'," The woman nodded to herself. "Might have to come here more often."

"We always welcome new customers," The bartender laughed. "With inflation, it's going to take more than these two idiots to keep me afloat."

"I'll keep that in mind." The woman paid her tab and left.

139

Andrew had come out of the bathroom shortly after the woman left, wiping his hands on a paper towel. He sat back down at the bar and almost tipped over. This time as he shot a leg tentacle out to steady himself it failed to catch him, and he crashed to the ground. Mike quickly got up to help his friend to his feet.

"Your friend just left," Mike informed his fallen comrade. "Said she liked the place so you might get a second chance."

"She said I might get a second chance?" Andrew questioned.

"No," Mike laughed as he pulled out his wallet to pay the tab. The owner of the bar just shook his head at the money and stated that watching Andrew all night was entertaining enough to pay the tab. "Just that she liked the bar."

"Cool," Andrew nodded his eyes starting to look glassy. "Second chance."

"Come on," Mike started to herd his friend towards the door. "Let's get you home."

The cold air nipped at the two as they stood outside. The two headed down the now empty street back towards Andrew's apartment. The snow had begun to fall heavily.

"Hey," Andrew smiled. "You live that a way. I know we both struck out tonight, but you ain't cuddling with me tonight."

"No dipshit," Mike laughed. "you struck out tonight. I'm making sure you get home safe."

"There's no need for that," Andrew waved him off. "I've made it home drunker than this. Plus, I have those fancy new superpowers. I'm good. I'm very good."

"You sure?" Mike asked and stopped when Andrew nodded towards him. "Look, just don't start thinking about shit and go and do what you tried last time you were pretty hammered. You got me?"

"Yes," Andrew nodded. "Though it might give me more superpowers."

"I don't want to take that chance," Mike laughed and hugged the man he considered his brother, then they parted ways. "Just make sure to sleep on your side tonight."

Andrew walked alone down the empty streets of New Hancock. They say that once you pop the seal when drinking, the

140

urination doesn't stop. This was still true for the man that had just got his superpowers a few months ago and just recently stopped a bank robbery. Andrew taking a cue from his friend found a dark alley, and a dumpster, unzipped and began to relieve himself.

"Hey," A familiar voice came from further down the alley. "Public urination is a crime, Squid Boy."

Andrew squinted as he looked down the dark alley. A brunette woman, with her hands in her pockets, stood at the end. He could hear the snow under her canvas shoes crunch as she walked towards him. As she passed under a building light Andrew got a good look at her. It was the brunette from the bar.

"I thought you told me no..." Andrew zipped himself up. "Wait... what did you call me?"

"Squid Boy." The woman took her hands out of her pockets and balled them into fists.

"Look," Andrew put his hands up waving them at the woman staggering towards him. "I don't know who you are, or who you think I am, but why would you call me Squid Boy?"

"Shut," The woman slurred. "Shut the fuck up, Squid Boy. You're the god damned Flayer. I would know your voice anywhere. That... that shitty whisper shit doesn't hide a thing."

"Ok," Andrew admitted as he staggered closer. "You got me. Do you want an autograph? I'll only sign your tits, maybe your ass. Going to have to do a little spin to let me see it first though."

"You talk too... too much," The woman got in Andrew's face. Andrew had maybe an inch or two on the woman. "I'm... I'm Sister Slaughter, and I'm gonna kick your ass."

"What?" Andrew couldn't believe what he heard. "But... but... you were taller."

"So were you." Sister Slaughter glared into Andrew's eyes. Drunkenly, the woman reached back and took a swing at Andrew. Who barely had to move as the woman began to fall forward. Andrew reached out, almost out of instinct and caught the woman from falling over. The woman got a shock in her eyes and quickly pushed him away. The missed punch must not have done much to help her drunken state as a retching sound began to come out of her. Andrew grabbed the woman's long hair and pulled it back gently as Sister Slaughter began to release the contents of her stomach on the snowy alleyway.

"Stop it." The woman pushed Andrew back again. The force of the push confirmed to Andrew that she was who she said she was.

"Look," Andrew again put his hands out showing that he was not going to fight. "You are really, really drunk."

"So are you." The woman wiped her mouth on her sleeve. Andrew reached in his pocket and pulled out the napkin the female bartender had given him with her number on it a few days prior. Sister Slaughter accepted it and used it to wipe her mouth.

"Exactly," Andrew laughed. "So, what's the point? I can't fight you. You see I kind of got a problem."

"What," Sister Slaughter cocked her head, "What's that?"

"I got," Andrew attempted to shoot out a few tentacles from his arms which promptly dropped to the ground. "E-tent-tile dysfunction; can't get them up."

"Fuck you," The woman began to laugh, and then snorted. She quickly covered her mouth embarrassed. "You're not supposed to be making me laugh."

"Alright," Andrew smiled at her. "How's this? You are fucking drunk. I am fucking drunk. Neither of us are going to remember this or a fight. We're both going to get sore and hurt and then wake up tomorrow with more than a hangover and no explanation as to why. So why fight? I got a better idea."

"A better idea?" Sister Slaughter sat down in the snow. "Ok, fuck it, shoot."

"I just got this killer weed from my buddy," Andrew told her. "Let's say, we go back to my place. Smoke the shit out of it and bury the hatchet. What do you say? No need to start off a new year with enemies."

"What?" The woman was confused by the proposition.

"Let's go back to my place," Andrew repeated, "smoke weed and relax. Hell, I'll even get you a cab to make sure you get home safe afterward."

"The fuck?" Sister Slaughter remained confused. "You fail to pick me up in the bar, so now after finding out that we've nearly killed each other twice, you still want to take me home and fuck me?"

"No sex," Andrew waved off the idea. "Just two people, sitting down, sharing some drugs and chilling. What do you say?"

Sister Slaughter had no idea what to say. She never in a million years would have guessed this was what was going to happen if she went out drinking with her friend. She would never have thought that attempting to jump a guy in the alley would lead to what was transpiring before her.

"Fuck it," With a bit of a laugh to see how this would all turn out, Sister Slaughter agreed to the most idiotic plan she had ever heard.

The walk to the apartment was silent. Sister Slaughter walked two steps behind the man she had fought twice before. Not once did he turn around to make sure she was still following him. As they approached the door she was amazed that she had not just taken a swing at the back of his head and bolted. Andrew only turned back to see her when he held the door open for the woman as they entered the building and again when they entered his third-floor apartment.

Andrew kicked off his shoes and took off his gray coat and hung it on the hook on the back of the front door. He then took Sister Slaughter's coat and hung it up as well. The woman took off her shoes and took a quick look at the apartment in front of her. She had never been in a superheroes place, and never thought she would be in one. It was much, much smaller than she had ever imagined.

"Want a drink?" Andrew asked as he walked into the kitchen that was separated from the living room by a counter. "I ain't got beer, but I do have store brand cola."

"Yeah," Sister Slaughter got brave enough thanks to the alcohol in her system and began exploring. A small hallway off the living room leads to the only two other rooms in the apartment. The bedroom and off that the bathroom. "Got to admit. Your place is small for what I would think a superhero's place would look like, Squid Boy."

"Yeah," Andrew laughed as he tried to pour two glasses of soda. "Can't really afford much on my salary."

"Thought you capes made a bundle fighting us bad guys." Sister Slaughter took a seat on the couch, and pulled her feet up off the floor, tucking them underneath her. "At least that is what I heard."

"I just found that out a few days ago," Andrew nodded as he handed her a drink. He took a seat on the couch next to her, but still kept his distance. Sister Slaughter sat there holding her drink and didn't partake of any until Andrew did. "Still haven't got paid for the bank robbery."

"Damn," Sister Slaughter laughed. "I was kind of curious how much I was worth."

"Hold on," Andrew reached into a pile of papers on the table and handed her the check from his rescue of Erin. "Nothing about a henchwoman on there though. Said the amount was so low cause I killed a bunch of people."

"Yeah," Sister Slaughter nodded reading the check. "Heard you all can't kill. Kind of why I was so ready to fight you each time. Ten-foot-tall squid man that can't kill me. Fuck it, let's see what he can do."

"Beat your ass." Andrew gloated with a laugh.

"Fuck you, Squid Boy," Sister Slaughter shared in his jesting. "That first one was a draw. I could have escaped and kicked your ass all over that strip club."

"Fair enough," Andrew admitted, as he pulled out a book from under the table and began to roll a joint from the contents of the hallowed out book. "Still won the second one hands down."

"You got lucky," Sister Slaughter took another sip of her drink and then set it on the table feeling herself become more relaxed. "did have to crawl through the sewer damn near naked though. Those were my good boots though."

"They're in the other room," Andrew pointed towards the bedroom, as he finished the joint and handed it and a lighter to Sister Slaughter. "You can have them back if you want them. Justice Hammer gave them to me as a trophy of my first victory."

"Really?" The brunette took a hit and passed it back to Andrew. "I can really just have them back?"

"Go for it." Andrew shrugged taking a hit of the joint himself.

144

"Bitchin'," Sister Slaughter felt herself smile despite herself. "So, tell me. How long did I lay you up for?"

"Excuse me?" Andrew's mind could get what she was talking about.

"We kicked the shit out of each other twice," Slaughter tapped the ash off the joint. "How long were you on the shelf?"

"A couple of days," Andrew took a drink from the soda. "I'm amazed how quickly I recovered. I think you broke a few ribs the first time."

"That healing time is nice huh?" The woman smiled.

"That what?" Andrew questioned.

"You really are green," Slaughter cocked her head. "Has no one explained that to you? Like how you're not feeling as drunk as you were when we left?"

"Not a word," Andrew shrugged. "Hell, I still don't know where the tentacles come from."

"Ok, Squid Boy," Sister Slaughter lifted her shirt to reveal her stomach. A flat toned stomach giving a hint of the muscle and lack of body fat underneath. "Not even so much as a bruise. One of the things I found out about all of us is we all can heal very quickly and extremely well. Including toxins in the blood. Makes getting drunk very expensive."

Andrew's mind was no longer focused on the question at hand. His mind had gone to imagine what the rest of her looked like under there.

"No shit," Andrew mumbled. The two were silent for a moment.

Sister Slaughter broke the silence. "Did my old boss really kill your dog? I heard some of the goons mention it back at the club."

"Yeah," Andrew nodded trying not to think too hard on that. "Butchered him."

"Asshole," Sister Slaughter cocked her mouth to side. "Dog was innocent. Should have left him out of it."

"Hell," Andrew grinned taking another hit and passing the joint back. "I was fucking innocent. Here's the story. My ex-fiancé's uncle took out a loan from that Martinano guy in my name. We go to clear it, he bolts and leaves me to his goons. So I waste

145

the guys, my dog gets murdered in revenge. The uncle sells his niece into sex slavery, so I go to rescue her."

"Fucking dirtbags," Sister Slaughter took a hit and passed it back to Andrew. Both had begun to start feeling the effects of the drug and both began to loosen up even more. "But fuck. I can't say shit, I work for assholes like that. Pays the bills better than my other job. So, what can you do, Squid Boy?"

"No idea," Andrew took a hit. "Living ain't free."

"Tell me about it," Sister Slaughter took a huge hit, which almost finished the joint. "So, what's your name?"

"I'm sorry?" Andrew was shocked by the question.

"You've already brought me to your squidly lair, shown me your actual face," Sister Slaughter untied the plaid shirt around her waist and tossed it on the chair next to her. "What's your name? I can't just keep calling you Squid Boy."

"Andrew," Andrew smiled killing the joint, and beginning to roll another one. "Andrew Mullen."

"That's plain as fuck. I think I'm going to stick with Squid Boy," The woman reached out to shake Andrew's hand which he accepted. "Jennifer Seeley, but everyone calls me 'Jen.' So, tell me, Mr. Andrew Mullen. What do you do when you're not stopping my crimes?"

"I'm an auto mechanic," Andrew hit the fresh joint. "You?"

"Hey, fucker that was my turn," Jennifer joked accepting the drug from Andrew. "You promise not to laugh?"

"No." Andrew blew out the smoke he had been holding in.

"Great," Jen hit the joint. "I work in a music store in the mall part-time."

"Hey," Andrew's eye lids began to get lower. "Girl's got to eat."

"Especially when an octopus thing keeps stopping her big paydays." The two laughed.

"So, what got you into all this?" Andrew asked waving off the joint Jen tried to pass him.

"Let's just say, Squid Boy, I had a really bad day and wanted to take it out on the world," Jen grew silent after admitted that. "You?"

"Felt I was becoming too boring and tried to kill myself." Andrew made a gun with his fingers, put it to his head and let his thumb hammer drop.

"Well, Squid Boy," Jen put her arms back on the top of the couch. "I can say you fixed that, huh?"

"Yeah," Andrew smiled. "I guess I did."

The two grew silent. Both relaxed and enjoying the high and the good decision Andrew came up with. Jennifer smiled as she finally figured that coming here was a really good idea.

"Hey, Squid Boy," Jen sat up, her legs curled up with her arms cradling them. "Crazy question, you wanna fuck?"

"I'm sorry?" Andrew stammered as he was caught off guard by the question.

Jennifer smiled a wicked smile, and slid over on the couch and threw a leg over Andrew, straddling him. Andrew wasn't sure whether it was the weed, the booze, or the fact that a rather attractive woman had her warm crotch pressed against his, but he felt himself get hard in an instant.

"Look," Jen stared into the man's eyes and spoke slowly. "You were right, this is better than fighting. Now, I'm coming down off the drunk, but I am high and I'm really fucking horny. Like you said, neither of us are going to remember this. So do you want to fuck?"

"Dear god yes." Was all Andrew could eek out with his heart racing.

Jennifer did not say anything. She only bit her lip in a twisted smile and slowly slid backward off Andrew pushing the table back as she went down. Andrew didn't even look down as he felt her unbutton his pants and pull his member out. Andrew's brain then went numb as all his body would let him feel was the hot moisture of Jennifer's mouth.

As he opened his eyes he could see the brunette's head moving slowly up and down and knew that it felt amazing. Without thinking, Andrew slowly extended a tentacle out from his chest and under his shirt. He maneuvered the tentacle down Jennifer's chest. This caused the woman to jump a little but not stop. He slowly slid the tentacle over her right breast feeling sliding across her nipple and the little metal bumps there and continued further south across her stomach.

Jennifer used a free hand to unbutton her jeans with a delighted mumble as she continued. Taking the hint, Andrew slid the tentacle down and between her legs, and moved it slightly, until he found a warm, wet hole. Then with an even gentler movement, the tentacle went inside. Jennifer gave a jump and looked up at the man.

"I thought you said," Jen stood up and Andrew straightened himself not sure if he did something wrong, "You had e-tent-tile dysfunction."

"Seems like you fixed that." Andrew laughed catching his breath.

Jennifer then headed towards the bedroom she found earlier, taking her shirt off as she went. She undid her bra and tossed both over her shoulder without turning around.

"Then come on, Squid Boy," Jen disappeared down the hall, "and show me what those tentacles can really do."

Andrew almost tripped over his own pants trying to rush towards the bedroom.

Issue 8

The sun had not even come up yet and Mike was already at work. Seeing his friend leave the bar drunker than he had been in a very long time, and with the knowledge of Andrew's last heavily drunken had put him a little on edge. That edge made it very difficult for Mike to sleep so he was up early and working early.

Working in the mechanic shop was always relaxing to Mike. He didn't need to do it. He owned a few buildings in the city and the rent from the places, that is from the tenants that paid rent, easily took care of his own condo. The buildings didn't even have mortgages on them as when his parents passed they left him a small fortune. So, he owned the mechanic shop more to give himself something to do and his best friend a job.

Mike struggled to loosen the rusted bolt holding a bar that held the windshield washer fluid reservoir. The wrench slipped, and he scraped his knuckles against another piece of the engine. A few of the now skinned knuckles began to let a bit of blood flow. He threw the wrench at a wall of tools and swore loudly to himself and at the unknown person who put the damn battery under the reservoir.

Mike sighed to himself and walked over to where he had knocked quite a few tools hanging on the wall off. He grabbed a pack of cigarettes and lit one. Then one by one he began to put the fallen wrenches back on the wall. He pulled the cigarette out of his mouth and scratched the top of his forehead leaving a long gray mark across it.

The doorbell rang in the back letting Mike know a customer had arrived. Confused, as the shop had not officially been opened for the day yet, Mike grabbed a large wrench and headed for the front. He didn't keep much money in the front register. In fact, the till had not even been put in yet for the day. Then again, Mike thought to himself, this was not the best neighborhood, and some people might feel the need to help themselves to some free wiper blades.

"Mike," Andrew's voice called out towards the back as he sent out a thick tentacle to stop anyone from robbing the shop. "You here?"

"Jesus, dude," Mike sighed for relief as he set the wrench down coming through the door to the front. "Why the fuck are you here so early?"

"Had to take the bus," Andrew admitted. "So, I didn't know how long that was going to take. Left way too early. Why are you here so early?"

"I couldn't sleep too well," Mike admitted. "Hadn't heard from you since we left the bar. Didn't know if you decided to try and give yourself more superpowers again."

"Nah," Andrew shook his head. "Had kind of a rough morning. Had to get permanent marker off my damn mirror in my bedroom."

"The fuck?" Mike got curious.

"Yeah," Andrew laughed. "You know how some girls will leave you a message in the morning in lipstick? Bitch wrote it in permanent marker instead."

"Hold up here," Mike threw his hands up stopping the story. "What woman? Where? When? We left just the two of us."

"That brunette at the bar?" Mike laughed. "Yeah, found her puking in the back alley and took her home with me."

"Bull shit," Mike laughed. "That girl not only shot you down but me too and I didn't even say a damn word."

"Hand to God," Andrew raised his right hand. "Shedidtrytokickmyassthough…"

"What was that last bit?" Mike pointed out. "That part you said really quick. You holding back on me, Andy?"

"I said she did threaten to kick my ass though," Andrew admitted.

"Andy," Mike faked shock to hide his curiosity and put his face in his dirty hand. "Did you attack that girl?"

"Wait what?!" Andrew grew shocked. "No, oh god no. Why…what…? I said she left me a message on my mirror in the morning. Gave me her number. Her name's Jennifer. Jesus dude."

"Then why would she threaten to kick your ass?" Mike questioned. "It's not like you did anything but try and pick her up. It's not like you did to that Sister Slaughter and wrapped a car around her."

Andrew was silent.

"Andy," Mike stood up. "Why aren't you saying anything? Andy…"

"Ummm…" Andrew couldn't find the words. "Turns out our previous meetings didn't go too well."

"Don't you fuckin' tell me." Mike's jaw hit the ground.

"Well…" Andrew kept working on finding the words.

"Seriously?" Mike still could not believe what he was starting to draw connections to in his mind.

"The brunette. The little grunge girl," Mike drew significant pauses between his words. "Was Sister Slaughter? Don't you fucking be lying to me, Andy."

"Yeah," Andrew chuckled. "She was."

"Bullshit," Mike leaned back in his seat, not believing a word Andy was telling him. "Probably just lying to get some attention."

"No," Andrew began. "She proved it. I held her hair back while she blew chunks. She shoved me off hard after that. Hard enough to make the point. Besides, she knew exactly who I was."

"How did she know that shit?" Mike asked now genuinely curious. "How did she know who you were? Or where you were?"

"Disguising my voice doesn't help too much," Andrew shrugged. "Other than that, don't know."

151

"Well," Mike laughed. "Let's ask her."

"What?" Andrew grew nervous.

"Call her up and let's ask her." Mike slid the phone over to Andrew.

"Dude," Andrew protested. "I'm not going to call her so soon."

"That's true," Mike thought out loud while standing up. "Still we do need to find out how she found out. Then again, it's not like you have kept who you are a very good secret. Hell, the only person I don't know the name of was the Choir Boy."

"Dillon Tyler," Andrew informed his friend. "Or at least that's what I have been told by my old pastor. Said he ran into Father Vasquez and Dillon a few times. Not sure if it's the same guy but most likely is."

Mike got that look on his face. Mike always made the same look when he was thinking too hard on a subject but really didn't want to say anything. His eyes would always look down and he would run his tongue over his front teeth, then to the back, find where he lost a molar in a bar fight and rub the empty gum till he was done thinking and that tongue was moving quite a bit right now.

"What are you thinking?" Andrew got brave enough to ask.

"Nothing," Mike shook it off. "I thought that guy looked familiar. Anyway, that's not important right now. I want to meet her, though."

"Who?" Andrew asked distinctly remembering that Choir Boy was a guy.

"Jennifer A.K.A. Sister Slaughter," Mike put his hands on the desk in front of him. "I want to meet her. Got to make sure she's good enough for my Andy."

"You're planning something," Andrew shot up. "I know you too well. You're fucking planning on something."

"Yeah," Mike laughed. "Say did you get your papers filled out yet for that woman?"

"No," Andrew shook his head. "I really haven't had time."

"I want those papers turned in," Mike was running his tongue again. "Don't come back to work until you do."

"Why?" Andrew shrugged. "I really don't know about getting into this whole superhero business."

"Because," Mike let a huge grin out. "I have a plan that could end up making us a ton of fucking money. So, get your paperwork turned in, and go give your new little friend a call. See if she wants to go have some drinks with us tomorrow night. Till then, head on home, Andy."

Andrew grew a skeptical look on his face. He never trusted Mike having that grin. Ever since they were younger, that grin usually meant either running from police or getting caught by the police. This time Andrew wasn't sure that he really wanted any part of what that grin was for.

Issue 9

Andrew tapped his foot nervously underneath the bar booth at Zeroes. He had called Jennifer the next night and only got an answering machine message for someone else. He still left one for Jennifer, but highly doubt she got it. Maybe she gave him someone else's number. Then again, he told himself, she did leave a message on his mirror stating that she wanted her boots back, and sure enough, even though he had pointed them out to her before he fell asleep that night, they were still there.

"You sure you called the right number?" Mike asked taking a sip of his drink.

"As far as I know," Andrew shrugged. "It went to an answering machine. So, it's not like she gave me the phone number to a Chinese restaurant."

It was only a matter of minutes from that point for Andrew to realize that the phone number he had been given was the correct one. Jennifer walked through the door to Zero's and scoped the crowd until she saw Andrew in the seat of a booth facing the door.

"Hey." Jennifer greeted Andrew as she approached the table. She took a backpack off her back and handed it to Andrew, who placed it next to himself. Andrew then moved over in the seat and made room for Jen. The woman shook her head and made a gesture for Andrew to get up, which he did, and Jen slid across the seat and placed her dusty military jacketed back against the wall, and her feet on the seat leaving enough room for Andrew to sit down.

"Jen," Andrew introduced her to Mike as he sat back down. "This is Mike, guy's practically my brother."

"Cool," Jen reached over and shook the tattooed man's hand. "Nice to meet you. Sorry, I was running late, just got home from work and found the message on the machine."

"Have we met before?" Mike asked. Andrew knew where he was going with this and tried to shake his head subtly.

"No," Jen shook her head. "Can't say that we have. You an ex of mine? I tend to forget a bunch of them."

"No," Mike rubbed his chin. "You're not my type. Where are you from? Might know you from there."

"Wyoming." Jen raised an eyebrow wondering where this line of questioning was going.

"Really?" Mike leaned back and took a drink of his beer. "You're wearing that dangly cross earring. You a religious girl?"

"Not really," Jen was starting to visibly not like the immediately being shoved with questions. "Just works as an accessory."

"Oh, so you were never part of a covenant. A nun, perhaps?" Mike felt a tentacle slam against his shin but chose to ignore it. Watching Jennifer start to sweat a little was giving him a bit of sick pleasure. "Hey, Andy, why don't you go get your lady a drink?"

"I'm not his lady," Jen snickered to himself, as Andrew got up. Jennifer tried to dig in her backpack for some cash, but Andrew waved it off. "But just get me something cheap, could you? It's been a rough day."

"Oh," Mike nodded as staring down the woman. "So, what do you do for a living?"

"I work in a music shop," Jen got agitated and her tone turned just this side of hostile. "I sell shitty pop music to shitty teenagers."

"Really?" Mike smiled. Every fiber of his being was loving the fact that he was getting a reaction of a woman that had

155

attempted to kill his best friend on more than one occasion. "I don't know. You seem more like the type to work in some place a little dingier. Say a slaughterhouse? You ever kill cows for a living?"

"You fucking told him." Jen caught on to exactly what Mike was getting at and turned her anger towards Andrew, as he sat back down with a beer for her.

"I didn't tell him shit." Andrew protested wrapping and unseen tentacle around Mike's leg and was driving a point rather hard into his calf, to which Mike gave no reaction. A canvas shoe propelled by a leg in loose fitting jeans shoved Andrew out of the booth and caused Andrew to let Mike's leg go, or reveal his secret.

"He's not lying," Mike informed her, finishing off his drink, and covered for his friend. "I actually had my suspicions who you were on New Year's. I have a very hard time forgetting a face, or a voice. You just confirmed everything for me more than Andrew did. All he told me was that that brunette he got shot down by in the bar tried to kick his ass afterwards."

Jennifer couldn't say a word. If everything Mike had just told her was true, then she couldn't hold it against Andrew. This did not stop her from shoving him back out of the booth when he climbed back in, this time not so much for telling who she was to his friend, but for bragging about what he probably referred to as his latest conquest.

"Besides," Mike smiled, "It was my idea to invite you here."

"Really?" Jen scoffed. "I thought Squid Boy just had my boots, wanted to have a few drinks, I'd turn him down for an actual date and we all would move on with our lives. You got them, Squid Boy?"

"Yeah," Andrew finally got back in his seat comfortably. "Back at the apartment. You want 'em, you got to come get them."

For the second time in this conversation, Jennifer had nothing she could say. She stared at the fledgling superhero for a second. Jen let out a solid laugh. Not a scoff, or a chortle, but a good laugh. She raised her glass in a cheer to Andrew who accepted.

"Well played, sir," Jen added after she drank.

"Wow," Even Mike felt a little impressed as he acknowledged his friend. "Someone dropped 120 pounds and grew a set of balls. Bravo, good sir."

"Figured," Andrew smiled. "What's the worst that could happen? She tries to kick my ass and I make the score 3-0."

"Oh, fuck you," Jen laughed again to the point where she snorted. She quickly threw her wrist up over her nose to try and prevent that from happening again. "That first one was a draw. We both know that."

"You were pretty tough," Mike recalled. "Until those bullets came at you."

"What? You don't move when bullets come at you?" Jennifer raised an eyebrow.

"Of course," Mike shrugged, "But I'm not as tough as you. I mean, a car getting wrapped around you is fine, but a few bullets are a no-no?"

"Busted, huh?" Jen took a drink and nodded. "My weakness it out. You're a lot sharper than you look Mr. Mike. Ok, since I don't think I'm getting choked by a tentacle anytime soon…"

"Unless you ask…" Andrew added quickly.

"Hold on to that thought. I still got to go get my boots," Jen pointed at Andrew without taking her gaze from Mike. "I'm pretty much invulnerable to anything over about the size of a finger."

"Does not say a lot for Andy here…" Mike added into the beer as he pulled it to his lips.

"May not hit the back door but it beats the hell out of one side…" Andrew laughed and took a drink of his own.

"Wait, should we even be talking about this here?" Jen finally wondered as she pulled herself up in her seat and looked around. After confirming no one she knew or had heard of was in the bar she slid back down.

"It's Zero's," Andrew informed her, "unless its booze, drugs, or cock, no one gives a fuck."

"Here," Mike stood up. "May I have everyone's attention please?"

No one turned around to Mikes announcement.

"I am the newest hero on the street Flayer!" Mike announced as loud as he could. Again, no one bothered to move at the announcement. Mike then sat back down and smiled.

"See?" Andrew pointed out. "No one gives a shit."

"Cool…" Jen let out slowly, catching on to how things worked there.

"Which brings up the next question," Andrew finished his drink and set the glass down. He then got up from his seat and headed to the bar. He then returned with a pitcher of cheap beer and glasses. "What is this idea you had for bringing her here?"

"Seriously?" Jen rolled her eyes. "You're not going to try and sell me on some pyramid scheme, are you?

"It's not a god damn pyramid scheme," Mike scoffed at the woman. "Think about this for a second. Andrew gets paid based on superhero shit he does, right?"

"I guess." Andrew nodded.

"Ok," Mike poured a drink and set the pitcher back down. "So, Sister Slaughter goes out and does bad shit. Flayer comes in and stops it. The League writes the Flayer a check and everyone goes on their merry little way. But what if, Sister Slaughter wasn't really beat? What if she, let's say, took a dive. Then Andrew comes up to Jennifer and gives her half the money from the fight."

"You want to defraud the god damn League?" Andrew almost spit the beer he was drinking out. "You want the defraud the god damn League?"

"Sounds like he wants to commit fraud on The League," Jen confirmed.

"Who's gonna know?" Mike shrugged. "Just the three of us sitting here."

"Yeah," Jen waved off the idea. "Until say some League spy sees the handoff. You know they have them out right? Keeping an eye on the bad guys."

"No, I didn't," Mike confessed.

"But they can't be spying on you," Andrew mentally put some facts together and found a flaw in her logic. "They have no idea who you are, Jen."

"Bullshit," Jen shook her head. "As much as I'm commanding for my henchwoman services. They have to have an eye on me."

"No," Mike recalled what Andrew was getting at. "They had no idea who Andrew was either. We ran into The Holy Frijole. Told us he was looking for both you two. So, no they don't know who you are. Does your side know anything about Andy?"

"Word around is that no one knows who Squid Boy here is," Jen shrugged her shoulders trying to hide that she felt a little dejected. "Aside from myself, that is. Then again, I'm the only person he stopped. So, no one really cares who he is."

All three sat quietly and contemplated the proposition brought before them.

"Wait," Jen finally spoke up. "Here's a problem. Someone once told me that you guys get paid based on the danger that the villains cause. If you keep stopping me on a regular basis, that means the amount that I can get paid goes down, and that the amount Andrew will get paid for stopping me goes down. So eventually we're back to broke."

"I could take a day off," Andrew rubbed his chin. "Then you can go do something that won't get on the news but will make your normal jobs still make you some cash."

"The news," Jen shook off the idea, "Is how we get the biggest exposure to clients. They see us getting away with it on the news reports and we can ask for quite a bit more moolah."

"But," Andrew protested. "If you do that. Then The League, who is looking for you, is going to be able to find you much more easily. Also, since it will look like I can't handle you, then they will come in and take over. However, I keep stopping you, then they see that I have the situation under control."

"Holy shit," Jen finished her drink, poured another one, and then downed half of that. "This might actually work."

"Wait," Andrew realized there was one piece still missing from what Mike was discussing. "Where do you fall into all this, Mike?"

"Me?" Mike leaned back. "I keep everything in tight wraps. I make the drops usually. That way in case we do get figured out,

159

then you two aren't seen together. All I ask is that Andrew finally starts paying his damn rent."

"How does that help you?" Jen questioned.

"He's my landlord," Andrew informed her.

"You don't pay rent?" Jen laughed to herself.

"I ain't gonna make this guy homeless cause he can't pay he is rent," Mike added. "Who would drink with me?"

"I have got to get me that sort of arrangement." Jen chuckled again. "Then again, I usually only pay my half when I can. Really surprised my roommate hasn't kicked me out."

"That her the other night?" Mike asked only vaguely interested.

"Yeah," Jen nodded. "She had an ad out in the paper and I replied."

"Probably keeps her from owning too many cats," Mike surmised, "That will probably eat her when she cuts herself too deep."

"Wow," Jen leaned back against the wall. "You're an asshole."

"A special kind," Mike raised his glass. "So, what are you two thinking about this? About my idea?

"I'm in," Andrew admitted quickly. "What's the worst that could happen? We just get chased by a different form of law enforcement than before? I can handle that."

"Why not?" Jen shrugged. "I am a villain after all. So, let's do this."

The three raised their glasses and clinked them together.

Snow had started to fall very heavily after the group parted ways. Mike headed his own way. While Jennifer walked next to Andrew headed to his apartment. She shivered as the wind kicked up the snow and pulled up the collar on her coat. A warm fleshy tendril gently wrapped itself around her neck. She wanted to push it away, but in the chill, the warmth felt too good to. Though, she admitted, that it was still an awkward feeling. The tentacles that had been used to do harm to her were now much more gentle, and almost friendly.

"Guess I should have brought your boots," Andrew admitted tucking his hands in his pockets. "Probably holding up better than those shoes."

"You could always just use your squidy powers and carry me back to your place." Jen joked.

"You don't think that would be a little too obvious?" Andrew had not understood that she wasn't serious.

"Relax, Squid Boy," Jen looked at her escort. "I'm fine. I've dealt with worse."

"Weather this bad back home?" Andrew asked.

"New Hancock is my home," Jen informed him. "I've been here since college and can't really imagine living anywhere else."

"Only a few years and you already decide that, huh?" Andrew questioned. He wasn't too sure how to feel still. Was an awkward silence good? Was it even that awkward? Should he be filling that gap or should she?

"Yeah, sure," Jen looked down at her feet. "Just a few years. What about you? Lived here your whole life?"

"No," Andrew admitted. "Just kind of landed here."

"Just kind of landed?" Jen pushed.

"Yeah," Andrew found that this was his turn not to look at the woman next to him. "Just kind of landed."

"Sounds like there is more to it than that" Jennifer pushed as she felt her interest in the question peak.

"It's not something I like to talk about," Andrew sighed. "Can we leave it at that?"

"Yeah," Jen nodded as she felt the tentacle that she had gotten used to slide back to its owner. "Sorry, didn't mean to offend you by prying I was just curious."

"Don't worry about it," Andrew shrugged and brought the two to a stop. "Do you hear something?"

It was only a few moments, and the phantom sound Andrew thought he heard was proven true. The two turned to see a lone person walking behind them. Within moments the figure bolted. Andrew and Jen nodded to each other and took off after them.

It wasn't long before the two had to give up the chase. The snow had picked up the pace in falling and had covered any tracks

161

that the two could have hoped to follow. There were no footsteps crunching in the snow.

"We were being followed," Jen confirmed for herself.

"Seems like it," Andrew agreed. "Might be a good idea if we cancel the rest of the night."

"Why?" Jen looked at Andrew. "It's like you guys pointed out at the bar. No one knows who I am. So even if it was one of The Leagues spies, they wouldn't know who I was. Anyway, we need to start talking about a plan."

"Are we really going to discuss a plan?" Andrew questioned.

"In the morning." Jen patted Andrew's chest and continued to walk.

Issue 10

New Hancock was cold in the winter nights, but this winter was especially bad. Snow and ice covered the city and vehicles left on the street. Luckily, for the woman staring down at the street below her from the fire escape of a nearby building, the snow was making a perfect cover for herself and the two hired goons that she had hiding in the nearby alley.

Two local gangbangers she had hired for this caper waited with cheap pot metal pistols in hand. Sister Slaughter reaffirmed in her head that the plan was solid, even if Andrew had to take a few bullets.

"You two know the plan." An electronic voice barked down at the two hired thugs. The two nodded in agreement as they moved to a darkened area of a downtown building. Sister Slaughter had made sure to go over with the two exactly what they were to do, and even practiced with them, move for move how to go about it. A kidnapping was dangerous in itself. The kidnapping of a high-profile judge, out for an evening stroll with his wife, and bodyguards left no room for error.

Sister Slaughter adjusted what was once a cheap corset until it had been fitted with numerous layers of bulletproof material underneath. Normally, she would not have been able to afford this on her own, but since working with Mike as well on the plan he offered to buy it to keep her safe. Though she wondered if he bought it to keep her safe, or to keep Andrew happy. Either way, she was grateful for the gesture.

Once Sister Slaughter was certain that her two goons were in place she dropped from her perch into a shadow to hide herself and began to listen. The crunching of snow was going to be a dead giveaway as to who was coming. All she had to do was wait for the sound of more than one pair of feet and that would be her target. Which meant it was time to play the waiting game.

As her wait began, she couldn't help but ponder three things. Her first thought was she dreamed of finding a material that was as thin and as flexible as what she had on but would keep her warm on these winter nights. Her second thought was where the hell The Flayer was going to be coming from, and if he was even close by. She had gone over the plan with him as much as she had with her goons, but something in her mind told her that the goons might be a little bit more experienced in this than The Flayer. Finally, why would that judge be taking a stroll tonight?

"Did you see something?" One of her goons asked the other. "I thought I saw something above us."

"Shut up," Sister Slaughter barked, "and get back in your hiding spot."

Then the crunching of feet came. Sister Slaughter felt her heart began to pound in her chest. She always loved this part. The rush of excitement, the feeling of not knowing how this was going to go over. Sister Slaughter licked her lips and was on the edge of her seat with anticipation. Sure enough, her prey had started to come along the street.

Sister Slaughter stepped out of the shadows just as an elderly couple with two younger men walked towards the alley where the three were hiding. The whole group stopped dead in their tracks and the two guards pulled their weapons. The two goons had made their moves perfectly timed and with a few quick blows to the back of the guards' heads, knocked them out.

"What is the meaning of this?" The elderly judge stammered realizing he was surrounded.

"You see," Sister Slaughter began walking around the couple. Her combat boots crunching in the snow with each step. The goons cocked their weapons and kept them pointed at the elderly couple's heads. Sister Slaughter wondered silently why her goons didn't have their weapons loaded in the first place. "One of my boss's kids is on trial. A trial you are presiding over right now. I'm here to make sure that trial no longer continues. To give the kid another shot. The best way to do that is to make sure you go missing, or so I've been told. I try not to question these things. So, we're going on a little walk. Well, a little walk for you guys, I still have to get home tonight."

"I'll give you anything thing you want…" The judge's voice quaked.

"You'll give me anything I want if I let her go," Sister Slaughter mocked the scared man. "Look here, your honor. She is seeing what's going on. She is going with us. Sorry, that's just the way this works. Maybe, just maybe though. If she's a good girl, I'll let her go. Got to get my name out there somehow. So, let's get moving."

The two thugs motioned for the two to move down the alleyway. Sister Slaughter took the lead and the two goons took up the rear, exactly as Sister Slaughter had shown them. Everything was going according to her plan. Even down to the muffled yelp, everyone heard as they made it about halfway down, a spot that had no security cameras for the businesses nearby. The woman in charge couldn't help but smile under her mask.

With a snap, everyone looked around to notice one of the hired thugs had gone missing. Sister Slaughter began to look to the top of the building. She never heard the ten-foot-tall tentacle monster slide down the side of the building behind her. She did, however, feel it lift her in the air and throw her against the wall.

The second guard wasted no time opening fire at the monster. The Flayer felt himself wince every time the bullet connected with his body. The robe he had on had been reinforced to catch the bullets, but the force still had to go somewhere and that somewhere was still into him. A tentacle whipping out of The Flayer's arm put a stop to this when the goon went to reload, only to have the firearm wrenched away from him and crushed.

The man who had been so brave before felt a warm liquid run down his leg as he was lifted into the air effortlessly by a tentacle coming out the hood of the monstrous Flayer. The gangster kicked for his life until a block of wood crashed against the tentacle monster causing him to drop his prey.

The Flayer shook his head trying to release the pain that coursed through him. Sister Slaughter came at him with the pointed end of the broken wooden piece and leaped into the air to get better leverage for a stab. A quick swat with a tentacle made short work of her attack and even landed her in a nearby dumpster.

"Go on," The Flayer motioned to the judge and his wife. "I'll handle these two. You two call the police."

The judge didn't have to be told twice as he grabbed his wife and ran for their lives.

The remaining goon began to crawl away as fast as he could, trying to escape the melee. That was until he felt a strong tentacle grab him around the leg and start dragging him back. The man reached for anything to grab on to. Unfortunately for him, everything on the ground he grasped had been made slick by the snow. The man eventually gave up when he felt his body being lifted into the air again, and he found himself once again, face to upside-down face, with the monster. It was only a matter of The Flayer extending his eye tentacles and beginning to wrap them around the man's head that caused him to faint.

With a shrug, The Flayer dropped the prey and turned his attention back to the dumpster. Sliding a tentacle inside he felt around. In the dark, it was too hard for him to see, but a gloved hand eventually found the appendage and used it to help its owner to her feet. With a gentle pull, The Flayer lifted Sister Slaughter out of the trash receptacle.

"Everyone is either out cold," The Flayer hissed. "Or gone."

"Awesome," An electronic voice crackled back. "That went well. It should take the cops about ten minutes to get here, less if there is a patrol car nearby."

"Go on," The Flayer turned around. "I'm going to go and make sure the judge and his wife are ok. I'll meet you at the spot."

166

"Bitchin'." The electronic voice added, and Sister Slaughter took off.

The Flayer slid around the corner to find that the elderly couple was huddled together down the way. He retracted some tentacles to make himself less imposing and allowed them to see his human hands.

"Are you two alright?" The monster hissed.

"Yes," The Judge nodded. "You're that guy from TV. The one who stopped the bank robbery."

"I am." The Flayer was trying to keep it short and sweet after he found out the two were alright.

"Thank you," the judge's wife added through the tears in her eyes. "Thank you."

"Don't mention it," The Flayer hissed at them. "I need to leave before the police arrive."

The sound of sirens finally started to come into hearing range and The Flayer took this as his cue to leave. Hopefully, he thought to himself as he made his way back down the alley, Jennifer had time to get changed before the police arrived. Fighting the hired goons was one thing, but the police were a different story altogether.

"Hey, Squid Boy," A voice called out from a fire escape away down the alley. In the darkness, the owner of the voice could not be seen. "Hurry up."

As Flayer got closer he could see Jennifer stood there, leaning on the railing with a gym bag sitting next to her. Her Sister Slaughter garb was probably neatly tucked away, and her normal look gave her the perfect disguise. The Flayer threw two tentacles over the railing and pulled himself up. Andrew retracted his monstrous disguise and with a bit of help from his friend pulled off the brown robe and started to pull on the clothes that Jennifer had grabbed from the bag for him.

"I didn't hit you too hard back there, did I?" Jen asked leaning against the railing as Andrew quickly threw his fresh set of clothes on.

"No harder than usual," Andrew Joked. "Gonna be sore for a few hours, but I'll be good."

"Damn," Jen smiled, and gave him a much gentler, joking punch in the shoulder. "I'll hit you harder next time."

The two jumped from the top of the building's fire escape. Jennifer landed on her feet and dusted off the kicked-up snow. Andrew landed gently on a set of tentacles he threw out to slow his descent. The pain of the impact was still there; however, the broken bones were not. Though to be honest, Andrew thought, the pain was getting easier and easier to ignore.

The two made their way out of the alleyway. Going in the opposite direction of where Andrew had left the judge and his wife seemed to be the best option for the two of them. Then without warning or gesture, Andrew felt Jennifer grab his hand. No sense of pulling or tugging as if to hurry him up. Despite everything Andrew had told himself, he couldn't help but get himself lost in that little bit of warmth on this frozen night.

A bright flashlight in Andrew's eyes snapped him back to reality. On that journey back, it also made him realize what her grabbing him was. Just another part of the disguise. Jennifer must have noticed the police officers looking around before he did and took his hand to help play up the story the two had created for themselves in case the two were noticed together.

"Evening you two," The officer stopped them. "You guys hear any commotion around here?"

"Heard some loud banging around a little bit ago," Jennifer threw on a look of concern. "Everything alright, officer?"

"We got a call that there was an attempted kidnapping," The officer informed them. "That a super-criminal dressed as a nun tried an attempted kidnapping of a judge tonight. Have either of you two seen her?"

"No," Andrew shook his head. "Did the judge fight her off himself? Guy's kind of badass for that."

"No," The officer turned off the light. "Word is The Flayer rescued him. So, you two didn't see anything? We were told they both went down the alley you two came from."

"Nothing," Jennifer continued. "We were at a friend's apartment hanging out. Heard some commotion and waited until it subsided. Then decided it was best to leave. Andy? What are we going to do if that woman shows up?"

"Don't worry," Andrew pulled his arm around Jen's shoulders not letting go of her hand, causing it to wrap around her chest. "I think I can take her if need be."

"Good," Jen rested herself against Andrew adding to the idea for the officer that they were just a couple on a night out. Andrew couldn't help but get a good whiff of how she smelled. She must have thrown on a perfume to mask the smell of sweat from the fight. To him the smell of the two becoming intertwined was intoxicating.

"Well," The officer smiled at the two. "Make it straight home, and you two have a great night."

"We will, officer," Andrew nodded. "And if we hear anything we'll be sure to let you know."

Andrew and Jen walked off, still not letting go of their position. Jen took one good glance over her shoulder as they turned the corner towards where they had parked the car Mike had lent them. After the coast was clear of cops, Jen pulled herself away and tossed the duffle bag in the back after Andrew unlocked the doors.

Andrew made himself comfortable in the driver seat, and then he started the vehicle. Jennifer plopped down in the passenger seat, slid the chair back and put her feet up on the dashboard. Andrew reached into the pocket of the grey trench coat and pulled out a pack of cigarettes. Andrew popped one in his mouth and drove off after pushing in the car's cigarette lighter.

The sound of the lighter popping out broke the silence between the two in the car. The cigarette lighter gave the car a red glow to contrast the green glow from the gauges and car radio. Andrew rolled down the window and let the smoke out of his lungs.

"Put that shit out," Jennifer scolded Andrew as she dug through the glove box. "I already smell like garbage and that will just make it so much worse. So hitting the shower when we get to your place. Mike got any good music in this car?"

"Could not tell you." Andrew launched the cigarette out the window.

"Eh," Jen gave up her search and turned around to the backseat. She returned with a cassette tape and shoved it in the radio. The song about making misery for people had the grunge sound that Andrew pegged that the woman sitting next to him

169

would love. "You should quit that shit anyway. Bad for your health."

"This is coming from the woman that has tried to kill me twice." Andrew laughed.

"No," Jennifer shook her head. "This is from Jennifer. Sister Slaughter has tried to kill you twice."

"Didn't realize you had multiple personalities," Andrew questioned.

"What do you mean?" Jennifer leaned her seat back and went down with it. "Wanting to kill you? Then not? Self-defense. I do occasionally have the urge to kill Mike though."

"No," Andrew shook his head. "Wanting to kill Mike is pretty normal. I mean not thinking of yourself as Sister Slaughter."

"Sister Slaughter is sitting in that bag back there," Jen placed her hands on her stomach. "Jennifer is sitting next to you. Are you and The Flayer the same person?"

"That's something I never thought about," Andrew shrugged. "I mean, everything I've done has pretty much been for me. I mean, rescuing Erin, stopping the bank robbery to get the Christmas parade going again. So, I guess, yeah, The Flayer is just a tool I use."

Jennifer didn't respond. Andrew debated whether to check if she was sleeping or not. He took a quick glance over at the side mirror and saw a glimmer of the street lights in her eyes.

"I guess it's how I deal," Jennifer finally broke her own silence. "I do a lot of bad things to people who have never done anything to me. They haven't even looked at me in a bad way. Most of them don't even know I exist. Jennifer isn't hurting them. Sister Slaughter is hurting them."

Andrew regretted saying anything. He didn't even bother to look down at the woman in the seat next to him. He didn't need to. When the two were like this, he thought, they weren't heroes or criminals. They were just people. She was Jennifer and he was Andrew. They weren't Sister Slaughter and The Flayer. Until this point, he had never questioned that. He never thought of Father Eduardo Vasquez. He only knew of The Holy Frijole. He didn't even question the Justice Hammer's life outside of the cape.

Andrew's mind immediately went to the other side of the coin. He joked about Jennifer trying to kill him, but on their first encounter he admitted to himself, he did try to kill her too. Not once did she even bring it up. Then Andrew's mind wandered to the gangsters who weren't as lucky to survive their encounter with The Flayer. He had just thought of them as obstacles, not as the people that they really were. The fathers, the brothers, the husbands, the people.

"You got quiet." Jen gently poked Andrew shaking the thoughts away.

"I just got lost in thought," Andrew admitted.

"No shit, Squid Boy." Jen put her hands behind her head and looked over at the driver.

"I was just thinking," Andrew continued. "About what you just said. About it being two different lives, and how thinking of yourself as two people helps to deal with the thoughts about what you do to people. Got me to thinking about those gangsters I killed. They were just doing what they do to feed their families."

"Andrew didn't kill those people," Jennifer helped him to understand the mindset. "The Flayer did. The Flayer just rescued a judge. Andrew is going to split the bounty."

"But those guys we just used," Andrew began to feel bad for them. "We just used them and let them take the fall for a job that they were never going to get paid for. Now they are going to lose their whole lives and even the innocent members of their families are going to suffer."

"Fuck those guys," Jen laughed trying to lighten the mood. "So, get this. When I first started this whole Sister Slaughter thing, I hired myself out to their gang. Went out and I got the job done. So, like any other job, I went back to their leader for payment. Son of a bitch told me that the only payment he was going to give me was a rock-hard dick, and to take it or leave it. Then I watched as every member of that gang pulled a gun on me, and that includes those two. So, I walked out. Told them I would be back and would get my payment then."

"Fuck those guys," Andrew laughed at the fate of the two gangbangers now that he knew this bit. "You ever go back?"

"Too many guns," Jen admitted. "I'm fist-proof, not bulletproof. Funny thing was, one of their guys got nabbed for murder one, and they called me to help them out. Had to wreck a few cars, and houses of jurors. Those guys must have completely forgot about me."

"Or got really fucked up and thought it would be a good idea to try and fuck you over again." Andrew shrugged.

"Eh," Jen laughed. "Now they got three to worry about losing. Anyway, enough of this somber shit. Let's go get this thing back to Mike. Like I said, I can really use that shower."

The car pulled up next to a curb by Zero's and after stopping the car the two made their way inside to have a drink and relax after their evening.

Issue 11

Hell. Mike only knew of one place in the known universe that he would consider Hell. Nothing in his life had ever compared to the horrors that he was now psyching himself up for. He was about to walk into that exact Hell.

Mike licked his lips and opened the glove box of his car. A shiny pistol sat there. For a brief second, Mike thought that there was a way out. He didn't have to go inside. He didn't have to face the nightmare structure before him. He shook off the thought and grabbed an envelope from underneath the weapon. He opened it, pulled out a wad of cash and stuffed it into his breast pocket.

The glass doors before him slid open and allowed him to enter the portal to hell. For a moment, Mike stopped, mustered all his courage and stepped through the door. He had spent the day before picking the door that would bring him to his destination and back out as fast as possible. Right now, he hoped all the planning was correct.

"Will you move?" An angry mother and her child shoved past the bald man and made their way into New Hancock Mall.

"Fuck off!" Mike shouted.

"Great language in front of my kid!" The mother didn't even turn around.

173

"Fuck your kid too!" Mike chased them with his voice.

"What's it mean to fuck me too, mommy?" A child's voice piped up as the two disappeared into the crowd.

Mike smiled to himself after realizing he did a good deed for the day in the field of education. He then made his way through the crowd with a sense of haste.

A small, failing, music chain store sat in the corner of the mall by one of the main department stores. A current pop song as bland as the beige paint on the walls, played over the loudspeakers in the store. A few teenagers stood by a high standing rack of the latest releases. One of them stared Mike up and down almost in awe of what must have been a rare sight for the kid. Mike overheard him whisper to his friend about checking out that guy's tattoos but quieted quickly when Mike made eye contact with him. What amused Mike was the way the kid jumped back when Mike feigned coming at him.

Mike made his way to the video section and started flipping through the porn section. Due to it being the pornography, there were no security cameras and Jennifer had told him that would be the place that they made the hand off. Mike reached in his pocket and pulled out the envelope, folded it and put it in the palm he was using to dig through the films.

"I'd really appreciate it if you didn't scare the customers," Jennifer snuck up on Mike with a fast food drink in her hand. "Ok, my assistant manager would appreciate it. Frankly, I don't give a fuck."

"Not my fault the kid is a little bitch." Mike defended himself without stopping his search.

"Whatever," Jen shrugged. "Looking for anything in particular? Anything I can help you find?"

"I'm looking for some really fucked up shit," Mike didn't even turn to her. "Got any snuff?"

"I bet you are," Jennifer sipped on her drink and crouched down and ignored the snuff comment. "Here, this is the cartoon shit. It's animated, so the creators do pretty much whatever they want."

Mike flipped through one and found one where scantily clad Japanese school girl was being surrounded, and restrained by

174

tentacles. Mike picked it up and handed it to Jen. Jen's fingers wrapped around the VHS tape and the cash Mike had placed behind it. She took both and set down her drink. She then palmed the money and slipped it into her front pocket.

"Bringing back fond memories?" Mike joked.

"Hey," Jen shrugged as she spoke softly, "Andy can control length and girth. Plus, a girl can't complain when that many holes are being filled."

"Alright," Mike shook his head. "That was way more than I needed to know. Really more than I needed to know."

"You picked up the porn," Jen smirked. "Figured you might like the details. Anyway, that box set your friend ordered came in. He called earlier and said you would be here to pick it up."

"Yeah," Mike nodded and followed Jennifer up to the counter. "He can't wait for the latest King Chilla movie. Something about a dude in a giant rubber chinchilla suit destroying a miniature Tokyo really puts a smile on his face."

Jennifer reached down behind the counter and pulled out a brown box with a handwritten sticky note on it that read "Andrew Mullen." It appeared to be a box set of a special edition of the King Chilla movie Mike had just mentioned. Jen then scanned the box's barcode with a hand scanner and pressed a few buttons. Soon after it printed out a receipt. Jen then bagged up the box and placed the receipt inside.

"Thank you for shopping with us," Jennifer recited as she handed the bag to Mike. "We hope to see you again soon."

Mike took the bag and made it back to his car as quickly as he could. Once he was inside, Mike took a minute to compose himself. He had always hated the mall, and even walking inside made him feel uncomfortable and itchy. The people, the smell, the mass consumerism, and the people; especially the people.

Mike quickly took out the box that Jennifer had given him and opened it up. Sure, he thought to himself. It had Andrew's name on it, but that wasn't going to keep Mike out. The brown box was heavier than it should be if it only contained the latest King Chilla film, so it could have been a bomb. Mike wasn't snooping, he was a hero.

175

A cracked porcelain doll mask with black eyes stared up lifelessly at Mike, and the nun's habit covered the back when Mike picked it up. A small black, plastic collar sat underneath. Smiling to himself Mike put the collar on. It was tight. Tight enough to press into his throat uncomfortably.

"This must be her voice box," Mike made the electronic box speak. "How does she fight wearing this thing?"

Mike put both down on the seat next to him and found that underneath was in fact a VHS of the latest King Chilla movie. The VHS sat on top of a piece of paper that appeared to be the back of a photograph. Mike rolled his eyes when he turned it over to find a picture of Jennifer sitting nude on a bed, hugging a large stuffed chinchilla to cover herself.

"Come get me, Squid Boy." Mike read the note on the bottom of the photo to himself, and then put it with the rest of the stuff. "I really should reconsider being a damn messenger."

The only other object was a piece of paper. Mike opened the folds and found that it was instructions to the next meet up. A fake robbery. Easy enough for Andy, Mike thought. He stuffed everything back in the box and started the car.

Andrew was in the kitchen when Mike let himself into the apartment. A box for a coffee maker sat on the counter that separated the living room from the kitchen and the smell of coffee filled the air.

"The fuck are you doing?" Mike asked setting the music store bag next to the coffee machine box.

"Trying to figure out how to work this thing," Andrew told his friend. "Everything comes out with grounds in it. I use the instant stuff and it comes out fine. I use these grounds, and everything comes out chunky."

"What kind of filter did you get for it?" Mike asked. "Is it too small?"

"Filter?" Andrew cocked an eyebrow.

"You know what?" Mike shook his head. "I am not even going to answer that. Got a package from your little girlfriend from the mall."

"Jen's not my girlfriend," Andrew walked away from his new machine slightly frustrated. "We're just friends."

"A friend that lets you stick a tentacle in her ass," Mike laughed. "That's a good friend there."

"I have never stuck a tentacle in her ass," Andrew shook his head with a smile, as he gave the idea some thought. "Good idea though."

"Dude," Mike threw his hands up. "I don't even want to hear about it, ok? Can you do me that one favor?"

"What's that?" Andrew started to open the box and go through the contents. "Why'd she give me the mask and voice box?"

"Just," Mike began. "Don't get too involved with her, dude. Not saying she's trouble, but you've been through too much shit recently. Just take some time to yourself."

"Thanks for the advice, Romeo," Andrew's eyes got bigger at the photo. "I think I have a handle on what's going on. We're good."

"Alright, brother," Mike turned around to leave. "If you think you have a good handle on this."

"Good enough." Andrew smiled at his friend as Mike walked out the door.

Issue 12

Shit. Shit, shit, shit, shit, shit, Sister Slaughter cursed to herself mentally and repeatedly. The cops arrived way too early. She couldn't show the goons she had hired that she was panicking and was very grateful that black hid the fact that she was sweating profusely.

"We have the building surrounded," The police bullhorn announced. "If you all surrender, we will not harm anyone. We want a peaceful solution to this situation. You have five minutes, or we send the SWAT team in."

"Barricade the doors," Sister Slaughter's electronic voice barked orders. "Barricade the windows. No one comes in or leaves unless in a body bag."

"Why would they come in in a body bag?" One goon asked the other.

"Don't question me!" Slaughter's electronic voice cracked. She had always hated to admit it, but she was never good at this when the pressure got too high.

This was supposed to be a quick smash and grab at a jewelry store. She figured there would be alarms. She figured there would be a guard or two. What she didn't plan on was that the 70-year old guard was going to put up a hell of a fight before being subdued and bound. In that time, the police were able to make it to the store and surround the place.

The lightly armed mercenaries quickly made every effort they could to barricade the place. Sister Slaughter knew it would slow down the cops, and hopefully, they were smart enough not to try and storm the building. Most likely, Sister Slaughter figured, they were going to try and wait them out. With no food or water, the police had the time advantage on their side.

Sister Slaughter looked up and checked the clock. Three minutes to midnight. Hopefully, she told herself, The Flayer was not going to be late. She had seen how many cars lined up to try and stop her. She had to dodge a few shots and get behind something to block the small arms fire from the first few cops that showed up. That was until her men had returned fire at the law enforcement officers.

"You," Sister Slaughter pointed at one of her guards. "Guard the door to the restroom. I have to take care of something."

The goon nodded and followed her. Sister Slaughter made it to the restroom and turned on the faucet. She sat down on the toilet with the seat down and began to tap her foot. She listened and hoped for the sound of combat. Let's get this over with. A few shots ringing out were the answer. Sister Slaughter wasn't sure if that was directed at the police, her men, or The Flayer had arrived on the scene.

"What's going on out there?" Sister Slaughter's voice crackled. There was no answer. That was the best answer she could have hoped for. With a smile under the mask, Sister Slaughter stood up and flushed the toilet just to keep up appearances. With a shove, the woman busted the door off the hinges. Within a second the door came right back at her. With minor effort, Sister Slaughter swatted the door towards a wall.

"Was wondering when your do-gooding ass was going to show up." Sister Slaughter looked around. Her guards had been knocked out cold in what looked almost like no fight at all. Then she looked to where the guard was and saw that he had been untied and was gone. The only thing standing in the room was a ten-foot-tall mass of writhing tentacles, vaguely in the shape of a human, donning a brown cloak.

179

The monster did nothing. Sister Slaughter began to circle the monster and found that the police had stepped back, presumably to allow The Flayer to do his thing. The Flayer did not even spin to consistently face his opponent. Sister Slaughter hated when he did this. She found this uncomfortable. Sister Slaughter couldn't tell if he was just staring straight ahead or spinning in his "suit". She made a mental note to ask if he could move personally in that thing.

"How'd you get in here?" Sister Slaughter whispered.

"Ate a lot of ammo trying to work through that barricade they put up." The Flayer hissed.

"How are we going to get out of here?" Sister Slaughter threw a punch that was much lighter than normal, allowing The Flayer to grab it and flip her over still landing on her feet.

"Fight a bit, then I want you to lift me off my feet and ram me through the cop cars. Use me to block any gunfire, throw me at them, and take off running after that." The Flayer explained to her. Both sighed in relief that no one could see their mouths move.

Sister Slaughter shot forward with a jumping spin kick. A quick tentacle shield blocked the attack, and his vision, so he didn't see the follow up low kick to his open lower half, which connected painfully. Sister Slaughter followed that with another, and another. The Flayer caught the third one and lifted the woman in the air and threw her against a wall.

Sister Slaughter righted herself in mid-air and used the wall to push off which added speed and force to her attempted tackle. The Flayer was a lot heavier than he looked, then again, a massive writhing block of meat would be a lot heavier than a normal man. Sister Slaughter began running as hard as she could and slammed The Flayer through the wall and out on the streets. She continued the run using The Flayer as a shield, until the two crashed into the police cars, spinning the vehicles they smashed through. Sister Slaughter then jumped a bit and drove The Flayer into the pavement. She then flipped off him and landed on her feet and continued to run.

"Take my hand." A police officer reached down to help The Flayer.

"I'm fine," The Flayer used a few tentacles to push himself up. "Which way did she run off too?"

"That way," The officer pointed towards an alleyway that Sister Slaughter had run down. "I'm coming to back you up."

"No need," The Flayer shook his mass of a head. "I can handle her strikes. You can't. I'll come find you when I defeat her. Go take care of the guards in the store."

"Yes, sir!" The officer ran towards where the knocked-out goons were as Flayer made his way down the alley.

The dark alley was silent as The Flayer looked for his prey. He searched around, hoping to see Jennifer standing on a balcony somewhere. The two were far enough away that it looked like a good spot for them to go back to their civilian clothing and make their escape.

"There you are Flayer," An electronic voice crackled in the dark. Sister Slaughter appeared from behind a dumpster and made a charge at The Flayer. "You've walked right into my trap."

Sister Slaughter took a playful swinging punch at her pursuer. The Flayer whipped out a tentacle and caught her fist. Quickly he slipped behind her and pinned her arm behind her back. Sister Slaughter then threw a slow elbow at the monster, who caught that as well, and with a little help from the woman, forced it behind her as well. Then the two moved towards the wall and The Flayer pinned her up against it, forcing Sister Slaughter to face him, with her arms behind her back.

"It appears you caught me," Sister Slaughter tried to coo, but the electronic voice ruined the effect. "Whatever will you do to me now?"

"Why don't I show you?" The Flayer hissed sliding closer to her. A few tentacles slithered out of from his cloak and began to run over Sister Slaughter's body. One found its way down her boot and began to make it way up Sister Slaughter's leg. Another found its way under her mask, around the back of her neck and gently in her mouth, where Sister Slaughter's tongue ran around the tip.

Sister Slaughter looked down after the tentacle left her mouth and saw the lumps of tentacles make it under the sports bra she was wearing and around her nipple giving it a twist, causing her to revel in the pleasurable pain, with the sound muffled by her biting her lip.

Forcefully, she was spun around and pressed against the wall. Two tentacles spread her legs apart. A pair of tentacles began to try and untie Sister Slaughter's corset and failed miserably.

"Having trouble back there?" Sister Slaughter crackled, between the hard breaths and moans caused by the tentacles playing between her legs.

"Yeah," The Flayer hissed. "Trying to get this damn thing off."

"Just rip my fucking body suit," Sister Slaughter commanded him. "Rip it open and fuck me, dammit."

The Flayer didn't have to be told twice. A tentacle lifted his robe, ripped a hole in Sister Slaughter's suit's crotch and Andrew thrust himself deep within her.

With each thrust, the two lost the world around them, and just let their lust take over.

Choir Boy was drawn to the commotion and the police scanner he carried in his satchel as a sidekick to a member of The League. He hoped that the name of Sister Slaughter and the Flayer was going to allow him to hit pay dirt and finally get some information about both people he was told to follow.

As he moved from rooftop to rooftop he was able to see the battle from the jewelry store, to the smashing through the cop cars. All lead to great pictures to help The League learn about these two people.

When he made his way over the alleyway that Sister Slaughter had ducked down he hoped to get some great shots of maybe whatever dark secret that her mask was hiding. When he saw The Flayer come down after her, he took even more shots that he hoped would help the fledgling superhero earn his way up to being a member of The League, as he photographed the apprehension.

What he found, however, and the shots he took of the two in their carnal act, were much, much more valuable to him. Choir Boy smiled as he used every last shot on the camera roll. To him, maybe it would be enough to even get himself a higher position in The League.

Issue 13

Mike and Andrew sipped their drinks watching the nightly news at Zero's, at the bar. The battle at the jewelry store was just the latest in the string of fights between The Flayer and Sister Slaughter, and the public was eating it up. Newspapers and magazines were starting to get in on the action as well and Andrew saw his horrific visage all over the media.

Andrew smiled to himself, he couldn't help it whenever he saw something on him. He would never have guessed in a million years that he was going to go so quickly from an average nothing about to have life just handed to him, to the city's latest craze. Andrew also hated to admit it, but he was loving every second of it.

"That Flayer guy is hitting it big," Mike said into his beer.

"Yeah," Andrew laughed, "I'm betting a movie deal and merchandise will be coming on soon. Then maybe The League will let him in, and bigger things will come his way."

"Is that what he really wants?" Mike laughed. "They might make him finally put that Sister Slaughter away. He seems so sloppy that he can't contain her."

"Oh no," Andrew got a hearty laugh, "I think he's got her number. It's like he's got built-in restraints. With the way she keeps coming back for more from him, I think she's liking it."

"Dude," Mike put his face in his palm, "you would think that would be too much information for that guy to be sharing though. Especially, when the idea of him sticking a tentacle…"

"Alright, alright," Andrew leaned back, "I'm shutting up."

"Thank you," Mike went back to his beer. "I bet he probably looks like you under there and I really don't want the idea of you plowing anything in my mind."

"Fair enough." Andrew motioned to the barkeep for another round of drinks.

"Still," Mike began to ponder, "It makes me wonder. He's only fighting her. Is she the only villain in this town? I mean, I was kind of expecting more. This town does have a superhero legacy behind it. Sure, they haven't been around for, what, since I was around five? I thought maybe he would bring them out of the woodwork."

"I'm sure there's more," Andrew shrugged. "If not, maybe all the exposure with how little hero presence there is will bring some in. Really make that guy wok for it, instead of using it as foreplay."

"Ok," Mike was obviously starting to get flustered. "Seriously, I know that you haven't been laid for at least two years. That was your fault though for dating Ms. Churchy. I'm glad your dick now has a smell to it, but can we please stop talking about it. Fuck man."

"Hey," Andrew smirked, "not my fault you're jealous."

"My friends," A male voice with a Hispanic accent interrupted their playful banter. "How are we this evening?"

Andrew turned to find Father Eduardo Vasquez standing behind them with a big smile on his face. Andrew returned the grin and offered his fellow superhero a seat. Much to Andrew's concern the man shook his head.

"No, no," The priest smiled at the two. "Why don't you have a seat with me and my colleague over in the booth. We would like to have a bit of a friendly chat with you two. My friend Dillon

185

and I got a pitcher. Since you two are familiar faces, and we're strangers to this bar, we figured you two would make great hosts."

Andrew looked over at Mike who gave a quick shrug and stood up his drink in hand. Andrew followed suit and the two went over to the booth. Choir Boy, now in street clothes, waited in the booth for them a pitcher of beer sat there with five glasses. As the group approached Choir Boy stood up and offered Mike to slide in between himself and the wall. Quickly, Mike shook his head no, which was met with a bit of a shove from the priest.

"Go ahead," Eduardo gestured. "Have a seat."

"Go ahead," Mike responded feeling the friendly drink turning threatening, "and politely fuck yourself. You don't tell me what to do."

"Fine," Eduardo smiled at Andrew, "Have a seat next to Dillon. He doesn't bite, and I got a pretty clear shot in case you do."

Andrew felt something in turn in the pit of his stomach. He had been in this position before with Mike. Two authority figures, blocking the two of them between themselves and the wall. This was a questioning tactic, and it was not good. It was not good at all.

Eduardo did have a point. If he was to fire a beam at Andrew, hopefully, he was not going to have the same reaction that he had before. Although, Andrew did not want to take that chance. The loss of his abilities, the pain, and the consistent horrible burning for the next few days did not seem like a pleasant idea. So, without much of a fuss, Andrew took the seat.

"Why don't you take the inner seat next to me." Eduardo gestured to Mike.

"I'll grab my own." Mike pulled a chair over from an opposing table.

"No," Vasquez shook his head and pointed a finger at Andrew, "That's not a very good host. Have a seat."

Knowing what was going to come next for his friend, Mike reluctantly did as he was told, but left his extra chair right where he had placed it.

"Leave the chair," Eduardo laughed to himself as he sat down trapping Mike in. "You never know who might show up and need it. Now, I don't believe you two have met Dillon Tyler, well as himself I should say."

"Hi." Andrew meekly let out. Fear had begun to take over him. He wasn't sure why the fear and anxiety had started to have that effect. Was it because of the power of the two trapping him? Could it be that with his weakness in front of him he was back to plain old Andrew?

"You look really familiar," Mike leaned on the table and pointed at Dillon. If there was one thing Michel was good at, it was staying calm under pressure, and Andrew could feel it coming down. "I know I've seen you somewhere before."

"I'm great with faces," Dillon finally spoke up, "Aside from stopping those attackers a month ago, I don't believe we've met."

"I never said we met," Mike leaned back, "just that you looked familiar."

"I'm sure we'll all have plenty of time to get to know each other better after we have our little chat." The Father spoke up.

"So, what do you want to talk to us about?" Andrew chimed in, not honestly wanting the answer.

"Well, Andrew," Eduardo began. "Do you take me for an idiot?"

"No," Andrew shook his head. "I've looked up to you and the members of The League ever since I was a little kid. A lot of respect. You're all the reason I've done a lot of what I've done."

"Good!" The priest let out a jovial smile. "I'm very glad to hear that. What about you Mike? Do you think I'm an idiot?"

"No," Mike shook his head as well. "I think you're probably a child rapist, but since you somehow talked your favorite into being your sidekick I don't think you're an idiot. I think he's an idiot."

Andrew had to stop a snicker at his friend's remark. The jovial smile was quickly wiped from Father Eduardo's face.

"Well," The father put his hands up, "I can assure you I'm not. In fact, recently, I feel that I'm part of the people getting screwed."

"So, you're a bottom," Mike finished the beer he brought over and refilled his drink. "That's cool. We all have our tastes."

"I came..." Eduardo tossed his hands up lightly in frustration over Mike's comments.

"Guessed it." Mike added.

"I came," The Father continued through his teeth. "Here to talk to you boys about a problem. Instead, I get insults. Maybe I should take my findings to The League. I'm sure they'd be happy to deal with you two."

"What findings?" Andrew questioned. His gut made him go mentally through anything terrible he had done.

"Well," Eduardo smiled. "You see, I was told to have you followed Andrew. To keep an eye on you and make sure you didn't get into too much trouble. Who knew? Maybe you could lead me straight to Sister Slaughter."

"Fuck." Andrew felt the pit of his stomach try and leave out his anus. He figured out what this was about.

"Fuck indeed, Andrew." Eduardo shook his head. "I can assure you, sir, The League does not like to be played for fools."

"What is he talking about, Andy?" Mike lowered his eyes at his friend.

"Here," Eduardo motioned to his sidekick. "Dillon, show Mr. Mike here the photos you took the other night."

Dillon reached into his satchel and pulled out a manila folder and handed it to Mike. Mike's eye widened at the photos as he flipped through them. Eventually, he tossed the photos on the table, and just glared at his friend.

"You two," Mike spoke slowly, "are the dumbest, most reckless, mother fuckers I have ever met. How fucking... I can't even... really? In your costumes?"

"I'm afraid so," Eduardo shook his head. "But there is a plus side. You see, I believe that love is a good thing. I believe that it can even transverse battle lines and bring two sides together. So, I decided not to bring these to the attention of The League. You see, I quickly realized what you two were doing. You two were working together to make a quick buck. Pretty smart. Don't know which one of you three thought of it but bravo.

"So, not being an idiot, I continued that line of thinking. You see, Andrew. I use my award money to maintain several schools and orphanages in South America. All over the continent.

So I thought, why not get in on this little game. In fact, why not up the money? You see, you get paid a pittance for 'beating' Sister Slaughter. Did you know if you actually lead to an arrest that the amount you make is much, much higher?"

"What are you saying?" Andrew said after rubbing his face with his hands.

"Simple," Eduardo smiled. "You help me apprehend Sister Slaughter. We split the money. No one has to know about your little tryst with her. The photos will just disappear. You're free to continue the life of a superhero. The orphanages stay open a little while longer."

"And if we tell you to shove your ideas up your ass," Mike scoffed. "Would you use lube or go in dry?"

"Actually," The priest nodded. "I would have to give those pictures to Ms. Claremont, and everyone spends time behind bars. A lot of time. If you three survive the encounter."

"Yeah," Mike ran his tongue over his teeth. "and what is to say Sister Slaughter doesn't spill the beans afterward? She's already in prison what does she have to lose?"

"Well," Father Eduardo looked up pondering that quandary, "the by-laws state that she just has to be taken into custody. Once an arrest is made, we are no longer held liable if something were to happen to her, say she dies in custody."

"You want us to kill, Jennifer?" Andrew almost shot up from his seat, nearly spilling the beer on the table. "Some man of the cloth you are."

"I said," Father Eduardo put his hands up in a mock defense. "If something were to happen. I didn't say we would do it. We were just a little bit rougher than we should have been. How were we to know? A very easy case to argue against the no killing rule, wouldn't you say?"

"Get fucked," Andrew tried to shoot up again, a finger from the priest made him sit back down. "Get fucked hard."

"Andy," Mike calmed his friend down. "Look at the reality of the situation. He's got us trapped. The photos are right there clear as day. Someone is going down if these get out. We really don't have much of a choice."

Andrew quickly caught on to the score. Father Eduardo, however, had the score pegged wrong. Andrew and Mike had in fact been these very booths, and in a very similar situation before. The two of them knew exactly what to do. The good Father was lucky enough to learn what Michael and Andrew had planned rather quickly as a right fist from Mike spun the tattooed man around to drive it home square in the priest's nose. A tentacle that Andrew had been making a commotion to get out unnoticed reached up and grabbed Dillon around the neck and slammed his head into the table twice, putting him out cold.

Mike grabbed the photos off the table as he jumped on it and took off out the door, while the father began to recover. Andrew shoved Dillon out of the booth and tried not to step on his body as he took off towards the door, all while kicking the extra chair in the Father's way.

Both stopped for a second in the cold night air after making it out of Zero's to catch their breath. A second was too much time however against a battle-hardened superhero. Father Eduardo burst from the doorway blood gushing a trail down his face. A quick shot came out of his hands and was directed at Mike who held the photos. A strike against the shooter's cheek from a tentacle made the shot go wide, striking a car and leaving a rather considerable smoldering dent.

Missing no opportunity, Mike dropped the photos and rushed the superhero landing a solid kick into a stomach that was more solid than Mike had anticipated. This left his foot aching from the impact. A smile was the only reaction from his opponent. Mike's attack was responded to with a kick in kind to his own stomach which dropped the man to the ground, gasping for air.

Father Vasquez stood over the collapsed man and warmed up another glowing blast from his hands. This one tended to be shot straight up into the air as a tentacle grabbed around his neck and pulled him back and onto the ground, kicking up a cloud of snow and slush from the street.

Mike regained his ability to breath and attempted to punt Father Vasquez in the head finishing the fight. Having the seen the move too many times and how sloppily Mike fought, the Father

190

was able to roll to the side and spin his leg into a sweep tripping Mike and causing him to land in the spot Vasquez just laid.

Andrew rushed over to his opponent, tentacle out ready to strike when a bright light caught him off guard. A sense of burning, and loss of vision, and the heat taking the air from his lungs from the shot that came out of the Father's hands caused Andrew to drop the ground and writhe in pain. The shot had struck Andrew in the chest causing the tentacles that Andrew used to protect his vital organs to fall off his body and writhe both under his shirt and on the ground next to him until they stopped moving.

"You stupid, stupid kids," The Father let out between breaths and stood over Andrew, "Do you really think that I didn't make copies of those photos? You do think I'm an idiot!"

"I think," A coughing voice came from Mike as he found his feet. "I think, you really need to get the cock out of your ears and look at me cause I'm still standing mother fucker."

"You?" Father Vasquez began to laugh and leaned down to get in the face of the hero. "You? You're going to stop me. Did you even listen to what I just said? Even if you kill me, those pictures are getting out. So, go ahead. Go ahead. Do your worst."

Mike knew it was a trap. Mike was certain of it, understood it, and found that this asshole had just blasted his best friend for the second time, and throwing him in so much pain he probably was in and out of consciousness. Mike couldn't leave him, he had to do something.

Mike rushed the man head-on. Again, as foolish as it was it had to at least buy some time for Andrew to come back and do something. However, it didn't buy enough time as Mike's body rocketed in the air and then skid across the street until he was stopped by a light post. However, the scrapes from the road and the light post were not the most painful part. The concussive blast against his chest and the burning sensation over his entire body was what really knocked it out of him. Mike rolled in the snow as much as he could to try and get the burning from the Father's shot to stop, but it was to no avail.

Father Vasquez turned his attention back to Andrew and pulled his limp body up by his shirt. Andrew's eyes tried the best they could to focus but failed miserably. A light spit of blood that had poured out of Andrew's nose, and a weak strike with a tentacle across the Father's face done in defiance caused no visible effect.

"You fail this, Andrew," The Father stared almost into Andrew's soul. "I will not only turn the photos in, I will personally lead the hunt for you, her, and your foul-mouthed friend over there. Now, if Dillon is hurt badly in any way, I'm coming back out here and making sure you won't grow another tentacle again. Do you understand me?"

Andrew did not answer. He did not even get the chance to answer. A gunshot blast roaring over everyone's head was the only sound that came out. A strong burly man held a sawed-off shotgun in his hand. Over his opposite shoulder, Dillon was draped still unconscious.

"You ain't doing shit, God boy," It was the bar owner Mitch. A man that had taken care of these two when times were very rough, and when they had bitten off more than they could chew. Right now, was no different. "Only thing you're doing is taking your faggy-ass little friend and getting the fuck out of here."

"You with the shotgun. You're are going to stop me?" Father Vasquez got a slight chuckle out of the idea. Slowly, however, that chuckle faded as every regular, everyone from the old members of a defunct biker gang, to the old bar flies that were usually only there to score some blow or blow some dude, exited the bar. Each one with some sort of a makeshift weapon in hand.

"Nope," Mitch laughed, dropped Dillon on the ground and loaded another shell. "But we will make you disappear. Fight ain't with us, but it's with some of our own. So, you walk away now. We all go back inside. You don't, you see how fast ten drunks with improvised weapons can make your night a living hell. So, do us all a favor, collect your friend, and walk away, bitch."

Father Eduardo Vasquez spat on Andrew and dropped him. Slowly and with open palms, he walked up to the bar owner. The burly man with one eye covered in cataracts simply stood there, unflinching as the two locked gazes.

"You gonna kiss me," Mitch licked his lips and leveled the shotgun at the superhero's chest, "or you gonna make the right choice?"

192

Without a word, Father Vasquez picked the smaller framed Dillon Tyler up in his arms and began to walk away. Every single member of the posse that had come out to help their friends watched and waited until the two were out of sight and then rushed to bring Mike and Andrew inside.

No one noticed a figure, bundled up in the cold come by and see the photos on the ground. A gloved hand reached down and picked them up. The hood on the coat hid their face. Fingers flipped through the photos, only stopping a second at the one with The Flayer waist deep in Sister Slaughter. With a feminine sigh, the figure put the photos in her coat pocket and walked off into the night.

Issue 14

Andrew knew two things when he awoke. The food being cooked smelled amazing and that whatever he was laying on was so horribly uncomfortable he was just glad to finally be awake.

Slowly and tenderly Andrew lifted the blanket off himself and checked out his surroundings. Wooden panel walls, a vomit green colored shag carpet, and all this was decorated about with a smattering of empty beer cans and overfull ashtrays. Andrew only had one guess who's place he was in, and lucky for Andrew he figured a light shooting priest would probably keep his living space better than this.

"Holy shit," A large, shirtless heavily tattooed man rushed into the room and gently helped Andrew to sit up. "Look who finally woke up. Hungry?"

"Yeah, Mitch," Andrew nodded as the older bartender helped him to sit up. "And I could use a cigarette too."

"Help yourself," Mitch sat down in a stained chair next to Andrew and tossed him a pack from the arm of the chair. Andrew looked around helplessly for a lighter until one was tossed at him. "Little Andy, having a smoke. Never thought I'd see the day."

"Yeah," Andrew chuckled as he lit the tobacco product in his mouth took a large drag and exhaled. "It's been a fucked few months. Just booze wasn't helping."

"Well, figuring the damn suicide attempt, and now whatever the fuck that light show was last night," Mitch laughed and lit one of his own after Andrew handed back the pack and lighter. "I can imagine."

"Kind of wish it all ended with the damn suicide part," Andrew said behind a smoky exhale. This was only met with one of the sternest looks that Andrew had ever received, as the old man got up to go and get whatever he was cooking on the stove. "I meant attempted. I don't mean the whole wishing I dead. Look, long story about how this has been. Anyway, what time is it?"

"3 in the afternoon. You've been out all day," Mitch returned with two plates of scrambled eggs. "Figured you'd want some breakfast when you finally woke up. Want something to drink?"

"What you got?" Andrew took the plate and began to gulp down the food.

"Water, pop, O.J. Wouldn't recommend that though. Shit's a killer." Mitch laughed at his own joke. Andrew didn't want to admit to the old man that it had already aged horribly.

"Pop's fine." Andrew placed his order.

"I think it has been a strange couple of months for you," Mitch returned with a drink for Andrew. "You lose Erin, Mike punches a priest, but on the plus side you're a god damn superhero now."

Andrew stopped dead in his tracks. The piece of egg on the end of his fork dropped off as Andrew stalled eating it.

"What do you mean?" Andrew tried to judge what his old friend of talking about.

"You're that Flayer freak all over the news," Mitch laughed. "Never would have thought you would be charging head first in to stop robberies and shit. Then again ever since you stepped in my place, you been itching for a fight."

"I have no idea what you're talking about." Andrew denied quickly.

"Kid," Mitch let out a hearty belly laugh. "I've known you since you and Mike showed up with the worst fake IDs I had ever seen. Since then, I've pulled your fat out of the fire so many times from bar fights, helped hook the two of you up with floozies that enter the place, and even kept you fed when you were homeless. I ain't got kids of my own, so like it or not you're the closest thing I got. Don't fucking lie to me."

Andrew stopped for a second. The old man was right, on all the accounts, even the ones that Andrew didn't like to think about such as being left homeless on the streets of New Hancock. Whenever bad things went down, Mitch was there for both Mike and himself. Andrew knew in his heart he never could thank the man enough, but at the same time, he also knew that he would never have too.

Deep down Mitch was a good person. Mitch had become the perfect example of how reformation can work when properly implemented in the federal prison system. Mitch had spent years behind bars for assault and battery on numerous people. Not for the simple bar fights that usually happened at Zero's. The police had hardly ever followed up on those. At one point in Mitch's younger years, he was a Neo-Nazi, and still had the tattoos to prove it, and when a few members of a minority gang decide that violence is the best way to make some extra cash off Mitch's mother, Mitch did the only thing he knew to do to deal with the problem. The police must have found the cracked skulls and bloody baseball bat a bit excessive. So they put him behind bars.

While Mitch went away, he had some time to think and change the direction his life was headed. His time wasn't like a movie about redemption or anything. No, Mitch's story was plain as could be. He did his time and decided he didn't want to go back. So, he stayed away from the violence unless absolutely needed. Even to the point of allowing himself to be robbed. He was still racist as all hell but just toned it down quite a bit. He opened his own little bar for the misfits of New Hancock and enjoyed a quiet life in his own little part of the world.

That was until two nineteen-year-olds entered his bar with bad fake Ids. Instead of yelling at them to get out of his bar, Mitch did the one thing that he guessed no one had done for the obviously troubled boys. He served them and listened to them. Never charged them for a drink until they were legal and was always there to pull them out of the fire when they bit off more than they were in over their heads. To him, they were his boys.

"What gave it away?" Andrew looked down at his plate.

"I found all these wiggly things around you when I pulled your ass out of the snow," Mitch flicked the ash off his cigarette. "Just kind of put two and two together. Who'd thought a fucking high school drop-out would be this city's superhero."

"Thanks, Mitch," Andrew laughed going back to eating. "Always got to bring that up."

"Until you get that god damn G.E.D. you bet your ass I will." The two shared a laugh. Andrew smiled to himself. After dropping out of high school and being kicked out of his home for his "behavioral issues," Andrew loved the fact that instead of having a blood family, he got to make his own. Every time something like this would happen, Andrew knew he made the right choice.

"And if you don't do it soon," Mitch got on him further. "I'm going to tell that little hot piece of ass you have been spending so much time with about it. Then you'll have both of us on you, and lord knows you don't want a damn woman up your ass about something."

"Yeah," Andrew nodded. "I just got that two-year stick out from there. Don't need another one up my ass."

"Amen, kid," Mitch put out the cigarette. "So, tell me. That why Erin dumped ya? Couldn't deal with the tentacles?"

"No, Mitch," Andrew sighed as he put his empty plate to the side. "I killed a lot of people that month. I killed people right in front of her. I mean, I did it all to save her, but it was the fact that I killed all those people."

"Huh," Mitch took the plates and put them in the sink. "Ain't an easy thing to do."

"Not like I wanted to do it," Andrew admitted. "Just lost control when they tried to kill me first."

"In that case," Mitch returned and sat back down. "Fuck 'em. So, What's Father Spic's story?"

"Long story short," Andrew leaned back. "He's a superhero too. His sidekick caught me fucking someone who I really wasn't supposed to. They are going to go tell the big league of superheroes that we were committing fraud with their pay system."

"What?" Mitch snorted up some phlegm and spit it into a random cup. "Ain't like you were fucking that nun looking chick you been fighting... Oh god damn it, Andy. You were, weren't you?"

Andrew didn't say a word. He knew he didn't have to.

"She that one that's started showing up here with you and Mike?" Mitch asked, and Andrew just responded nodding. "She got nice tits?"

Andrew just laughed at the old man grinning.

"Fucking amazing, Mitch," Andrew smiled thinking of Jennifer as a person and not just the pair of tits that Mitch seemed to be focused on.

"Good pair of tits are worth a lot, Andy," Mitch cocked his head to the side. "Well, till about thirty then they start to get all saggy and shit."

"On another note," Andrew looked around. "How'd Mike fair last night."

"Like Hell," Mitch informed Andrew. "He left a bit earlier. Said he had to go to the mall and talk to someone."

198

Issue 15

Mike made his way into the mall. There was no stopping him this time. No worry about noisy teenagers and no worry about dealing with shitty mothers. He had a goal and he had to make sure it was executed. The restrooms that were hidden in the parking garage where rarely used and he needed to make sure that he had the cleanest bathroom in the place.

After the fight a few hours ago, nothing in his body had worked as well as it should. He hoped it was all just bruising and that he would be fine. However, the shots he took seemed to have rustled up his internal organs enough to cause them not to hold things like they used to. He figured that having a doctor look at it later would be his best bet, but that would be something he would have to put on hold.

After finishing, Mike made his way to the only other place in this mall that he would go. He needed to talk to Jennifer. He had to tell her what was going on. As much as he didn't really want to deal with this and probably should let Andrew do the talking, having the two of them even close to each other was not the best of ideas. It also didn't help that because of the pained screaming due to Father Vasquez's shot, Andrew's voice would probably would be out for a few days.

Mike saw Jennifer as soon as he walked in. She stood next to a rack of cassettes putting them back in proper alphabetical order. He tapped her on the shoulder twice causing her to spin around.

"How can I…" Jen responded in her apathetic retail voice, which changed when she saw who stood behind her. "Hey, what's up?"

"We got to talk." Mike was straight to the point.

"I'm working," Jennifer waved him off and began to whisper. "So, unless you got some money for me I don't have time for you."

"Andrew and I were attacked last night," Mike informed her.

"So?" Jennifer shrugged. "Squid Boy ok?"

"No," Mike shook his head. "He's not. Guy was screaming in so much pain he might have lost his voice. Was still out cold when I left him."

"Hold on one second," Jen's face turned to hidden panic. She turned to her co-worker. "I'm taking my 15."

"You just took your 15." The co-worker shot back.

"I'm taking another one! Unless you want me to go change my bloody fucking tampon in the back room." Jen yelled at him.

"Jesus," The man waved her off. "Go, just go, and watch your language. We do have customers in the store."

"Come on," Jen rushed out of the store with Mike quickly behind her. "Where are you parked? I'm not discussing this shit out in the open."

The two made their way to the parking garage. Jennifer then instructed Mike to take the car to the top floor and park in a secluded corner of the garage.

"So, what the fuck happened?" Jennifer turned to Mike as he threw the car in park. "Who fucked you two up enough that you had to come to me for help?"

"I didn't say I was here for help," Mike lit a cigarette and rolled down the driver side window to let the smoke out. "I'm letting you know what's going on. We got attacked by this priest dude. Ok, to be fair I broke the fuckers nose first."

200

"If I've heard of a faster one-way ticket to Hell…" Jennifer laughed.

"Shut the fuck up for a second," Mike protested. "Guy goes by the name of the Holy Frijole, I think. Shoots these light beams out his hands. They hurt like a son of a bitch."

"Yeah," Jennifer nodded, "old school League guy. I've heard of him. I've never seen him though."

"Well," Mike looked around into the parking garage to make sure no security guards were sneaking up on them. "You sure it's safe to talk here? No one's coming up here?"

"This mall's not that busy," Jen shrugged. "So security trusts the cameras up here and doesn't come up. Hell, this is where I usually bring guys to fuck."

"Yeah," Mike puffed air out his nose. "Next time, bring Andy somewhere this secluded. Then maybe you won't get caught next time."

"What do you mean?" Jen raised an eyebrow in concern. "So, what if someone saw us fucking it's not like they caught us in… Oh dear god, someone caught us fucking in costume the other night. Way to go Jennifer, really good idea you had there."

"Yeah," Mike finally turned to her. "Your bright idea blew the whole thing wide open."

"So," Jennifer put two and two together. "The Holy Bean put everything together in his mind and is going to blow the whole idea wide open."

"No," Mike shook his head. "He's making Andrew help him bring you down, and he's going to beat you to the point that you probably will get arrested but not survive. He's basically forcing Andy to kill you."

"Squid Boy wouldn't kill me," Jen waved off the idea. "He can't even if he wanted too. Which he doesn't, right?"

"Of course he doesn't want to kill you," Mike shook his head. "But if he doesn't help him we all go down, hard. I'm talking not just cops after us. I'm talking the god damn league after us."

Jennifer stopped for a second. She leaned her head back on the chair of the car. She shut her eyes and tried to make sense of the whole situation. She had seduced Andrew into having sex in the alleyway after their caper. Jen felt the costumes would add a little danger of getting caught, and the role-play would be fun. She never thought they would have been caught. Now here she was, her mistake bringing her newest friends problems. Jennifer cursed herself in her head. Sometimes she felt that was all she was good for, causing the people she cared about more problems than she was worth.

"Tell him to do it." Jennifer finally spoke.

"What?" Mike looked over at the woman.

"Tell Squid Boy to help The Bean Man to bring me down." Jennifer nodded looking straight ahead.

"You're kidding." Mike protested.

"No," Jen shook her head, and climbed out of the car, and leaned in the still open door. "This is my fault. Tell Squid Boy to give him all the relevant information to stop me. My weakness, all of it. I fucked up this plan. You two shouldn't have to pay for it. Give me a week to get some shit in order. I'll plan a heist somewhere, and I'll do it alone. They can be big superheroes."

Jennifer closed the door to the car and began to walk away. Mike turned the car on and followed her.

"Jen," Mike pulled the car up next to her and kept it going at her pace. He could see a few tears letting themselves out of the corner of her eyes as she walked away. "You're not the only one in this. Andy fucked up too. We can find a way to handle this."

"Go," Jen didn't turn towards the car following her. She couldn't bring herself to face Mike. "This is what's got to happen. So fucking go."

"Jennifer!" Mike yelled at her. "The fuck is your problem? This isn't the first time things have gone wrong in your career. You got out of those, and we'll all get out of this. I have an idea. Listen to me!"

"Go!" Jennifer turned to the man in the car. She put her foot on the car and gave it a quick shove turning the vehicle away from her by around 30 degrees. Her face red and what eye make-up she was wearing started to run down her face. "You don't go I'm going to do some real villain shit and throw this fucking car out of here!"

Mike paused for a second and looked at the woman that he had started to consider a friend. Nothing he could find in his mind that he could say could change her mind. He did the only thing he could and drove off. However, he looked back in his rearview mirror in time to watch Jennifer lean on a support, turn, and throw a hook straight through it.

Issue 16

Mike took his normal spot at Zero's. The spot happened to be next to Andrew who had been there a while before he arrived. Not a word was spoken between the two as he sat down and ordered a drink. The two sat in silence for a few minutes, neither saying a word just staring at the wall of liquor in front of them. Each person both wondering what their friend was thinking and possibly trying to figure a way out of the situation.

"Jen," Mike finally broke the silence. His mood was not somber but instead just thoughtful. "Jen didn't take the news too well."

"Could you really blame her?" Andrew responded in the same flat tone.

"She feels this whole thing is her fault." Mike continued to inform his friend.

"You tell her it's not?" Andrew questioned. He already knew that Mike was good enough to try and remind the woman that Mike had come up with the plan, and that Andrew also had his part in it. He knew that Mike would stress that Andrew having his part in it more as a joke, but would and currently was feeling just as responsible.

"She threatened to throw my car and me off of the parking garage." Mike took a sip of his drink and decided that he needed something a little stronger to keep his mind working. He looked to the female bartender that he had worked so hard to get Andrew her number and ordered two shots of the strongest whiskey that they had. The woman quickly obliged.

"Sounds like Jen." Andrew got a little chuckle.

"You need to learn to stop fucking around with crazy chicks," Mike told him after the two took their shots.

"Crazy in the head," Andrew realized his friend was trying to keep him calm and lighten the mood a little. "Crazy in bed."

"Well," Mike said. "To be honest this has been the happiest I've seen you in a few years. So, we got to find a way to keep that smile on your face."

"Yeah." Andrew quickly felt the mood die down.

The silence between them grew again.

"She wants you two to bring her down," Mike told Andrew. He hadn't wanted to deliver that news and hoped that he could find a plan for at least get something off the ground before telling him that.

"Why is she taking all the hits in this?" Andrew pondered to himself. He felt that deep down he truly did not want the answer.

"Tell me something," Mike swirled his beer in his glass absently, very lost in thought, "What do you think of her? Been sleeping with this one for a bit. You two got a thing going on? Or what's the story?"

"It's just sex," Andrew informed him. After a pause added. "I think"

"Is that what she said or what you thought?" Mike pushed the question.

"Does it matter?" Andrew laughed a little. He had already tied a few on and was slowly losing his ability to care about the course of future events.

"No," Mike thought. He knew Andrew well enough that he already had the answer he needed, but still had a question for his friend. "Andy, do you trust me?"

"Yeah," Andrew nodded. "Why would you even need to ask a question like that."

205

"Do what Jen said. Bring her down," Mike stood up from the table. "Try and get a hold of Jen. Maybe spend some time with her."

"Mike," Andrew looked over at his friend, "What are you going to do?"

"Something's been bothering me," Mike took some money out of his wallet and threw it on the bar counter. "I'm going to get an answer for it."

"You're not going to do anything crazy are you?" Andrew's voice began to show some concern.

"It's me, Andy," Mike smiled as he turned away. "Of course I am. Now try and get a hold of Jennifer. She's not taking this as well as you or I am. I am starting to think this is the first time the chips have really bee stacked against her and she needs someone right now. Might be good for the both of you."

Andrew just sat in silence wondering what his friend had in mind. Andrew knew deep down that this was something that he really shouldn't just let go. At the same time, however, he knew that he had to let Mike do his thing. Mike had come to the aid of Erin a few months ago without ever being asked. Now here he was again, about to do something so stupid that Andrew knew if he heard the plan he would stop him. Andrew found that he just couldn't. He had to let Mike do Mike.

Andrew hated being alone. The only thing that really kept his mind at bay during this time was alcohol and he already had a ton of that in his system. However, his new healing was starting to make that go away. Much to his surprise, what was left of the booze wasn't keeping anything calm. The recent events ran through his head like they were running a marathon and they still had 25 miles to go. So, to Andrew the only possible solution was to try and drown them as best as he could.

Everything kept bouncing on the idea of how things could have gone differently. He could have told Jennifer that banging in a back alley in their attire was a bad idea. He could have never agreed to Mike's idea of committing fraud against The League. All the bad decisions he made. All the reckless ones he made. There had to be a way to get everyone out of this. All Andrew had to do was think of it.

Killing The Holy Frijole was out of the question. The thought had crossed his mind a few times on the way home. The career hero had a leg up on him though. For some reason, any shot Andrew took from the man burned like the fires of hell had already laid claim on his soul. Not to mention he had years of experience on him. Another thought hit him. What if he took out The Choir Boy? Tell the priest that if he doesn't drop it, he'll kill him? No, Andrew concluded, the man was basically innocent in all this. Probably just doing his job.

Either way, it didn't matter. Andrew still thought of himself as a superhero. Heroes don't kill. Sure, he didn't do much heroing. Sure, he was currently on the hook for fraud. Sure, he was sleeping with the closest thing he had to a supervillain. All things considered though, Andrew Mullen still thought of himself as a superhero. After this is all done, he decided, he was going back to being legit, and cleaning up the streets of New Hancock. Even if that did bring him to going toe to toe with the villain known as Sister Slaughter.

How was she holding up? Andrew thought to himself. He didn't admit it to Mike at the bar, but over the past couple of days, he had been trying to get a hold of her. However, all he would get an answer from was either her roommate saying she'll leave a message or the answering machine. That was making all this just so much worse in his head. Jennifer was out there caught up in this mess, and she had chosen to isolate herself from it all. Part of him just wanted to just be there and comfort his friend.

His friend. That was the thought that bounced again in Andrew's mind. He thought they were just friends. Something in Andrew felt that something more might be nice. He never expected, nor did he want to feel this way. It was just something about her. Something fun. Something that made him feel a little alive. Something he never felt with Erin. Was it the danger of her being a bad guy and him being a good guy? Andrew shook the thought from his head. That was either the reason or that was she was the first woman that made him feel more than safety in the past few years.

Andrew's train of thought had was interrupted however when he heard the bedroom window slide open. His instincts shot a group of tentacles to cover both arms as he stood up. There it was, the one thing that more than anything else made him glad his superpowers didn't allow him to kill himself. That rush of adrenaline. However, Andrew's heart rate died down, and his tentacles slid back into wherever they came from when Jennifer walked out of the hallway leading to his bedroom.

The two stood there for a second. Neither moving, neither saying a word. Jennifer looked disheveled. She looked as if she had not done anything with herself for days. No make-up, no sleep and had just let her hair go. It looked like she was in her pajamas that she probably had not taken off for days. At least that's how she smelled.

Instantly, Jennifer regretted her decision to show up. The man across from her probably hated her for the idea that she thought would be fun. He probably didn't want to see her, and that she really, really should leave. Quickly, she turned around to make the hasty retreat that her mind was telling her to make. When she felt something, a hand on her shoulder. Jennifer spun around to find Andrew standing there. He stood there with a look on his face that said that he wasn't holding up any better than she was.

No words were said. All he did was pull her close and wrap his arms around her. Jennifer hated to admit it, but just this small act was enough to try and force herself not to let tears come out. Jennifer was strong. She was one of the top villains this city had seen in a while. Villains don't cry when they're in trouble. They fight.

This time was different, though. She wasn't Sister Slaughter. The man holding her wasn't The Flayer. They were Jennifer and Andrew. Two people locked in a problem, together, and both willing to help hold each other up. That was the one thing that Jennifer was missing. Right now, Andrew was holding her up, and right now he probably needed to be held up as well. Jennifer freed her arms from between her and Andrew's chest and returned the embrace.

That was when Jennifer made what she considered her next mistake. Jennifer freed her right hand and placed it behind

Andrew's head. Gently she pulled his face close to hers and pressed their lips together. What the young woman didn't expect was Andrew to accept so willingly. Jennifer had always felt that she was good at making mistakes, but sometimes, and right now she hoped this was one of those times, they worked out.

Issue 17

Andrew awoke from a heavy, dead sleep. The bright light of the television shone with too high of an intensity to make anything out. He looked over to find that he was alone in the apartment. Jennifer who had fallen asleep pressed up against him was nowhere to be found. For a moment, Andrew wondered if he had just fallen asleep and dreamed the whole thing. Frankly, he figured as he got up to use the bathroom, he didn't care.

"We have interrupted the currently scheduled program as we have breaking news from downtown," A news anchor read off. "It appears that the supervillain known as Sister Slaughter has begun a rampage downtown. We are getting reports of parked cars being thrown into buildings, street lights destroyed, and businesses being broken into and set on fire. Luckily, no fatalities are being reported."

Andrew cursed as he rushed into his bedroom and threw open his closest. In a small boxed marked "Memory box," Andrew found his cloak and threw it on. He quickly rushed to the bowl by the door where left he keys and memory decided to catch up with him. His car was still not running. In the haste of everything happening in his life, Andrew had failed to get his vehicle up and running.

After a dose of more corrosive language, Andrew rushed to the phone. His fingers flew so fast dialing Mike's phone number that he had to try calling the man twice.

"This better be good," Mike answered the phone.

"It's Andy. Turn on the TV," Andrew commanded. "Jen's going nuts downtown right now."

"The fuck?" Mike gave a bit of pause. "Stupid bitch said she was going to give us a week to figure this shit out! Mother Fucker! How fast can you get down there?"

"Car's still down," Andrew informed his friend, "and it's not like I can exactly take the bus."

"Alright," Mike set the phone down for a second, "I'm on my way. You ready?"

"I'm dressed," Andrew affirmed. "Hurry. We got to get down there and stop her before The Frijole gets a hold of her."

"Be waiting outside," Mike said and hung up the phone.

"We have word now that a member of The League has appeared on the scene," The news reporter continued as Mike turned up the radio of the car. "It appears to be The Holy Frijole. He is currently getting a situation update from the police."

"He's stalling." Andrew broke the silence in the car. "He's got to be. Doesn't know what he's up against and is waiting on me to show up and help him."

"You sure of that?" Mike found a spot to ditch the car in an alley so the two would not be seen exiting.

"Why else would he not just rush in?" Andrew shrugged as he got out of the car. Quickly, the mass of tentacles that changed Andrew Mullen into The Flayer covered him from head to toe. "He's a member of The League, for god sakes. She's a street level criminal. This has one-punch knockout written all over it."

"You got a plan?" Mike asked also climbing out of the car.

"No," The Flayer's tentacles stood still and stoic as he shook his head underneath. "Didn't for Erin either. That seemed to work out. Where are you going? Aren't you going to wait with the car?"

"No," Mike shook his head. "I'm coming too."

211

"The fuck you are," The Flayer was not about to let his friend get hurt. "You're a civilian. You'll be recognized in an instant."

"I didn't say I was going to be helping you." Mike opened the trunk and pulled out a small box.

"What's that?" The Flayer asked.

"Like I've been saying," Mike turned a knob and with a crackle and some radio static it came to life. Mike put a pair of earphones in the jack on the front and clipped it to the belt. "I've got this hunch. I'm going to follow through with it. You go do what you got to do."

With that, Mike took off running down the alley. The Flayer had no time to question and took off in the opposite direction towards all the flashing lights and commotion a few blocks away.

"Well," The Holy Frijole greeted The Flayer with a hand out. His armor was beautiful and as shiny as the last time the two met in costume. Only this time the sense of admiration and awe that Andrew had felt was replaced with disgust. "Look who decided to come help. Come, my friend, the news will want a shot of us together for their papers and broadcasts. Let's the people at home know that everything is under control."

The Flayer did not say a word.

"Play ball, Mullen," The helmeted man said under his breath so only the two could hear. "Or this whole thing goes wide open. You understand that right?"

Without a sound, The Flayer extended a tentacle and shook the senior superhero's hand.

"As you can see people of New Hancock," The Holy Frijole announced, "With his experience of dealing with her and my aid, together we shall finally bring Sister Slaughter to justice! We don't know how dangerous this battle will be so we ask that all news cameras and police stay back. This is League business."

The crowd erupted in a cheer. The Flayer surveyed the crowd and tried to take it in like he had done during the bank robbery. He wanted to feel the pulse of the city again. He wanted to feel like the big damn hero one more time. This time, however, he felt nothing but regret.

212

"Now, good people of New Hancock," The Frijole continued. "We are off to make the streets safe once again. The way God wills it!"

The Flayer could hear the crowd cheer again but couldn't bear to see them so alive, so he turned around and began to head to the sounds of destruction.

"So," The Holy Frijole began as he finally caught up with The Flayer. "How do we defeat her? What is her weakness?"

"Fuck off." The Flayer hissed back.

"Do you think I'm playing with you?" The Holy Frijole was starting to get annoyed. He had expected some resistance from The Flayer, but what he had received was starting to get a little more than he really wanted to handle. "Between the broken nose and now this, it's almost as if it would have just been easier for me to let you be handled by The League."

"Probably," The Flayer shrugged not even bothering to look down at the man below him. "Besides, I don't know what her weakness is. If I did, my victories over her would have been much more decisive. I tended to just get lucky against her."

"Let me explain something to you, Mullen," The Frijole pointed a gloved finger at the tentacled monstrosity. "This thing better go off without a hitch. If you're holding back on me and I die during this, you're in even bigger trouble. See that window over there? Across from the park? Choir Boy is in that window watching over this. That's my dead man switch so to speak. I go down, and he releases those photos. He sees you lay one finger on me to stop me, he releases those photos. This isn't a game, boy."

The Flayer went silent. He had nothing he could say to the man that would satisfy him.

"Fine," The Flayer sighed. "She's invulnerable to anything but strong wide hits. Her invulnerability has a limit. Hit her hard and as much of her body as you can. That's all there is to it. I can only sometimes hit her hard enough. So you'll want to crank up the heat."

"See?" The holy superhero patted an arm tentacle, "Was that so hard to tell me?"

"Don't touch me." The Flayer let out a warning as the two began to approach the park where Sister Slaughter awaited them.

Sister Slaughter couldn't help but smile under her mask when she watched the two superheroes approach where she was leaned up against a tree taking a small break from her wanton destruction. Her plan had worked, do enough damage and the good guys come out to stop you.

"Like moths to a flame," The electronic voice crackled out of the voice box. "I do enough damage and out you come. Two of you though? To stop little ol' me? Have to say I'm flattered."

"That's enough, Slaughter," The Holy Frijole began. "Come with us and we can make sure this all goes very easy on you."

"Really?" The porcelain head tiled to the side, and a finger wagged at the Holy Frijole. "Not what a little birdy told me, Vasquez. That little birdy told me you're here for one purpose. To make sure I die tonight."

"I'm a superhero," The Holy Frijole responded. "We don't kill. We'll turn you over to the proper…"

"Oh, give me a break," The electronic voice laughed. "Squid Boy's friend told me everything the other night.

"Jen," The Flayer slid closer to Sister Slaughter. "If you surrender to me, his whole plan goes out the shitter. You're my prisoner then, and I won't let him touch you."

"Why, Squid Boy?" Sister Slaughter shook her head and shrugged her shoulders. "He isn't going to drop this. We all know it. That's why we're all standing here. Frankly, I was hoping you were still asleep, so it would just be me and him."

"We're in this together," The Flayer dropped his mask and stared into the glass eyes of the doll mask's eyes. "Mike was trying to tell you that. Like I said, we can end this right now."

"He's right," The Holy Frijole confessed. "Only downside is, we'll do this dance over and over and over. I'll make more and more money. I like this plan."

"Fuck you, Bean," Sister Slaughter adjusted to a more defensive stance. "And fuck you too, Squid Boy, for even thinking I would go along with that."

"Well, Mullen," The Holy Frijole let out a shot in surprise to both the other combatants. Sister Slaughter flew from the attack

214

and slid along the ground. "Looks like she made her choice. Why don't you go get some too?"

"Like hell, I will!" Andrew threw the mask back on and started to rush The Holy Frijole when the man waved a finger at the fledgling superhero.

"That wasn't a request." The Holy Frijole pointed to the window from earlier.

The Flayer snarled at The Holy Frijole. Then realized he had no choice. He made a quick move over to Sister Slaughter as she was hunched over. The Flayer caught the one thing he didn't expect when he went over, the sound of labored breathing. The Flayer had purposely told The Holy Frijole the wrong weakness for Sister Slaughter but didn't count on the fact that he was right.

"So much burning," Sister Slaughter coughed, loud enough for only the two to hear. "Can't breathe."

The Flayer wrapped a tentacle around Sister Slaughter's throat, not tight enough to choke her but enough to pull her back to her feet. He could see where her outfit was not ripped but was, instead, starting to scorch. The impact didn't hurt her, he figured, the burning sensation from it did. The heat from the blast must also be eating the oxygen around her as well.

The Flayer then caught something else. A boot straight to the midsection. Enough to send him flying across the way and over a park bench, but strangely enough, not enough to seriously hurt him. It was more of a shove that looking like a kick than an actual kick.

"Come on, Flayer!" Another light blast threw Sister Slaughter to the ground again. "Hit her like you mean it!"

The Flayer rushed in again. Mike had asked Andrew how much he trusted him. Did he have to trust Jennifer the same amount? He knew he had to. The Flayer wound up a large tentacle swipe and slammed it against Sister Slaughter who was now kneeling. That was when The Flayer caught on to what was happening.

"Hit me again." Sister Slaughter whispered as The Flayer loomed over her. The Flayer lifted her in the air with a free leg tentacle and Sister Slaughter was then ripped from his grip from a light shot straight to her head from The Holy Frijole.

215

The Flayer looked down to see a scorched piece of her mask lying at his feet. He looked over to see Sister Slaughter gasping to air ten feet away from him.

"This was easier than I thought it was going to be." The veteran superhero laughed as Sister Slaughter tried to climb to her feet and failed. The Flayer knew that he had to keep the pressure on her so that she could catch her breath. However, another shot sent her tumbling away from an outstretched tentacle hoping to grab her.

Sister Slaughter made it to a knee. She couldn't breathe. The impact was a ton worse than she had been anticipating and the oxygen being burned away from her was making it so hard to breathe she couldn't mount an offense. Her legs were almost too weak to get her to her feet. When she finally got to them, another blast of light was right there waiting on her. She couldn't do anything to save herself. The Flayer couldn't keep up with the way that she was being shot all over the park so she couldn't rely on using himself to act as a buffer between her and the shots. Sister Slaughter could feel the strength being sapped from her with each missed breath. The next thing she felt slipping was her consciousness as it faded in and out.

Sister Slaughter threw the broken remains of her mask to the ground. She coughed and spit on only one knee. The broken edges of the mask had cut her face rather deeply as she would skid across the ground with every shot she took. Everything looked like a mixture of dark life and crimson from the blood-drenched eye. Stupid small edges, she cursed, as she felt the darkness, grow more and more around her. Finally, Sister Slaughter found there was no other alternative. She rested on her knees and shut her eyes for one final time.

Mike had moved quickly after he heard the location of Choir Boy. Planting a miniature microphone in The Flayer's robe had been a godsend this time. He knew that The Flayer was going to need back up at some point and he needed to be there and be able to hear when it happened. Right now, happened to be that time.

Breaking into the building had not been a problem, and Mike figured that if Choir Boy was in the building that there couldn't be an alarm going off. So, smashing a glass window on the ground floor was a great way to get into a place wouldn't alert anyone of his presence. Again, he was right.

Choir Boy sat in a chair in an attic watching the battle unfold in the park below through a pair of binoculars. Mike smiled to himself as he knew one thing about everyone, whether they were a super sidekick or not. Everyone in the world is brave and willing to fight for their lives until a pistol is put to the back of their head, and they hear that distinct sound of a hammer cocking.

"Don't say a word," Mike informed the sidekick. "Drop whatever microphone you have, because you and I are going to have a little chat."

Sister Slaughter thought that was the last time she was ever going to close her eyes. She felt the heat. She felt an impact. She was ready to die. The heat wasn't as strong. The impact was only the air around her. She opened her eyes to see Andrew's now non-tentacled body slide through the snow, grass, and dirt before her.

Sister Slaughter didn't know if she screamed upon seeing Andrew now lying there. This body motionless almost twenty feet away from her. She knew her vocal cords hurt, and her jaw moved. She wanted to rush over to him and make sure her friend was ok. However, the lack of movement already told her the answer.

"Fucking Mullen!" Sister Slaughter heard the Holy Frijole curse. "God damn it! Choir Boy get down here. We have another friendly fire. Hurry!"

"Dillon ain't going anywhere." A new voice entered two-way radio in the Holy Frijole's helmet. The superhero felt everything go cold in his body when he heard Mike's voice. "You fucked with the wrong batch of assholes. Oh, don't worry he's still alive. We had a very nice little chat. Turns out, I had seen him before. Who'd thought that? I was actually right about something. Anyway. You might want to come get him. He is a little hurt. A little scared. Happens with a few bullet holes. Also, you may want to turn around."

The Holy Frijole slowly turned around. He expected a woman with super strength to be fast, but as The Flayer had learned, he wasn't expecting the woman with a crimson mask to be that fast. He also wasn't expecting to be hit that hard. In fact, in all the battles he had ever been in, he was never hit that hard.

The fist ripped right through the body armor that the Holy Frijole wore and struck him in the bulletproof vest he wore underneath. He lost his footing and flew like a rocket through the cold, early morning air. Being a man of God, he prayed. He prayed to land against a park bench. His prayer was answered as his legs struck against one and began to spin him end over end. He prayed for a bush. He blew right through the bush. He then prayed for the worse thing he could pray for, a building. A building was right there, only the brick and mortar did not stop his movement. He bounced to the ground once as he crashed through to the other side of the building. He then only prayed for the strength to get up. This prayer went unanswered as he fought to stay conscious and lost.

Sister Slaughter rushed to Andrew's side. Small tentacles writhed around him, but none were attached to his body. The stinging on her head and the burning sensation on her body went away as the sting of tears began to escape from her face. She picked him up gently and felt a wet, viscous fluid come over her gloves. Blood and a lot of it. Sister Slaughter began to check the damage. A hole in Andrew's chest cavity reviled a small grey lump moving in a rhythmic pattern. Instantly fear took over her as she realized she was looking at Andrew Mullen's lung inflating and deflating. Fear turned to hope as she realized that meant one thing. Andrew was still alive.

Sister Slaughter took off running to an alleyway, then another. She began to follow the same course of action as The Holy Frijole. Sister Slaughter, no Jennifer, prayed. She hoped that Mike had brought a car or something. Just as Father Vasquez's prayers were answered so were hers. Mike's car pulled up to the closest street.

"The fuck happened?" Mike asked as Sister Slaughter threw open the back-seat door. A lot of the bleeding had stopped. She made sure Andrew was secure, and looked at the wound one more time and found that she couldn't see inside of it. Small tentacles had come together to make a makeshift bandage and hold the wound closed.

"Fucking drive!" Jennifer's actual voice yelled over the crackling of the broken electronic voice box.

"Drive where? What the fucking fuck is going on?!" Mike began to panic after seeing Andrew coated in blood.

"St. George's," Jennifer sat in the passenger seat and ripped off the sleeve of her outfit to make a makeshift bandage for her head. "You don't move this car Andrew is going to fucking die. Now move!"

Mike did as he was told and sped off into the night.

"I'm going to Saint's Pass," Mike informed Jennifer.

"Go to St. George's," Jennifer screamed at the driver.

"It's been closed for ages!" Mike yelled back.

"No," Jennifer shook her head sending a small smattering of blood over the glass in the car. "It's a place for people like us. They specialize in treating people like us. It's run by The League."

"Ok," Mike found a chuckle. "Sister Slaughter all over the news is going to waltz in there with her enemy and demand treatment for him. Great fucking plan."

"I need your clothes," Jennifer told him as she looked in the mirror to see if the bandage had stopped the bleeding. Her face now drenched in her own blood.

"What?" Mike asked as the car started to get closer to the supposedly closed hospital.

"Park in the alley, and I need your clothes," Jennifer retied on her bandage. "You're right, Sister Slaughter can't take him in there. Jennifer can. Or would you rather he dies?"

"Fuuuuccckkkk!" Mike slammed the car into park in an alley and climbed out. He quickly undressed and tossed Jennifer his clothes. Jen quickly changed and tossed her tattered costume in a nearby trash can.

"Car keys," Jen demanded.

"Are you serious?" Mike stood in his boxers feeling the cold in the night air.

"I'll be back to get you. Just please, Mike." Jennifer felt herself begin to beg.

"Hurry," Mike tossed her the keys. "Make it quick."

"As fast as I can," Jennifer called out as she slammed the car into drive and speed off.

Mike stood in the cold. His feet starting to ache from snow he was standing in. This was not how he imagined his night to go.

Issue 18

Jennifer was true to her word and a few minutes later returned to pick Mike up. Jennifer had made him drop her off out by the warehouses that Mike knew from Andrew's first stint as The Flayer. Back when four unlucky gangsters tried to murder a future superhero.

The next morning came too early for Mike. Never the less, he got in his car and headed to the auto shop. The past few nights of snow, that Mike had neglected, had to be cleared off the front steps in order to be let inside.

Mike flipped on the lights and noticed that there were a few messages on the answering machine. He took a deep breath and with everything going on in his life he considered just closing the place down. Andrew, if he survived, had a new job as a superhero. Mike had enough money to live on doing whatever he wanted. He then sighed and realized that the only thing he wanted was to spend his time with his best friend.

Mike walked into the back and opened a garage door. An old car that Mike had tried to sell the parts off for some extra cash sat there. Mike grabbed a handful of wrenches off the wall and began throwing them as hard as he could at one of the autos. He laughed slightly to himself. The car had been named "car-tharis."

Since it didn't run he declared that it was alright to damage that car when either he or Andrew had become frustrated. He wanted to feel better with each clank but only felt emptier. It was almost as if he wanted to break down.

When Jennifer had returned from the hospital to pick him back up, she informed him that they had given her no news and had only told her to leave. She claimed to be a civilian that found Andrew and fought off someone to rescue him. They just turned her away telling her this was not a place for her, and to go get looked at Saint's Pass. So sadly, she had no news on Andrew's condition.

Mike stopped throwing wrenches when he heard the doorbell ring in the front.

"Fuck off," He shouted not caring who it was. "We're closed."

"Good thing I'm not here to get my car worked on." Jennifer walked in the back. Her forehead stitched up, rather messily Mike noticed. Jennifer had her hands tucked in the pockets of an old military coat as she walked closer to Mike.

"Nice stitch job." Mike pointed out.

"Kind of hard to do in a mirror," Jen shrugged. "Really wish the whole invulnerable thing worked for small things too."

"How'd you find this place?" Mike asked grabbing more wrenches from the wall. After a thought, he handed some to Jennifer and pointed out the car he was throwing them at. Then launched one at a broken windshield.

"Frankly," Jennifer followed suit and threw one. With a clang, it drove through the hood and got stuck inside the car. "Sorry."

"If I can't get it back I'll buy more. No biggie." Mike shrugged.

"I called a bunch of auto shops in the area and found which one only opened in the afternoon." Jennifer smiled throwing another wrench.

"Good guess." Mike tried to toss his in the whole Jen had just made but missed.

"You're pretty predictable." Jen threw.

222

"I bet." Mike trotted out to the car to dig wrenches out of the snow.

"You hear anything about Squid Boy?" Jen asked. Her voice was too somber even for her.

"Nothing yet." Mike returned and handed half the dug-out wrenches to Jen.

"Yeah," Jen threw one through the front tire. "What happened last night? Helmet head turned around like he was listening to something when he called for support. Where was his support?"

"Knocked out," Mike confessed. "Turns out I did know that guy. Kind of a long story. Rather not get into it. Had a little chat with him, then clubbed him over the head with a gun knocking him out. I told The Frijole I shot him."

"Why didn't you?" Jen laughed.

"I still need him." Mike smiled. "I'm going to use him to put a certain priest in his place."

"How?" Jen grew slightly concerned.

"Long story. Rather not get into it." Mike repeated.

The wrench throwing stopped when the doorbell went off again.

"Fuck off," Jen called out. "We're closed."

"Good thing I'm not here to get my car worked on," Ms. Claremont walked through the door of the garage and turned to Jennifer. "I don't believe we met."

"Jennifer," Jen introduced herself. "Jennifer Mullen."

"Family?" Ms. Claremont looked the woman up and down.

"Sister." Jen eyed up the older woman to determine if she was going to have to take her down. Then again with what she had just gone through she doubted she might be able to. She then looked to Mike for some sort of clue, and he just shook his head.

"If you're asking about family," Mike's hopes began to rise. "Then this is about Andrew."

"You would be correct," Ms. Claremont turned to Mike. "May we speak in private?"

"If you can talk in front of me," Mike shook his head. "Then you can talk in front of her."

"Fair enough," Ms. Claremont shrugged. "I just wanted to say that Andrew made it out of surgery fine. He's stable. Due to his… status… his body heals rather rapidly. We're moving him to Saint's Pass this evening to have them keep an eye during the recovery process and so that you can go see him."

"What happened to Andy?" Jennifer played along and looked at Mike. "What status?"

"Oh dear," Ms. Claremont chuckled. "I believe you may want to have a discussion with your brother."

"Yeah, I think I will." Jen nodded.

"That's all I needed to say. I'll excuse myself." Ms. Claremont began to leave.

"Actually," Mike stopped her. "I have a question. Have you heard anything from The Holy Frijole and Choir Boy?"

"No," Ms. Claremont shook her head. "I'm afraid they have gone missing after their failed attempt to stop Sister Slaughter last night. We tried to check the footage from the news cameras as to what happened, however, the cameras shut off after The Holy Frijole told them to turn them off."

"Who's the Holy Frijole?" Jen played dumb again.

"Ask your brother," Mike turned to her. "Thank, Ms. Claremont."

The older woman took her leave.

"Well played." Mike complimented Jen. The woman stood in silence. She began to smile and then a single tear escaped the side of her face.

"Squid Boy's ok." Jen softly said to herself.

"Looks like." Mike nodded. "You gonna go see him tonight?"

"Are you?" Jen asked.

"No," Mike shook his head. "I'm going to get ready for my meeting with the priest. I need to find out when he has confession. I doubt he would want to miss that."

"Didn't take you for the religious type," Jen joked when she couldn't help herself but smile.

"I'm not," Mike threw another wrench for good measure. "But I like to do my homework."

224

Saint's Pass was on the other side of town from Jennifer's apartment. The drive wasn't too terrible if she took the highway. However, her old beat up rust bucket of a car couldn't make it over 50 so that added some time to the drive.

Jennifer checked with the front desk as she walked inside and took the elevator to floor Andrew was being held on. Due to how well Andrew was doing it appeared that they had moved him to a normal bed and they were allowing visitors. She didn't want to admit it, but this was music to her ears.

The door to Andrew Mullen's room was shut. Jennifer stopped for a second. Does she knock? Does she just barge in? What does she say? Fuck it, she told herself and just opened to door and walked in.

When Jennifer heard that Andrew was doing well, this was not what she had expected. Andrew laid in the hospital bed not moving. As still as the moment she picked his body up out of the snow. Machines beeped all around him. At least those told her he was alive.

Jen walked over to the bed and took a seat in the chair next to it. Andrew was motionless and out cold. Jen reached out between the bar of the rail and took Andrew's hand. It was cold and clammy. Jennifer felt tears begin to well up in her one more time. Of all the things she wanted to do when she became a villain, hurting the people she considered friends was not one of them. Now, here she sat next to one that she had let rather close to her and he was hurt worse than she could have hoped.

The tears stopped however when she felt the hand squeeze back. Jennifer stood up and slowly Andrew's eye flickered to life.

"You couldn't have been more clichéd if you tried, Squid Boy." Jennifer let a smile out.

"Eh," Andrew gasped from under the ventilator mask he had on. "Not as bad a villain who has a name like Sister Slaughter."

"Fuck you, Squid Boy." Jennifer laughed a little.

"Not now," Andrew tried to wave weakly. "Too much morphine in my system. Later though."

The two were still and not saying anything. Jennifer was just glad to see Andrew was alright. Andrew just glad to see she was alright.

225

"So, it worked?" Andrew asked. "I was able to keep him away from you enough to get a miracle."

"Yeah," Jen nodded. She didn't have the heart to tell him the most he had done was hold her still to be shot. "Mike distracted him enough for me to knock him out."

"He still has the pictures though," Andrew sighed. "He has probably already gone to The League."

"A woman stopped by the shop and told Mike and I that they haven't heard from him. Probably too embarrassed after losing that one," Jen made a punch in the air. "And Mike says he's going to finish this. Says he did know that guy from somewhere, but he won't tell me where."

"Who knows," Andrew tried to shrug and only managed to wince in pain. "It's Mike."

"Good way of putting it," Jennifer went silent again. "How did he manage to hit you?"

"I saw you needed to catch your breath, so I jumped in to try and throw you. That was the last thing I remember. Aside from a lot of burning." Andrew gave Jennifer the rest of the story.

The two went silent again.

"I don't think we should do this anymore." Jen finally spoke up after a few minutes off quiet between them that felt like an eternity.

"What?" Andrew raised an eyebrow. "After you stopped by and kissed me and everything?"

"What are you talking about?" Jen got inquisitive. "I was talking about the fraud thing. I've never kissed you."

"But the night before we fought. You said you were there. I remember it." Andrew protested.

"I came in," Jen filled in the blanks for him this time. "You were passed out on the couch watching some giant chinchilla destroy Tokyo. So, I grabbed my boots and left. I'll be honest and with how emotional I was who knows what I might have done, but no we never…"

"Oh, I am so sorry," Andrew felt himself grow pale in embarrassment. "I am going to just blame this on the painkillers."

"I'll allow it." Jen smiled at him.

"Can we still keep the sex part?" Andrew laughed this time it really was the painkillers making him loopy.

"What?" Jen laughed. "Yeah, oh fuck yeah. Shit, you're my own personal tentacle monster. Never knew I had that fetish."

The two shared a smile. Then more silence between them.

"I really should get going." Jen stood up and began to head to the door.

"Jen," Andrew called out before she left. Jennifer turned around. "You should ask for more money for the henchwoman side. You beat the best upstart superhero in the city and a veteran member of The League in one night. You said that the notoriety was how you all charge. Hope that helped."

Jennifer smiled. Had he done this to save her from the Frijole? Had he done what he did to help her out with her work? Or had it been a little of both? Jennifer didn't care. This man had just sacrificed his health and almost his life to make her life a little bit better. This man that only a few months ago had to wrapped a car around her to stop her from trying to kill him.

Jennifer walked back to the bed and lifted Andrew's mask off his face. She gave him a quick peck on the lips and put his mask back on.

"There." Jennifer smiled. "You got one, Squid Boy. Happy now?"

"How do I get another?" Andrew laughed.

"I'm chalking that one up to the painkillers I'm on," Jennifer smiled and walked out of the room. "So don't push it."

Issue 19

Mike was never one for churches. He had hated the smell, the look, the obvious obsession with torture. Ok, Mike admitted, the torture part was kind of cool. Made for some amazing metal album covers.

A few people waiting in line in front of Mike as he stood waiting for his turn in the confessional. One by one the people took their turns and then left. Mike looked over at a pew in the back of the room and saw Andrew and Jennifer sitting there, chatting away about something that Mike couldn't hear.

Ms. Claremont was correct, about him being in good condition. Andrew's body did heal amazingly fast. Jennifer had explained to Mike that it was one of the perks of having these superpowers. As she showed off that the stitches that she had were gone by the next day and any marks were gone by the time Andrew was released from the hospital.

Andrew was almost as healthy as Jen was, though he did need to keep a cane to catch himself if he started to fall over. Apparently, the shot from The Holy Frijole destroyed his body armor but the high-powered skidding and crashing into things had broken his right leg in numerous places. Still, after a week, he had healed up enough to be released from the hospital. Best guess was from Jennifer who said he should be one hundred percent by the end of the month.

Mike finally had his turn at the confessional. He stepped inside the little dark room and knelt on the little bench.

"Forgive me, Father," Mike began. "For I am about to sin."

"I'm sorry?" A very familiar yet unseen voice spoke from the other side of the confessional. "You can choose not to my son."

"No, Father Vasquez," Mike couldn't help but smile to himself at the fact that it was Vasquez on the other side. "I'm about to piss off a priest rather badly."

"You…" Father Vasquez's voice grew dark and hateful. A small light could be seen shining through the mesh window.

"I wouldn't do that," Mike loved being the dick in situations where he knew there was nothing anyone could do about it. "How's Dillon? I didn't hit him too hard did I?"

"What do you want?" Vasquez growled.

"I want you to take a look at this," Mike opened the door to the confessional and gestured for Vasquez to do the same. Mike then handed the Father a closed envelope. "Like them?"

Father Vasquez trembled in anger as he opened the envelope and pulled out a set of pictures. The pictures very clearly showed himself in what appeared to be a nightclub kissing another man. Not just any man. He was kissing his side kick Choir Boy.

"You're really getting your tongue in there ain't ya?" Mike laughed. "What can I say? After we all have been through I can hardly keep those two apart either. You can go ahead and keep those. I made plenty of copies. I'm sure your bosses would love to see those."

"The League already knows about us." Vasquez prided himself on being able to answer that.

"Oh," Mike laughed. "I'm not talking about The League."

Vasquez finally understood what Mike meant. Anger and fear welled up inside him, the light grew again.

"Wouldn't do that," Mike wagged a finger at the mesh. "Andy is right outside the door as is Sister Slaughter. You kill me, they'll go to the fucking Pope to get you brought down."

"What do you want?" Vasquez took a deep breath.

"Two things. One, you destroy your other copy of the pictures of Flayer and Slaughter and never bring this up again," Mike counted off on his fingers. "Two, I want you to recommend

League status for Andy. You keep that up, and we stay shut up. You got it?"

"Mike," The priest let out a deep sigh. "I won't lie to you. Not in a house of God. Those pictures that night were the only ones. There were no copies. So, you can consider that proof of my silence. However, I can not recommend League status for Andrew. He is too green and not well enough known. He will never get it."

"Doesn't hurt to try," Mike stood up. "So, what's my penance, Father?"

"Go fuck yourself." Vasquez snarled under his breath.

"Atta boy." Mike left the confessional as he could hear Vasquez flipping through the photos again.

"You done?" Andrew asked turning to Mike.

"Yup," Mike nodded. "He ain't saying shit to anyone anytime soon. He might just storm out of there in a few seconds... Oh wait, there he goes."

Father Vasquez stormed out of the confessional and didn't even make eye contact with the two men and the woman waving at him as he walked by.

"Cool," Jen looked down at her watch and stood up. "Let's go get some dinner. I want to show you guys something tonight."

"Pull in over there." Jennifer directed Mike down an alleyway in a gang-ridden part of town. "Ok, everyone out of the car."

"My fucking tires are going to get stolen." Mike protested.

"You'd be the first," Jen laughed as she led the way. Realizing the two men were having a bit of trouble keeping up, she ran back to them and hooked her arms through theirs. Giving Andrew much needed extra support. "Come on, slowpokes. This will be cool, I promise."

The snow crunched beneath them. Jennifer had dressed up herself, as much as she felt still went with her style for the occasion of celebrating Andrew's release from the hospital. Her excitement was almost too much for Mike to bear and all he could think about was if she got any happier he might have to throw her in a snow bank to cool her off before she explodes. Then he realized tentacles and a super strong woman would be after his ass.

231

The three stopped outside of a non-descript door after sticking to the alley for a few blocks. Jennifer knocked on the door and an invisible window slid open. Jennifer didn't say a word she just pulled a trinket out of her pocket and slid it in the small window. After a few seconds, the trinket came back out. The woman then slid her arm in and pulled it back out a few seconds later.

The woman then turned to the two men and made a zipper motion with her hand across her mouth and motioned for them to do the same thing she just did with her arm. Andrew shrugged and went first. He felt the small pinch of a needle in his arm, then felt his arm get shoved back out by an unseen hand. Jennifer then motioned for Mike to do the same thing. Mike let out a yelp of surprised and to reach in and grab whoever was poking him in there, until Jen shoved him back, saving him from the little window slamming down in his arm.

The woman gave him a scornful look and shook her head.

"The fu…" Mike began until Jen threw her hand over his mouth and put an index finger to her lips. The three then stood there. After 10 minutes of waiting in the cold, the door swung open to the inside to a dark room.

Jennifer walked in first and pulled Andrew behind her. A little old lady sat behind a counter labeling the three vials with numbers and putting them on a shelf. Then returned to her game of solitaire on the table. Jennifer smiled and waved at her and the old woman nodded and gave her a smile back.

"How you doing, Slaughter?" The old woman greeted her.

"Not too bad, Bloody Mary," Jennifer motioned to Andrew and Mike. "These are my new mercs. We just got back from a tough job, figured I'd show them a good time."

"Yeah," Bloody Mary got up off her seat and offered both her hand which both shook. "I heard through the grapevine that you kicked the crap out of those two heroes. Way to go, girl, that's gonna up your pricing."

"That's the hope." Jennifer smiled.

"Well, you three go have a great time," Mary pressed a button and a door slid open letting the sound of a heavy bass through the room. "Give her the old Eiffel Tower tonight, guys."

Andrew looked confused as Jennifer pulled him down a dark hall and closer to the music. Andrew and Mike followed Jennifer down a hallway where the music grew louder and louder. When the light finally broke the darkness, Andrew found himself on a balcony overlooking a nightclub. The lights shone on people of all shapes, sizes and to Andrew's surprise, costumes getting their groove-on on the dance floor. Booths lined the wall which resembled brick foundation blocks. A bar sat on each individual level and dancers danced in cages hung from the ceiling.

Jennifer stopped and turned to the two men. She leaned on the railing and smiled at them.

"Figured it might be a bad idea if priest boy tried to get some revenge for me to ever really go back to Zero's. So, I figured I'd bring you two to my hang out spot. Welcome to Heroes! See you two downstairs." Jen then rolled backward off the railing. Both men walked to the railing and watched as Jennifer landed on her feet and walked off.

"I ain't fucking jumping down there." Mike pointed over the railing and began to look for the stairs.

Andrew began to look around and noticed what made the nightclub so special. In one corner, a man took a woman's drink and frost began to cover it. A woman sat in a booth next to a man who was staring at a projection of her dancing seductively on the table. Another man, or that was Andrew's best guess, had a few small gremlins sitting next to him which he kept trying to keep control of. A woman on the dance floor was bending the light to her will for her own personal light show. They all had powers and were all using them in the open.

"I smell weed." Mike interrupted Andrew's train of thought. "Andy, they got weed here."

"I would wager a guess that there's other stuff too." Andrew smiled as his friend took off.

It took a quick question from Mike to the bartender about where the stairs were and Andrew found himself on the edge of the lower level dance floor. He looked around for any sign of Jennifer and found none. Out of the darkness a pair of hands reached out and pulled him off his feet onto the dance floor. Jennifer wrapped her arms around Andrew's neck and began to move and shimmy against him to the music. Andrew did the best he could to keep up, but the damage to his leg was still too painful. Luckily for him, whenever he would lose balance the woman with super strength keep him on two feet.

"Jen," Andrew looked around, or tried too, with the way Jennifer was moving against him he found it hard to keep his eyes off her. "There are people with…"

"They're like us, Squid Boy," Jen smiled as she turned her back to him and slid up and down him. "This is neutral ground. Then again, not much to be neutral about anymore."

"What's that mean?" Andrew cocked an eyebrow.

"You don't know?" Jen turned back around to him and stopped dancing.

"I'm starting to feel there is a lot I don't know." Andrew scratched his head.

"Found the weed." Mike interrupted the two of them. Jen gently gave him a push off and pointed to a booth with bean bag chairs in it. To which he scurried off.

"Then, Squid Boy," Jennifer smiled and looked into his eyes. "I'll teach you. Now, you go have fun and bring us some drinks. Take your time, throw those tentacles up, live a little. I need to talk to Mike. Ok?"

"Yeah." Andrew nodded and made his way to the bar. What was Jennifer talking about? There was no need to be neutral anymore? What else didn't he know?

"The heroes are gone, sweetie." A woman sat alone at the bar. "Sorry, I'm a telepath. I didn't mean to invade. Your thoughts were just too loud, and I have trouble controlling my filter when I drink. You're new here. I'm Mystic Mary. League member. You are?"

"And…" Andrew found that he couldn't finish his sentence.

"No real names here, sweetie." Mary made a hand gesture at a guy sitting next to her. The man abruptly left. "Very long story. There's The League, and then there's you. Looks like he's letting you little guys come back. I'm afraid of why."

"What? Who's letting us come back?" Andrew asked.

"I don't have to read your mind to know who you are," Mary sipped her drink. Andrew tried to get a good look at the woman, but the light, or the woman kept playing tricks on his eyes. Andrew gave up trying to decide which it was. "You're new, Flayer. You're going to need a teacher. Sister Slaughter over there offered. I would take it if I were you. Also, don't worry about Frijole… see there I go again probing minds… your friend has him in checkmate. Welcome to the game, Flayer."

"What can I get you?" The bartender asked.

"He'll take a pitcher of something expensive. Three glasses and put it on my tab," Mystic Mary lit a cigarette. "A celebration to your new world."

"Here you go." The bartender returned with the pitcher.

"Go enjoy yourself," Mary smiled at Andrew. "I have a feeling we'll be seeing each other soon."

Andrew, still stunned from his encounter, began to slowly walk back to the booth of bean bag chairs where his two friends had a pair of large smiles of their faces and were passing a joint back and forth.

"So, it's cool if I smoke this in here?" Mike asked Jennifer as she headed towards the booth.

"Only if you share it," Jen plopped down and leaned her head back. "No law here. Plus there's no one here that is going to enforce it. That's just asking for a fight. It would make the Zero's bar fights look like a toddler slap fight."

"Awesome," Mike lit up the joint took a large puff and handed it to Jennifer.

"I need to ask you something." Jen took a hit and passed it back.

"I was going to say the same thing." Mike took a hit but did not pass it back.

"You go first." Jen looked slightly concerned.

"More of a statement," Mike didn't even look at her. "You hurt Andrew, I hurt you. Clear?"

"Crystal," Jen nodded. "It's just fun. We've discussed it."

"It gets too much for him, you knock it off," Mike's serious tone continued. "I came damn close to losing my best friend a few times already. I will not let that happen again."

"Fair," Jen admitted. "Wounds are still raw from that Erin chick. I get it."

"Good," Mike passed her the joint and she took a big hit. "Your turn."

"You are a resourceful mother fucker," Jen complimented him. "With balls of steel. You want a job?"

"Doing what?" Mike passed the joint back.

"My price is going to skyrocket after the other night. I could afford a permanent henchman. Start running more of my own heists and shit. Might some extra cash. You want the job?"

"I got the auto shop…" Mike began to scratch his head.

"Mike," Jen laughed. "Andy is going to be busy doing super stuff. That would just leave you."

"Not like he's going to get all the hero work," Mike tilted his head thinking of an excuse to say no. "There's probably so many out there."

"There's not," Jen admitted. "Aside from The League which only do photo ops now. He's alone. He's going to be very busy."

"What?" Mike questioned.

"I don't know the details," Jen shrugged. "But he's it."

"I'm not going to fight, Andy." Mike shot back.

"Neither am I." Jen took a hit of the joint.

"Do I get a cool costume?" Mike raised an eyebrow,

"We got to theme it," Jen suggested. "And since I lost my face plate in the fight. I might have to come up with something new too. Was kind of digging the look of my face covered in all the blood."

"Arrgghh…" Mike groaned after a minute of silence between the two. His brain going over any counter argument it could find. It found none. "Fuck it, I'm in."

"Bitchin'" Jen smiled at her new partner. "Next question. How did you know Dillon? How did you get those photos?"

Mike leaned back in his seat.

236

"I took the photos," Mike smiled proud of himself. "I'd seen him a few times before."

"Where did you see him that made that big of an impression on you?" Jennifer's curiosity grew.

"At that club," Mike admitted. "I'd seen the two of them there before. Kissing, making out, the whole thing."

"Funny," Jen shrugged. "Figured most places you would frequent would kick people out for being gay. That would make that a ...oh... oh shit... Mike... are you?"

Mike didn't say a word and nodded slightly, laughing a little at Jennifer's realization.

"Yup," Mike said as a matter of factually. "Damn proud of it. Didn't recognize the priest, but the sidekick had been there a few times. I think he shot me down once. I doubt Andy knows, though. I never told him and really don't feel like explaining it to him. Having an ex-nazi as a father figure might not be too compatible."

"I doubt Andy would care," Jen told him. "But I won't say a thing. Haha, now I'm the one with the dirt that could ruin people."

"Bitch," Mike laughed.

Andrew returned to find the two laughing, which just added to his confusion. Jennifer took the pitcher from Andrew and Mike took the glasses. Jennifer moved over to have Andrew join her on her bag and pressed herself closer to him.

"Hey Andy," Mike laughed as he poured the beers. "You're fired."

"What?" Andrew was not liking all the confusion.

"I'm closing the shop," Mike passed him a drink. "I'm working for Sister Slaughter. I'm a henchman, and that's gonna become our hideout. Put a big sign out that says 'No Heroes Allowed.'"

"I don't want that shitty auto body shop," Jen could feel the weed hitting her now. "I need like a hollowed-out volcano."

"I got money," Mike laughed. "I ain't got that kind of money."

"If some fucker would have paid his rent." Jennifer laughed and pulled Andy's arm around her.

A woman approached the table. A look of sadness filled her eyes. Her face was painted like a Day of the Dead skull. She bowed

237

slightly and placed an envelope on the table. Jennifer motioned for the woman to join them and offered her a beer. The woman shook her head, turned and walked away.

"That's funny," Jen's tone changed. "She's usually very accepting of a drink."

"Who was that?" Andrew asked.

"A friend...ish," Jen shrugged her shoulders. "Goes by the name Sugar Skull. Never talks but is always very willing to listen."

"What did she drop off?" Mike reached for the envelope and opened it. His eyes grew wide as he started placing the photos of The Flayer and Sister Slaughter having sex in the back alley on the table. "How'd she get these?"

Andrew shrugged. Jennifer Shrugged. Mike hit the joint again. To them, it didn't matter as all was well that ended well.

Acknowledgments

A personal thank you goes out to everyone who helped make this. Ashley for running over it so many times and encouraging me the whole way. Everyone who helped in one way or another. Jack Daniels for making some amazing whiskey that helped this thing get done. Most importantly is my Mom who first told me to try putting pen to paper and did more for me than I could ever properly thank her for.

Thank you, everyone.

About the Author

Before writing even entered his world, Joshua Koehn loved comic books. He always found a love in the horrible 90's "extreme" schlock. Comics where every man was a brooding figure of darkness and every woman was a badass supermodel. This led to finding the beauty in all things terrible.

Now he sits at home, drinks too much, writes terrible books, pets his terrible lump of pup, and plays terrible video games. Always looking for his next adventure.